UPROOTING
Ernie

Books by Pamela Burford

Jane Delaney Mysteries
Undertaking Irene
Uprooting Ernie
Perforating Pierre
Icing Allison
Preserving Peaches
Simmering Stu
Liquidating Larry
Scrapping Scarlett
Jane Delaney Humorous Mystery Series: Books 1-3 Box Set

Romantic Suspense
Snatched
Going Commando
Storming Meg
A Case of You
Twice Burned (Double Dare book 2)

Contemporary Romance
Rags to Bitches
In the Dark
Snowed
Too Darn Hot
The Boss's Runaway Bride (a novella)

The Wedding Ring matchmaking series:
Love's Funny That Way
I Do, But Here's the Catch
One Eager Bride To Go
Fiancé for Hire
*The Wedding Ring Matchmaker Series: Complete Four-Book
Romantic Comedy Box Set*

UPROOTING
Ernie

A Jane Delaney Mystery
Book 2

Pamela Burford

RADICAL POODLE
PRESS

for Pat, the Good Twin

1

Nothing to See Here, Folks

IF I WEREN'T so darn honest, I wouldn't have been the one to find him. And then I'd have been spared all the messy stuff that happened afterward.

Or not. Messy stuff seems to seek me out. I'm the trailer park to its tornado.

And okay, as for honesty, I admit I've been known to bend or even sucker-punch the truth, but only when the occasion really warranted it and the white lie was for the better good and all that. But when it comes to my paying clients, I'm practically always sort of mostly very honest. If I tell you, *This is what I'm going to do for you and this is when I'm going to do it,* you can take that to the bank. I mean, in a business like mine, you have only your reputation, right?

Which is how Sexy Beast and I found ourselves squelch-squelching across the sodden turf of Whispering Willows Cemetery on that windy midsummer afternoon, slogging through drenched leaves, willow limbs, and other post-storm detritus. Yeah, I know dogs aren't permitted in the graveyard, but I was the only idiot willing to venture outside so soon after the monster nor'easter that had just pummeled Crystal Harbor and environs, and I do pick up after him, so no harm no foul.

Plus, Sexy Beast—SB to his nearest and dearest—being the high-maintenance, neurotic toy poodle he is, doesn't even qualify as a real dog in the eyes of many of our neighbors, so I figure it's, you know, okay to bend the rules a little.

Just driving there had been a white-knuckled obstacle course around downed branches and live wires lying in the streets. But I had a job to do. In more than two decades I'd never failed a client. Well, okay, once, but she'd come to an untimely end before she could learn that I'd let her down, so that didn't count, did it?

Anyway, I'd made my perilous way to the local boneyard because of that reputation thing I mentioned before. Plus I'd already spent my client's prepaid fee on a one-year membership to dog-loving-singles.com, and issuing him a refund would have stretched my anemic budget past the breaking point.

Chip Wentworth, a local golf pro who'd relocated to Austin a few months back, had paid me a hundred bucks to empty a three-liter spigot box of white Zinfandel on his mother Dorothy's grave on the occasion of her third birthday in heaven. Dorothy had been fond of cheap rosé—perhaps too fond from what I hear. And I hear a lot. People tell me things. It's a mixed blessing.

That honesty thing meant my doing this particular job on this particular day as required by the client, nor'easter or no nor'easter. I'm like the post office that way—neither snow nor rain, yadda yadda.

"All right, all right, hold your horses," I muttered as SB strained at the leash. I unhooked him. "Stay near Janey."

We were crossing one of the cemetery's open rolling lawns, dotted with graceful weeping willow trees and stone benches. At some point in the future, when they run out of room where bodies are currently being planted, this unused space will become occupied, as it were. For now, it's corpse-free, a necropolis-in-waiting.

The sky was clearing, but the wind was still strong enough to whip long strands of my reddish blond hair into my face. I yanked the hair tie from its usual spot on my wrist and pulled my hair back into a messy bun.

Sexy Beast began high-stepping through the sodden debris, sniffing up a storm—hey, it's not that bad a pun!—as his gazillion olfactory cells catalogued every drowned bug and damp, irritable chipmunk hunkered in its burrow. We crossed the cobblestone footpath separating the sprawling lawn from the neat grid of tombstones. The cemetery's map was permanently etched into my brainpan, so it took me no time at all to locate Dorothy's final resting place.

I set the wine box on the spongy ground, lifted a whippy willow limb off the grave, and used it to rake wet leaves and blades of grass from the polished granite stone. I'm a full-service Death Diva—an unfortunate but durable nickname long ago bestowed by the locals here in Crystal Harbor, the well-to-do town on the North Shore of Long Island where most of my clients reside. It doesn't hurt to do a little basic grave maintenance whenever my assignment takes me to a cemetery.

Okay, I know it's killing you, so let me get this part over with right now. My name is Jane Delaney and I make my living performing tasks for paying clients. Those tasks involve loved ones who have gone on to their final reward. A typical workday might find me delivering flowers to multiple gravesites (I take Memorial Day reservations months in advance), tossing ashes out of a hired plane, choosing an outfit to coordinate with a satin-lined casket, or inventorying the contents of a deceased person's home—not to mention running the tag sale, sprucing up the house, dealing with the broker, and arbitrating the inevitable family skirmish over inheritance rights to, in one recent case, Grandma's deep freeze crammed top to bottom with T.G.I. Fridays Cheddar & Bacon Potato Skins.

The list of Death Diva assignments is endless. What's the most bizarre death-related chore you can think of? Oh please, I was doing that before I could vote—use your imagination! All right, that's more like it. I've done that. Come to think of it, I've done that more than once.

I stood back to examine Dorothy's neatened-up grave. "So what do you think, SB? Will it pass muster?"

The apricot poodle's dark little eyes flashed to mine. He licked his lips. I didn't need the Dog Whisperer to read his one-track mind. *Did you say mustard? Where are the hot dogs?*

I gave him scritches and a small cube of cheddar from my shoulder bag. "Don't worry, this shouldn't take long. Then we'll be back home and you can have a nice Vienna sausage."

He responded by lifting his leg to mark a neighboring headstone before I could stop him. Oh brother. I glanced around to double-check that we were still alone, then squinted at the words etched into the befouled stone. "Sorry, Mr. Parmentier," I muttered to the gentleman who'd reposed in that spot since May 15, 1955.

"Let's get this over with before you take a dump on the poor guy." I opened the spigot and held the heavy box of rosé over Dorothy's grave.

Sexy Beast yipped at the sight of the pink plonk watering the grass. This was the most exciting thing that had happened to him all day, since he'd snored peacefully through the roaring, window-rattling, power-outaging, record-rainfall-dumping nor'easter. Cautiously he inched his way toward the sweet-smelling stream.

"Nope. Nope. Nope. Nope." I tried to block him with my foot, but he's an agile little brat when he's motivated, and he managed to wet the tip of his tongue before I could shoo him away. "You're going to regret it," I warned him. Some things, one had to learn from grim experience. I knew that better than most.

SB licked his lips, thought about it a moment, then shook his head violently and sneezed.

"Like I said."

He made a dainty hacking noise, sneezed again, and perched on his haunches to observe the action from a safe distance.

I tilted the box, hoping to speed things up. No such luck. I studied the curved top of Dorothy's headstone and debated the wisdom of balancing the wine box on it to give my arms a rest. The rosé would, after all, be aimed more or less at her mouth, and wouldn't that be a nice plus?

But that would be cheating. Don't ask me why, it just would. So I stood there and held the box high as it gradually lightened and the wet ground underfoot became even wetter. Meanwhile I stared across the footpath to the normally manicured lawn I'd crossed minutes earlier, now looking like a prom queen after a rough night and rougher morning.

I squinted into the distance. I frowned. Was one of the willow trees tilted? It was hard to tell because of the wind whipping its dangly limbs. None of the dozen or so willows on that lawn had ever been tilted. I knew those trees by heart, had sat under them countless times, contemplating mortality, the infinite, and insanely adorable YouTube sloths.

Yeah, that's right, I finally got a smartphone. Are you proud of me? Irene McAuliffe had bequeathed a bunch of money to me so I could support her beloved Sexy Beast in style, and I used an infinitesimal fraction of that dough to buy the phone. No, it's not cheating! The thing's GPS and web access and all those fun gadgets will help me better care for Irene's precious pet. Like, um, if I have to find my way to the animal emergency center or, um, order SB's dog-breath biscuits (they don't work, alas). And yes, Sten Jakobsen approved the purchase. If Irene's lawyer and executor said it was legit, who was I to argue?

But I wasn't thinking about Irene or Sten or my new electronic toy at that moment. I was thinking about that one willow tree on the open lawn about thirty yards off that was definitely, no doubt about it, listing like a drunkard. I almost expected to see it stumble and right itself. As I watched, it gradually leaned farther, ever so slowly.

"Holy cow," I breathed, "that thing's going to fall."

Sexy Beast picked up on my mood and began barking in alarm. I stared dumbfounded as the tree continued to lean. That's when I saw the emerald turf behind it start to bulge as the roots lifted.

I gasped and SB went on high alert, all six pounds eleven ounces of him, prepared to protect me from any and all sources of danger. He followed my wide-eyed stare and the ominous creaking sounds, clearly audible over the sustained wind. In a flash he took off toward the doomed tree.

"SB, no!" I dropped the wine box and sprinted after him, screeching at him to *come!*—a command he usually obeys. Not this time. He turned on the juice, leaping gazelle-like over downed limbs and other obstacles while I struggled to catch up. In no time at all, he stood directly in the path of the killer tree, tail raised, barking as if his life depended on it.

Which it kinda did, since those long, wind-whipped branches soon swept the ground, obscuring his tiny form. I could hear him, but I couldn't see him. My sandaled feet kept slip-sliding on the wet leaves, causing me to waste precious seconds imitating one of those inflatable waving tube men you see at car dealerships.

I thought about the flowers I still delivered every Sunday to three little graves at the Best Friend Pet Cemetery—in perpetuity, as dictated by Irene in her last will and testament. The beneficiaries of those memorial arrangements were Sexy Beast's deceased poodley predecessors: Dr. Strangelove, Annie Hall, and Jaws. I had no intention of adding a fourth bouquet anytime soon. SB was only three years old, and he was going to live to be a crotchety old canine if it killed me. Which, I reflected, it very well might.

The toppling tree gained speed as Sexy Beast continued to scold it from somewhere inside that mass of greenery. The heaving ground behind the tree swelled alarmingly as if an interred corpse had decided that on second thought, he'd rather not spend eternity in that particular spot. Of course, I knew no bodies were buried under this broadloom lawn, but SB's plight sent my imagination into overdrive.

The creaking turned to rapid-fire cracks, each one a gunshot aimed at my darling, dumb little Sexy Beast. I raced to reach him in time, watching the carpetlike sod stretch, then split in a rough semicircle behind the tree as its root system broke free, stealing the trunk's last anchor to the earth. I called on my deepest reserve of strength, diving headlong directly into the path of the collapsing tree.

My body coasted on the wet ground as if I were sliding into home plate, my eyes squeezed shut against the lashing limbs. I made a blind grab toward the sound of SB's frantic barking and snagged a handful of curly poodle fur. Taking advantage of my forward momentum, I tucked Sexy Beast to my chest and rolled away from the center of impact as the percussive energy of the crashing tree shook the ground.

I lay in a gasping heap on the wet grass, clutching SB while my heart did its big drum solo. The dog barked like a maniac. It was the most beautiful sound I'd ever heard. I kissed his damp, furry head.

I managed to make it to my feet, wet, wobbly, and covered in scratches. Sexy Beast gave himself a vigorous shake. He yawned. Just another day protecting his alpha female. Said alpha female saw things differently.

"You know," I grumbled, plucking a willow leaf from my lip, "I almost got killed rescuing your pathetic little butt."

Which demonstrates how much that pathetic little butt means to me, considering the fact that once SB ascends to Doggie Heaven, I'll be free to sell the huge house in Crystal Harbor that Irene willed to me, plus the valuable artwork and furnishings, and to keep what remains of the million and a half smackers she left for the upkeep of the house and her cherished Sexy Beast.

He found the downed tree enthralling, and in truth, so did I. I'd seen uprooted trees before, including one on the way to the cemetery that very day, which had fallen across the road and forced a detour. But I'd never actually witnessed the dramatic event in all its glory. All things considered, it was an experience I could have lived without. Which was closer to the literal truth than I cared to acknowledge.

I followed SB to the base of the willow, thinking that if he sniffed any harder, he'd turn inside out. The tree's underpinnings had erupted from the ground as an intact mass of soil and roots nearly my height, carpeted in pristine sod on the flip side. The contrast was stark: choir practice upstairs and a meth lab in the basement.

The smell of raw earth bombarded my nostrils as I gazed at a part of the tree never meant to be gazed at. This tangle of broken roots represented the death of a living thing. I dealt in death on a daily basis, made my living from it in fact, but this was different. There's something about trees that speaks to the human soul, and the sudden, violent demise of this stately weeping willow left me awestruck.

And no, I didn't haul out my phone to snap a few pictures. I just gaped at the upended jumble of dirt and roots, from cables as thick as my arm to dangling shoestrings. A few rocks peeked out, along with a handful of outraged earthworms. One rock was as big as a good-size cantaloupe, held in place by roots that had snaked through a couple of holes in it.

Reflexively my mind played connect the dots, seeking patterns as if I were lying on my back contemplating stars or cloud formations. I noticed several curved roots that ran parallel to one another. Below those, a straight root seemed to connect, end to end, with another one and finally with a cluster of small, irregular stones.

I stepped back, tilting my head this way and that to take in the whole picture. "Well, this has been vastly entertaining," I told the dog, "but I think I've had about as much fun as I can stand." I hooked the leash to his harness. "Let's finish what we came for and get out of here."

I trudged back to Dorothy's grave, lifted the mostly empty wine box, and pressed the spigot. I stood staring at the headstone but without seeing it. Inside my cranium, roots and rocks played bumper cars, coming together in intriguing ways, coalescing into a whole…

"Nope." I shook my head. "It's preposterous."

Sexy Beast cocked his head at me.

"Insane." I cocked my head right back at him. "Right, little man?"

He gave a sharp, interrogative bark.

"There we go!" I shook the box to ensure it was indeed empty, then turned to the headstone. "Cheers, Dorothy. Enjoy it in good health. Or… oh, you know what I mean. Come on, SB. There's a Vienna sausage in the fridge with your name on it."

I flattened the wine box underfoot, tucked it under my arm, and led Sexy Beast back across the cobblestone footpath to the lawn. I had to pass the downed tree on the way to my car, which was parked on a side street. Deliberately I detoured around the top part of the tree, striding with brio, determined to not so much as glance at those stupid roots. I refused to humor the flight of fancy that had taken the rational part of my brain hostage.

I made it to the cemetery's gate before my brisk pace slowed and finally ground to a halt. I closed my eyes and threw back my head, bemoaning my lack of willpower. I knew I was being ridiculous, but I also knew that if I left without one more peek, I'd never be able to let go of the fantasy that I'd seen something I hadn't.

Which is why I retraced my steps and planted my feet in

front of the upended roots of that defunct weeping willow. SB explored the ground near my feet, managing, as always, to wrap the leash around my ankles.

"All right then." I let out a gusty sigh, exasperated and a little embarrassed by my own foolishness. "Nothing to see here, folks. Move right along."

At first, as I stared at the head-high mass, I saw only random roots poking through the soil, punctuated by a few rocks here and there. I concentrated on the parallel roots I'd noticed before, the ones my imagination had turned into the side of a rib cage. The big rock sat above them. The longer I studied the rock, the more its root-choked holes came to resemble a human skull's eye and nose openings.

Automatically my gaze slid down to an irregular shape that sure looked like the side of a hipbone poking through the dirt. Then came those straight roots, the ones that seemed to connect at an angle, terminating in a cluster of small shapes whose names I'd memorized in Mrs. Deluca's high school biology class.

Metatarsus. Phalanges.

I heard a low, throaty *"No no no no no..."* and realized it came from my own throat. I swallowed hard. SB, exhibiting his customary pack-member empathy, propped his front paws on my legs and whined.

The skeleton lay in a reclining position on his—her?— side, held in place by the tree roots that had grown around and through it. At the end of a bent arm, fisted finger bones clutched a gnarled root. Or so it appeared. Distractedly I realized the root must have grown through the fist. Bits of rotted cloth flapped in the breeze.

My voice was a quavering whisper. "Who in the world are you?"

2

It's Ironic!

"I KNOW WHAT this is." Officer Geri Marvin gave a decisive nod, her stubby arms crossed over her chest. "I saw it on the Science Channel."

Her partner, Howie Werker, quirked a dubious eyebrow at her. "You watch the Science Channel, Geri?"

She rolled her eyes. "I saw it somewhere. I'm telling you, this is one of those, like, antique guys. Like Kennedy Man. This stiff is thousands of years old."

"Kennewick Man," Detective Bonnie Hernandez corrected without taking her eyes off the skeleton tangled in the upended root mass. She leaned over the cratered ground in front of it to get a better look. "And you're jumping to conclusions, Geri."

It was the first time I'd seen Bonnie's feet shod in anything other than designer pumps. In deference to the post-storm mess, she wore practical but fashionable flats with a taupe pencil skirt and a sleeveless, cranberry-colored shell that appeared to be finely knitted silk. Her short, dark hair was tucked behind her ears, displaying a pair of elegantly understated garnet earrings. Next to her, I looked like pre-pumpkin Cinderella in ratty old cargo shorts and a pajama top.

Now, hear me out! Technically it was a pj top, but it was

styled just like a T-shirt. Not that any of my real tees are patterned with lots of fluffy cartoon sheep jumping over lots of little cartoon fences. It was an ironic purchase! Anyway, I'd let my dirty laundry pile up and this was my last clean top and I didn't expect to run into anyone today and…

Oh, shut up.

Conspicuously absent from Bonnie's neat, businesslike ensemble—conspicuous to me at least—was the four-karat engagement ring Dominic Faso had placed on her finger last Christmas. She'd called off the wedding in April, although Dom claimed he'd been the one to pull the plug. I knew him well enough to call BS on that one. He and I had, after all, been friends since middle school. Plus I was, you know, married to him once.

Okay, the divorce was a long time ago, seventeen years to be precise, and I regretted the split from the instant I signed the papers that turned me from Jane Faso back into Jane Delaney. It's an old story. I wanted kids. He didn't. I never got over Dom and never satisfied my maternal instinct, even as he cycled through two subsequent wives and three—yeah, you guessed it—kids. What can I tell you? I'm a slow learner.

Naturally, the instant I finally decided I could live without Dom was the exact same instant he decided he couldn't live without me. That was three months ago, and he'd spent those three months wooing me.

I like the sound of that. I don't think I'd ever been wooed before. I could get used to it.

Howie nodded toward the skeleton. "What if this guy's an Indian? Native American, whatever. If we're standing on an old Indian burial ground, some tribe will get its panties in a twist and the town'll have a nasty fight on its hands." Howie was a tall, good-looking, dark-skinned man whose neat beard sported a dusting of gray. I figured he must be close to having his twenty years in and wondered if he was planning to retire from the force anytime soon.

"Yeah, well." Geri reached behind her police cap to tighten her brown ponytail. "I'll bet you a pitcher at Murray's that this guy's some kind of ancient caveman." Murray's Pub was a local watering hole, the most downscale and therefore coziest bar in town. That evening, as on every Wednesday, the pub would be packed for the weekly trivia contest.

Bonnie didn't respond to the wager. Somehow I doubted she was a beer drinker. Howie, however, was all over it. "Add a plate of spicy crinkle fries and you've got yourself a bet," he said.

"So what now? We call in an archaeologist or what?" Geri stepped into the raw crater to get a better look at Crystal Harbor Man.

Officer Howie Werker and Detective Bonnie Hernandez shouted at her to get out of there.

Geri hopped back. "What?"

"This is a crime scene," Bonnie said. I could tell she wanted to add, *you moron.* When Geri opened her mouth to object, Bonnie added, "Until and unless the ME determines otherwise, this immediate area is to be treated as a crime scene."

The young cop blew a frustrated breath. Clearly she wasn't accustomed to reining in her tongue.

A voice called, "Nice day for a dead body!" I turned to see Mayor Sophie Halperin slogging across the lawn. She wasn't alone. Dom was with her. SB howled his warbling welcome, turning excitedly from his beloved Dom to me to announce the momentous event.

In the past, my heart would have done a little flip on spying my ex. Not that I wasn't glad to see him. I still considered him a good friend, though perhaps no longer my closest confidant, and for sure no longer the man I ceaselessly pined for. It was progress, I knew, but after seventeen years, it felt strange to be on the receiving end of unrequited longing. A nagging voice deep inside told me I should jump at this long-awaited chance to tie him down before some other woman beat me to it. Dominic Faso never stayed single for long. It was now or never.

Sophie and Dom offered cursory greetings to the rest of us before moving to the edge of the crater to view the phenomenon for themselves. Their perplexed frowns remained fixed in place as they scrutinized the mass of roots. They weren't seeing it. After a minute, their eyes widened in unison.

"Wow," Dom said.

"I'll be damned," Sophie said.

Dom looked his fill, then left the mayor standing there gawking. He approached me and went in for a lip-lock. I turned and let his kiss graze my cheek. Out of the corner of my eye I noticed Bonnie noticing her ex-fiancé's affectionate attentions toward Ex-wife Number One.

He took in my bedraggled, scraped-up appearance. "You look like you've been rolling around on the ground."

"It's called boneyard aerobics. You should try it sometime."

Dom was tall, with curly dark hair and deep espresso eyes that nearly always held a corner-crinkling smile. He gave my back a little rub, then took note of the garment under his palm. "Are those sheep, Janey?" he asked. "Is that a pajama—"

"It's ironic," I snapped, shrugging off his hand. "What are you doing here?"

He squatted to give SB some love. The dog bowed his head in abject submission, his customary posture in the presence of those more alpha than he. It was not an exclusive club—Sexy Beast is content with his self-appointed position at the bottom of the pack and has zero ambition for higher office.

"I was meeting with Sophie about the street fair when the call came in about our bony friend here."

Dom was a major donor, organizer, and food supplier for the annual Crystal Harbor street fair, which was the following Sunday. He owned a bunch of health-food restaurants called Janey's Place. Yep, he'd come up with the name back in the Pleistocene when we were still dating. The flagship store was located on Main Street here in Crystal Harbor, but over the past two decades Janey's Place had grown into the most successful health-food chain in the New York metropolitan area. My ex was a millionaire many times over.

Good thing I divorced him while he was still poor. Wouldn't want any of that pesky alimony compromising my scrappy, can-do attitude and proud self-reliance.

Yeah, more irony. Sue me.

Sophie was a short, well-padded woman in her mid-fifties, with graying hair and a spooky way of knowing everything that went on in her town. She was a friend of mine as well as a regular client. She'd be up for reelection next year, and as a new resident of Crystal Harbor, I'd finally be able to vote for her. If it were up to me, Sophie Halperin would be mayor for life.

She turned to the detective. "What are your thoughts, Bonnie? Don't see any crime-scene tape."

"There's a chance it's an ancient burial. I'm reserving judgment until Cliff gets here." Dr. Clifford Reddy was the medical examiner. He'd be the one to determine whether Geri would drink free at Murray's that night.

Sophie indicated the skeleton's position. "Guy looks pretty relaxed. Like he's lazing around with a good cigar." She turned to me. "You found him, huh?"

"Yep." SB was eager to investigate the crater, but I kept him close to me with a shortened leash. I didn't need him doing his business on what might turn out to be a crime scene. "The tree went down and there he was. Or she." I shrugged.

"Well." Sophie propped her fists on her ample hips and addressed the bones. "How the heck did you end up here, fella? That's what I want to know."

She was interrupted by a distinctive deep rumble, which grew louder by the second. Geri squinted into the distance. "Does the ME ride a motorcycle?"

Sophie snorted. "That, I'd pay money to see. Cliff Reddy makes me look like a famine victim."

I followed Geri's gaze to the footpath. I recognized that big honkin' Harley. My heart did its overdue flip, though I managed to keep my expression neutral. "It's Martin McAuliffe," I announced.

"McAuliffe," Dom sneered. He wasn't smiling now. "Perfect."

Detective Hernandez eyed Martin with distaste as he rolled to a stop on the cobblestones a few yards away. "Where's his priest getup?" she asked. The first time Bonnie had met him, Martin had been impersonating a man of the cloth. He'd also been advising me to keep my trap shut during her interrogation of me as a murder suspect, much to her annoyance. I just knew the lovely detective was looking forward to the day she could pin something serious on him. She turned to Howie. "Go guard the entrance. Don't let anyone else in except Dr. Reddy."

Howie took off at a trot as Martin dismounted and removed his helmet. No helmet hair for the padre, whose sandy locks were shorn close to the scalp.

Geri swaggered over to him, gesticulating. "This path is for pedestrians, sir. Vehicular traffic is not permitted."

His response was a dazzling, flirtatious, blue-eyed grin. "Good afternoon, Officer."

Unmoved, she hitched herself up to her full five one. "Sir, I must ask you to leave at once. This is a crime scene."

"Absolutely, Officer," he said, while striding toward our little group.

Bonnie greeted him with, "Let me guess. You have a police scanner." Her slight Dominican accent had grown more pronounced, a reliable barometer of her irritation.

"You're a vision today, Detective," he said. "You should wear red more often."

Geri stalked up to him, her little hand on her holstered gun. "Sir, I'm not going to tell you again—"

"Geri," Bonnie interrupted, "go help Howie secure the gate."

"But we can't let anyone just—"

Bonnie silenced her with a look. Grumbling, the cop trudged after her partner.

Martin and Dom exchanged barely civil nods. Neither offered his hand. Sophie gave Martin a warm hug. She walloped his back. "Haven't seen you in ages. Where've you been keeping yourself?"

I could have told her, at the risk of embarrassing Martin. He lived with his mom in a working-class neighborhood on the South Shore. I knew little else about him except that he tended bar at an upscale Irish pub in Southampton. Or at least he did three months ago when I first met him. His easy familiarity with criminal subterfuge, police procedure, and oh yeah, breaking and entering offered tantalizing hints to his background.

Despite the fact he was a riddle wrapped in a mystery inside a… well, inside a damn fine package, Martin and I actually had a history. No, not that kind of history, so don't even start. We came close to buying the farm together a few months earlier. The dirt farm, as in six or more feet under. That kind of shared close call should bring two people closer together, but the fact is, I'd seen almost nothing of the padre since then.

"Hey, Jane." He bent to greet a fawning Sexy Beast, while giving me an appreciative once-over. "Cool top."

"Go to hell."

"I'm working on it." He strolled to the upended base of the willow tree. All eyes homed in on him in anticipation of a lingering scrutiny followed by the inevitable *aha* moment. Instead he took one brief glance and casually announced, "He's wearing a ring."

"What?" Bonnie said.

"Check it out." He pointed, and the rest of us gathered at the edge of the potentially evidence-rich crater to look.

"Not seeing it." Sophie squinted. "Oh, wait…"

"I think you're right," Bonnie said. "It's crusted with dirt, but there's definitely something there."

I saw it too, now that I was looking for it. Dom stood

closest to the finger bones. He leaned over and started scraping dirt from the ring.

"Stop!" Bonnie cried. "This is a crime scene, Dom!" Sexy Beast barked, reinforcing her point.

He straightened, palms raised in apology. "Sorry, I just—"

The finger bone plopped into the crater at our feet. Bonnie cursed, spearing her ex-fiancé with a look guaranteed to shrivel his soul. Or something.

The five of us stood staring at the little bone, still encircled by the dirt-clogged ring.

Proximal phalanx, that's what it was. Mrs. Deluca would be proud.

"Oh, what the hell." Sophie bent with a grunt and reached for the bone. "Scene's already compromised."

I saw Bonnie stiffen at this further violation of protocol, but Sophie was the mayor, and alienating her would not be politic, and it probably didn't matter anyway. So she gritted her teeth and watched Sophie straighten, pull a tissue out of her pants pocket, and scrub away at the ring.

The rest of us gathered around her, eager for a peek at the long-buried artifact. If handling a human finger bone grossed Sophie out, she gave no indication, not that I'd ever known her to be squeamish. As she rubbed, the glint of yellow gold emerged.

The wide ring wasn't smooth. Some sort of design was carved into it. Sophie concentrated on a section, at one point spitting on the tissue to get into the grooves. Bonnie gave a longsuffering shake of her head, but really, it's not as if the crime lab was going to get usable DNA from a ring buried under a tree for who knew how long. I think.

Abruptly Sophie stopped scrubbing the ring. She just stood

there staring at it. The patch she'd cleaned bore an abstract openwork design that resembled leaves on a vine. The rest of us leaned in close. For some reason, Sexy Beast whined, pawing Sophie's leg.

Bonnie spoke first. "I think it's safe to say we're not looking at ancient grave goods."

"Or Native American," I added. "I guess Howie and Tina will have to split the bar tab."

"Better keep an eye on McAuliffe here." Dom gave me a secret half smile. "Wouldn't want this piece of jewelry to walk away."

An inside joke. Well, hardy har har. I wish I'd never told him about the incident last spring when Martin strolled out of a wake at Ahearn's Funeral Home with a brooch he'd filched from the occupant of the casket. But only because I didn't get to it first.

"Probably engraved on the inside," Martin said. "Hard to fence. Not that I know about such things." He smiled sweetly at Bonnie, whose baleful expression told him to enjoy his smart-ass freedom while he could.

Sophie had remained silent. I now saw that her summer tan had lost a good deal of color. Her lips were white. SB continued to whine, and I realized his agitation had to do with Sophie's emotional state. There are times I would swear that animal is telepathic.

"Sophie?" I placed my hand on her shoulder. "What is it?"

She shook her head, still staring at the ring. She opened her mouth to speak, but no words came out. I tried to take the finger bone from her, worried she'd drop it in the grass, but she wasn't letting go. Her hands felt like ice. She looked a little unsteady on her feet. Dom put his arm around her back, clearly prepared to catch her if she headed south.

She shook her head again and looked into my eyes. "It's not possible," she whispered.

I glanced from her stricken face to the ring and back again. "What's not possible, Sophie?"

"It's not possible," she repeated. "He's dead."

The rest of us looked from her to the skeleton. Yes, he was dead, no doubt about it.

"He killed himself. Drowned," she said.

Bonnie squeezed her arm. "Who are you talking about, Sophie? Who killed himself?"

"Ernie." Slowly Sophie reached into the neckline of her polo shirt and withdrew a thin gold chain. Hanging from the chain was a ring identical to the one in her hand, but smaller. "My husband."

3

Dumb Little Virgin

"MARIA THOUGHT YOU could use some nourishment." I set the tray on Sophie's tile-topped patio table and watched her toss a leafy limb onto the growing pile of storm debris in her backyard. "And a pitcher of mojitos."

Sophie barely glanced my way as she picked up a rake.

"It's guacamole," I said, hoping to tempt her away from the yard work she'd been at for two hours, according to Maria. Sophie had never been able to resist Maria's locally famous guac.

I stood on my friend's sprawling, charmingly freeform slate patio, feeling helpless to do anything for her. I'd known little about her two marriages, aside from the fact that the first one had ended when her young husband had committed suicide and that she was divorced from husband number two. Never had kids. Sophie was a dynamo, perpetually grounded in the present while working hard to shape the future. She didn't dwell on the past, which I'd always considered a favorable quality. I admired her for it.

I wished she'd do some therapeutic dwelling now. Maria was concerned about her employer's state of mind, and so was I. I crossed the lawn to where Sophie yanked the rake through the pristine grass. She'd already picked up every loose leaf and twig from yesterday's storm. What she hoped to accomplish at this point was beyond me.

I grabbed hold of the rake, forcing her to pause. "Sophie, come on. It's hot. You need a break."

She looked around the large yard as if seeking something else to do. "The cats."

"You already cleaned around the cats." And the cats had sat still as stone while she'd done so because, well, they were carved from stone. Marble, to be precise. A pair of life-size memorial statues patiently sitting out eternity in the shade of the house and about a zillion fluffy hydrangeas. Sometime in the far distant past, a white cat and a black cat went to their maker, and their owners—aka their staff, as the old gag goes—placed these statues in honor of them.

The white cat reclined as if on a divan, licking her paw. After a century and a half or so, you'd think it would be clean by now. The black cat crouched, preparing to pounce, its gaze fixed on a hapless, invisible sparrow. The statues were lifelike enough to scare away real sparrows, as graceful and softly curved as the long-gone pets they memorialized.

I said, "And you've cleaned the pond, too, I see. Why didn't you leave all this for the gardening service?"

It was close to seven in the evening, the sun still strong in the cloudless western sky. Sophie had shown up at her office in the Town Hall as usual that morning. I'm told she'd thrown herself into her work, not stopping to rest or even eat lunch. Now here she was, red-faced and sweating from exertion. I was afraid she'd keel over from a heart attack.

"All right, that's enough." I wrested the rake from her as gently as I could and steered her toward the patio, shaded by a striped awning. The farmhouse it was attached to was one of Crystal Harbor's historic homes, dating from the 1830s and built for a scion of the town's founding family. It was large, homey, and venerable enough to have a name: Nevins House. "Let's go attack that guacamole," I said. "Have you eaten today?"

"What? Sure. I guess."

"Uh-huh." A pair of padded chaise lounges occupied part of the patio, with a small side table between them. I adjusted one of the chaises to a semi-reclining position and made Sophie sit back and put her feet up. I moved the food tray to the side table and perched on the edge of the neighboring chaise.

"Here." I handed her a paper napkin to mop her sweaty face while I poured two tall mojitos and passed one over. "Drink up."

She did as ordered, then sank back against the chaise with an unhappy sigh. Her eyes were closed. I gave her a couple of minutes while I piled guacamole and homemade tortilla chips on a small plate. When she opened her eyes, I handed her the plate. She let it rest untouched on her lap, which more than anything indicated her state of mind.

I scooped some guacamole on a chip and shoved it into my mouth, which proceeded to have a guacgasm. Maria had not lost her touch. Sophie had hired her three months earlier after the murder of Maria's longtime employer, Irene McAuliffe. Sophie had as much as admitted to me that Maria's guacamole had played an outsize role in the decision.

I laid my hand over Sophie's on the arm of her chaise. "I've been thinking. Isn't it possible someone else had the same exact ring that you and Ernie did? Maybe it's not him."

She shook her head. "Ernie's mom had a jewelry artist

design them exclusively for us. Only two exist in the world. Besides…" She closed her eyes again. "They checked his dental records. It's him."

Conflicting facts bounced around my brainpan like ping-pong balls. I gave my head a little shake to clear it. "Okay, then… his suicide… ?"

"Faked, obviously." Sophie looked from the untouched plate in her lap to her drink. She lifted the drink and took a healthy swig. "By whoever killed Ernie and shoved him in that hole thirty-two years ago."

I shivered, though it was easily eighty degrees. A mosquito touched down on Sophie's ankle. I batted it away. "Eat," I said.

Sophie stared at her plate with unfocused eyes. "Massive blunt-force trauma to the cranium. Someone caved in his head." She looked up. "This is confidential info, by the way— Bonnie's keeping the details hush-hush for the sake of the investigation. I only found out 'cause Cliff Reddy blabbed it to me before Bonnie could muzzle him. So no spreading it around."

"Of course." I laid my hand on hers again. "I'm so sorry, Sophie."

She gave a little shrug. "Happened a long time ago."

I didn't need to state the obvious. It's one thing to recover from the suicide of your young husband. It's another altogether to discover he was murdered. A thing like that was sure to trigger a renewed bout of grieving.

She said, "They found the suicide note on his boat… drifting in the ocean off Montauk the morning after he went missing. Thirty-foot cabin cruiser. We spent a lot of time on that thing…" She trailed off.

"Obviously his body never turned up," I said.

"Cops figured he tied some kind of weight to himself."

"Was Ernie depressed?" I asked. "Were you surprised by his supposed suicide?"

Sophie took a deep breath. She looked at me levelly. "Ernie was troubled—I found that out later—but he never showed it, and I never imagined he'd off himself. Wasn't that kind of guy." She shrugged. "But there was that note. No one questioned it. Except Teddy."

"Teddy?"

"Ernie's mom." Sophie grimaced. "Theodora Augusta Waterfield. Mother of the freakin' year."

"She was suspicious?" I asked.

Sophie nodded. She finally seemed to notice the plate on her lap, and dipped a chip. "She couldn't believe her Ernie would take his own life. We all thought she was in denial. Turns out the old witch had the right idea. Who knew?"

"What about Ernie's dad? Did he share his wife's suspicions?"

"He died when Ernie was two years old," she said. "Teddy raised him as a single mother."

I tried to swat a mosquito dive-bombing my arm, and missed. "Is she still alive?"

"Far as I know," Sophie said.

"Where does she live?"

"Here in Crystal Harbor. Out at the edge of town on Wallings Drive."

That surprised me. "How come I've never met her?"

"Keeps to herself," Sophie said, around a mouthful of guac. "Which is fine by me."

Maria emerged from the house. "Are you okay out here?"

Sophie turned to look at her. "We're fine, Maria. You

should have gone home hours ago."

Maria shooed away her employer's concern. "There's some fried chicken and grilled veggies in the fridge, when you're ready for them. More than enough for two. You can eat it cold or nuke it, either way. And there's still some tres leches cake left."

I groaned in anticipated pleasure. I'd tasted Maria's tres leches cake.

"Thanks, hon." Sophie looked her housekeeper in the eye. "I'm all right, really. And Jane is here. She'll make sure I don't waste away." She patted her ample gut. Maria was about to take her leave when Sophie said, "You know what I could use? Cigar. Skeeters are out in force tonight." As Maria retreated into the house, she told me, "Smoke helps keep the bugs away."

"You smoke cigars?" I shouldn't have been surprised.

"Only outside the house. Fella I was seeing last summer got me into the habit. Thanks, hon," she said as Maria set a wooden humidor, heavy crystal ashtray, and cigar paraphernalia on the side table.

Sophie almost never alluded to her dating life. She knew everyone and everything going on in town, but also knew how to keep the flow of juicy information from becoming a two-way street.

"I'll see you in the morning," Maria said. "If you need me to come earlier than nine, or if you can think of anything you'd like me to pick up—"

Sophie took her housekeeper's hand and squeezed it. "I'm fine, Maria. Really. You go home and take care of that fine man of yours."

I caught Maria's eye and nodded, silently letting her know

I'd stick around and see to Sophie's emotional well-being. Maria smiled her thanks and bade us good-night.

Sophie set her half-full plate on the table. She flipped open the humidor and made a help-yourself gesture. I answered with a no-thanks gesture. The appealing scent of expensive tobacco competed with the green and flowering perfumes of midsummer.

She chose a midsize cigar with a dark wrapper and clipped it. "Bonnie stopped by the office today. Asked a ton of questions and, get this, requested that I not take any trips while the investigation is ongoing."

My mouth sagged open. "She considers you a suspect?"

Sophie shrugged. "Guess so." She placed the cigar between her lips and fired up the lighter, expertly turning the cigar as the tip started to glow.

"But… but she was there when you recognized that ring," I said. "You were practically in shock. What, she thought you were faking it?"

Sophie sagged back on the chaise and blew a smoke ring. The smoke smelled good, like earthy incense. A fine cigar like that probably cost what I spend on a pair of shoes. Granted, I shop clearance sales, but still.

"Bonnie's a detective working a murder case," she said. "Detectives need suspects. Guessed she looked around and figured I'd do."

"For starters, maybe. 'Don't leave town,'" I mocked. "Who does she think she's talking to? You're the mayor! You're on her side!" I nodded toward Sophie's thin gold neck chain. "For crying out loud, you still wear the wedding ring Ernie gave you."

Sophie drew the chain out of her neckline. It was bare. No

ring. "Bonnie needed it for comparison. She'll give it back," she added as I drew myself up to renew the rant. "Proud to have you in my corner, Delaney. Don't go storming the police station yet. Bonnie's only doing her job."

I exhaled a frustrated sigh. "I suppose it can't be easy with a thirty-year-old murder. Where do you start?"

"At the obvious place." She spread her arms. "The deceased's spouse."

"Did Ernie have life insurance?"

"That was her first question." Sophie shook her head. "We were kids. In our twenties. Didn't think about stuff like that."

"Well… and if you don't want to talk about this, it's okay—"

Sophie waved off my polite concern. "Fire away."

"Was Ernie well off? Did you inherit big when he died?"

Despite the fact she'd just given me carte blanche to ask questions, she looked uncomfortable. "It's complicated." She'd drained her glass. I refilled it. Maybe a little more rum, in combination with the calming effect of the cigar, would keep her talking and keep that rake out of her hands.

"I was a poor kid from Colorado," Sophie said. "Ernie came from old New York money. His family had been in Crystal Harbor since before the Revolution. I'm pretty sure they were on the wrong side of that one, by the way. Anyway, I met him a few months after college graduation. A Halloween party. He wore a skeleton costume." She winced.

"Was it love at first sight?" I asked.

"For me it was. I know you'll find this hard to believe, but I was about as naïve and innocent as they came back then. Shy as hell."

I choked back a laugh. "You?"

She shrugged, smiling. "Late bloomer. What can I tell you? I'd had two dates before I met Ernie, both disasters. I wasn't the glamorous sexpot you see before you today."

"And Ernie was, what, this sophisticated, experienced hunk who showed you the ways of the world?"

Her smile softened. "Not exactly. He was… well, he was a good friend. Kind. Fun to be with. I was this dorky kid from the sticks and he introduced me to New York. Broadway. The museums. Jazz clubs. He used to take me on these walking tours of bright, beautiful Manhattan. I ate it up."

"When did it become more serious?" I asked. "You said you were just friends at first?"

"Ernie knew how I felt about him. How could he not? I didn't know anything about manipulating men or masking my true feelings—none of those games. I was always afraid that today would be the day we'd have The Conversation." When I gave a quizzical look, she continued, "You know. 'You're a sweet kid, Sophie, but I don't think about you that way. Have a nice life.'"

"But…" I prompted.

"But that spring, when we'd been hanging together for seven, eight months, suddenly he kisses me." Sophie's expression softened in reminiscence. "Wasn't much of a kiss, but to me it was everything. I was over the moon."

I grinned. "Little Sophie from the sticks had a boyfriend. A *rich* boyfriend."

"Things moved pretty fast then. Before I knew it, we were engaged. I met his mom."

"Did you get along with her?"

"If you call being too terrified to speak 'getting along.' After a while I realized it wasn't just me. Teddy intimidated everyone. First person I met who just plain didn't give a crap what others thought of her. I'll say this for the old bitch—she taught me an important lesson. You don't have to be liked by everyone. That kind of neediness keeps you from being effective, getting things done."

"Well, maybe you didn't learn the lesson all that well," I said, "because I don't know anyone who doesn't like Sophie Halperin."

"Didn't say it's bad to be liked. You treat people decently, with respect and compassion, most folks will think you're a swell person. Teddy was smoking in the girls' room when they covered that chapter." Sophie raised her glass in salute. "To Theodora Augusta Waterfield. And keeping out of her crosshairs."

"So Ernie left you well off," I said. "I figured it had to be either husband number one or husband number two."

Sophie looked like she'd bitten into a sour apple. "Husband number two is a deadbeat loser. Always has been. Spent his whole adult life in a series of crappy jobs. At the moment he's selling used cars in Sandy Cove."

I knew Sandy Cove well. I'd rented a basement apartment in that blue-collar South Shore town before inheriting Irene's five-acre estate in Crystal Harbor.

"Why'd you marry him?" I asked.

She offered a self-deprecatory smile. "The lure of the bad boy. What can I tell you?"

"'Nuf said." I knew all about that particular brand of attraction, thanks to Martin McAuliffe.

"Fell for Dean right after Ernie died," she said. "Should've given myself more time. But I was a dumb little virgin and he knew just how to play me."

"Uh, wait a minute." I made a time-out *T* with my hands. "I assume you're using 'virgin' in the figurative sense?"

"That would be 'virgin' in the literal sense," Sophie said. "As in Ernie and I never did the deed. As in I had no inkling he was gay when I married him."

"Oh boy." I sucked air through my teeth, my expression pained. "So he didn't even, you know, go through the motions?"

She shook her head. "I always suspected he was holding a torch for someone else. If so, it was a guy."

"And Teddy knew her son was gay?"

Sophie nodded. "Never accepted it, though. Never accepted *him*. Insisted that once he found the right girl and settled down... well, you know. All that 'the love of a good woman will cure you' crap. Really messed him up. Anyway, since you ask, Ernie wasn't the one who left me well off. Once he'd graduated from college, he was on his own financially. Aspiring songwriters don't exactly rake it in. I was barely supporting us on my paralegal's salary." She'd worked for Sten Jakobsen's law firm back then.

"So if you didn't inherit from your first husband, and your second husband was a deadbeat loser..." I left the sentence hanging.

Sophie looked me in the eye. "I accepted three million dollars from Teddy Waterfield to remain married to her son."

My mouth worked, but no sound came out. Finally I managed, "Does he have a gay brother?"

She smiled. "Ernie was an only child, his mother's little prince until he 'decided' to break her heart by becoming a homosexual." She hesitated before adding, "Want you to know it wasn't an easy decision for me. To take her money. Once I discovered my new husband was gay, I figured, hell, I had to divorce him. Not that I didn't still love Ernie, as a friend. I loved and respected him."

"Even though he married you under false pretenses?"

Sophie puffed her cigar. That thing was smelling better and better. "Yeah, well, that mother of his, she did a real number on him. Not that he gets a free pass or anything, but you have to look at his actions in context. Anyway, when I examined my options, it came down to either—" she raised two fingers in turn "—spend my life with my best friend and three million smackers, or divorce him and hope to find a 'real man' I might like half as much while spending the rest of my life scraping out a living like I'd done up till then."

I laid my hand on hers. "Sophie, I don't think less of you for the decision you made."

She stared off into the distance. "Sometimes I do, but it's done. No calling it back."

"At least you were able to quit your job, right?"

She shrugged. "I could've if I'd wanted to, but I didn't want to. Sten needed me and I liked the work. I'm not suited to filling my days with shopping and white-glove lunches. It's not me."

I tried to imagine Sophie Halperin donning a pair of delicate white gloves. Perhaps at gunpoint.

Back to the issue at hand. "You mentioned that Ernie was troubled?"

She hesitated. "There was a… an incident, something that happened when Ernie was in college. Didn't know about it when I married him. Teddy hushed the whole thing up. You can do that when you have enough dough. And Ernie… I guess he was too ashamed to tell even me. It all came out after he killed himself—*supposedly* killed himself, I mean. The fake suicide note said that Ernie's guilt over this incident drove him to end his life."

I waited. She took a healthy swig of her drink and said, "It was your basic stupid prank gone wrong. There was this guy Ernie knew in college. Tim something. Ernie took him out on his boat one night. They were both loaded. Tim dove into the ocean for a swim, and apparently Ernie thought it would be funny to head back in and leave his friend to swim to shore. They were less than a mile out, and Tim was on the swim team." After a moment she said, "His body washed up the next day. Blood alcohol level was off the charts."

"Was Ernie just as drunk?" I asked.

"Who knows? Took a while for the authorities to ask around and find someone who spied his boat in the vicinity around ten p.m. By the time they pounded on Ernie's dorm door, he was sober. Didn't try to deny it. Thought Tim had hitched a ride and made it back to campus okay."

"Where did they take the boat out?" I asked.

"Montauk. Ernie's mom used to have a little summer place out there, and that's where he kept the cabin cruiser."

"Which brings us back to his murder," I said. "Whoever killed Ernie took the key to his boat."

"And then left it out in the ocean with the fake suicide note and, what, rowed a dinghy back to shore?" Sophie said. "Also, the killer used Ernie's typewriter. Cops were able to determine that the note was typed on it."

"Not handwritten?" I asked. "Isn't that strange?"

"Not for Ernie. He typed everything. Miserable handwriting. Used this big old antique typewriter that belonged to his dad."

I gazed at the house. Couldn't help myself.

"Yeah, I know." Sophie's expression was bleak. "He was probably killed in there since the killer used his typewriter and boat key. If so, the guy cleaned up after himself."

I shuddered, thinking about the mess that would have resulted from bashing someone's brains in. Sophie had always loved her rambling old home. Now she'd never be able to enter a room without wondering if something unspeakable had taken place there thirty-two years earlier.

"You know," I said, "maybe I will try one of those cigars. A little one."

She grinned. "I've corrupted the Death Diva. My job here is done."

"A *little* one," I repeated as she reached into the humidor. The cigar she handed me was petite, with a pale wrapper. I put it to my nose and inhaled the pleasant, mild scent. Sophie showed me how to clip and light it and warned me not to inhale. I leaned back against my chaise, sipping my mojito and smoking my cigar. It felt deliciously decadent.

"So when did Tim drown?" I asked. "You said they were in college?"

"Beginning of Ernie's senior year. Peconic University out on the east end. He would've gotten kicked out—hell, would've gone to jail probably—if Teddy hadn't stepped in. Hired a world-class lawyer. Donated a new library to the school. Managed to hush the whole thing up and keep it out of the news."

"What about Tim's family? How could she keep them quiet about it?"

Sophie's look said, *How do you think?*

"Oh." I nodded wryly. "She bought them off." Just like

she'd bought off Sophie to stay married to her son.

"She bought them all off." She shook her head in disgust. "Her specialty."

"You said the fake suicide note blamed it on guilt over Tim's death?"

She nodded. "Guess the killer figured there'd be fewer questions if it looked like Ernie could no longer live with himself."

"Then whoever did it had to have known about the Tim incident despite Teddy's cover-up," I said.

"I know, I thought about that."

I puffed the cigar, trying without success to make smoke rings like Sophie's. "How much time elapsed between Tim's death and Ernie's?"

She thought for a moment. "Three years. Almost. Meanwhile I met Ernie and married him. Had no inkling about the Tim thing till Ernie died."

"The story got out then?"

She nodded grimly. "Hit the news big-time. It was right there in the suicide note, like I said. Reporters dug up all the grisly details—including how Teddy hushed it up, the whole gay thing. That more than anything gave her fits, that now the world knew her precious Ernie played for the other team. The press spun it into this big, sordid story, with little regard for the facts. Claimed Ernie had a thing for Tim and killed him out of rage at being rejected."

I had to ask. "Was Tim gay? I mean, were he and Ernie…"

Sophie was already shaking her head. "Just college pals. Tim was straight. Left a pregnant girlfriend, as if this story could get more tragic. You probably know her. Lacey Vargas. Owns the lingerie store next to Janey's Place."

I gasped, which turned out to be not such a good thing while puffing a cigar. My coughing fit took me out of action for a minute. Sophie shoved my drink at me. It didn't help. Finally I managed, "Lacey? I had no idea. I mean, not that I knew about any of this, but…"

Over the years I'd occasionally shopped at Lacey's store, called UnderStatements. Those purchases of pretty, pricey undies always coincided with a hot date. Considering the pitiful state of my checking account and the even more pitiful number of said hot dates—due to my beyond-pitiful longing for my ex-husband—my collection of fancy unmentionables would fit in a shoe box. With the shoes still in it.

I said, "So Tim and Lacey were from Crystal Harbor too?"

Sophie shook her head. "Some working-class town in Jersey. Tim got a scholarship to Peconic and that's how he met Ernie."

I frowned, knowing UnderStatements had been in that spot on Main Street for decades. "You'd think Lacey would want to avoid the man responsible for her boyfriend's death, not open a business right here in his town. Wait. I never knew her last name. You said it's Vargas? Is she related to Porter Vargas?"

Sophie tapped her cigar on the ashtray. "His wife."

"Ah, so that would explain… but some coincidence, huh? She meets and marries a guy from the same town as—"

"Not really," Sophie said. "Porter and Ernie grew up together here in Crystal Harbor. Lifelong pals. Both ended up going to school at Peconic. When Tim drowned, Porter went to the funeral. Felt bad for Tim's family. Told me that later, after Ernie died. Said Ernie felt bad for them too, but of course, he wouldn't be welcome at the funeral of the fella he..." Her expression was bleak. "Ernie was such a sweet, sensitive guy. The guilt had to be eating him alive."

"So Porter went to Tim's funeral," I said, "and that's when he met Lacey. But you said she was already pregnant with Tim's baby?" I noticed the inch-long ash on my cigar and swung it toward the ashtray, only to watch the ash plop into Sophie's drink.

She laughed. "There are more subtle ways of telling me I've had enough."

"Sorry." I started to rise. "I'll get you another one."

"Forget it. I really have had enough." She grabbed my arm and pulled me back down. I sat on the edge of my chaise. "Yeah," she said, "Porter and Lacey got married within a couple of months of meeting. Guess her pregnancy hurried the courtship along. Things were different back then. Unwed motherhood was still stigmatized and all."

"Porter's fairly well off," I said. "His grandfather started Vargas Sporting Goods, right?"

"Yep. When he met Lacey he was already the heir apparent of a wildly successful multinational retail empire."

"That kind of thing's got to grab a girl's attention," I said. "Even one who's grieving for her baby daddy. Though I assume Teddy paid off Lacey as well? To keep her mouth shut about how her boyfriend died?"

Sophie nodded. "Everyone close to Tim who'd been privy to the truth got a little windfall. In return they had to sign an airtight nondisclosure agreement drawn up by Teddy's dream team."

My cigar was short now, the smoke hot, so I figured I'd had enough and set it on the ashtray. "You said Teddy never believed her son committed suicide."

"She was convinced from the get-go that Ernie was murdered." Sophie reached for her glass and made an oh-yeah face when she spied the cigar ash swirling in it. "By yours truly."

"Wait, what?" I sat up straight. "Teddy thought you killed her son?"

"Sure did. Tried hard to get me arrested back then," Sophie said. "Probably hectoring Bonnie this very minute to slap the cuffs on me now that the body's turned up."

"Why on earth does she think you'd do a thing like that?"

"Remember the three mill she gave me? Well, I had to sign a contract. If I divorced Ernie, I'd forfeit the money."

"But if he died?"

Sophie shrugged. "The widow gets to keep the cash. Teddy was only concerned with my leaving him. Got it into her head that Dean had been in on it, too, once we got hitched."

"She thought your second husband helped you kill your first husband?" When she nodded, I asked, "Um, were you and Dean… I mean, did you two get involved—"

"Before Ernie died?" Sophie said. "Nope. Dean tried, of course, but I was a married woman and I didn't cheat, even under those circumstances. Try telling that to Lady Theodora. She sees the worst in everyone."

"So Teddy had you and your supposed lover conspiring to eliminate your gay husband so the two of you could live happily ever after on her three million bucks."

"That's about the size of it."

"Did Dean get any of your money in the divorce?" I asked.

"Nah, we were married less than a year," she said. "I bought him a house, though."

"Wow. That was generous."

"Not really. I own the place, I just let him live there. It's over on Iris Street." The flower-name streets were in the least desirable section of town, where you didn't need to be a millionaire to live. "Dean was a poor kid from some one-horse town in Ontario. More than anything, he wanted a Crystal Harbor address. I wanted a swift divorce with no drama. In the end we both got what we wanted."

"You bought his cooperation, in other words," I said.

"Hey, I was willing to do whatever it took," she said, "once I realized what a schmuck I'd gotten myself tied to. Anyway, now my problem is Teddy Waterfield and her renewed vendetta. I'd thought all that was long over. Turned out it was just lying dormant, waiting for Ernie to turn up under a tree."

We sat in silence as yesterday's harrowing discovery replayed itself behind my eyes. I shook off the memory and said, "Apparently the ground was oversaturated from the storm. A bunch of trees fell over, not just that one."

"I remember when they planted those saplings at the cemetery," Sophie said. "Next day they discovered Ernie's boat drifting in the Atlantic. Until yesterday, it never would have occurred to me to connect those two events."

"The killer must have snuck into the cemetery that night, pulled up one of the newly planted saplings..." I stopped, thinking Sophie might not want to hear my mind's grisly meanderings. But she picked up where I left off.

"He'd have had to enlarge the hole." She deposited the stub of her cigar on the ashtray. "Which meant sneaking not just a body into the cemetery, but some kind of shovel as well."

"Maybe he had help," I suggested. "It could have been more than one person."

"Anything's possible. We're talking about a thirty-two-year-old crime. Detective Hernandez has her hands full with this one."

"Was Bonnie even born when it happened?" I calculated Dom's ex-fiancée to be in her early thirties at most. "Let's just hope she doesn't focus solely on the most obvious suspect."

Sophie waved her hand as if to say, *That would be me.*

"Yeah, hello to you too," a grumpy male voice called. I turned to see a man approach us from around the side of the house. He was middle-aged, moderately tall and of average build but soft around the middle. He wore a short-sleeved white shirt and tie over gray dress slacks. He did not look happy.

Sophie groaned. Out of the side of her mouth, she muttered, "Speak of the freakin' devil."

The man stalked up to Sophie, gesturing toward the house. His spicy cologne overpowered the lingering cigar smoke. "I'm standing out there on your front porch ringing that damn doorbell for ten minutes, eh, like some idiot. Where's that Puerto Rican girl you had working for you?" I detected a Canadian accent.

Sophie gave him a flat stare. "That 'Puerto Rican girl' is a forty-seven-year-old Mexican-American grandmother who's been a U.S. citizen for decades. And she goes home to her own family at the end of the workday." She turned to me. "Jane, allow me to introduce my ex-husband, Dean Phillips. Dean, this is my good friend Jane Delaney."

Dean was about to dismiss me with a quick nod, but my name caught his attention. "Hey, you're that Death Diva girl, right?"

"'Fraid so."

"Huh." He studied me a moment as he extracted a lighter

and pack of cigarettes from his shirt pocket. I studied him back. Dean's head bore the aftermath of what had to be the world's worst hair transplant. Reddish brown crop rows marched back from a severe, slightly lopsided hairline. The whole mess had been meticulously blow-dried and sprayed in a swept-back style more appropriate to the 1980s.

He tapped out a cigarette. "You make money doing that?"

"Why, yes I do," I said. "That's kind of the point of it." That's the number-one question I get asked.

"What's the weirdest thing you've done, eh?" The number-two question, right on schedule.

Sophie interrupted. "Cut to the chase, Dean. This is about Ernie, right?"

"You know he turned up?" He lit his smoke and took a drag. "His bones, I mean."

"I'm the mayor. What do you think?"

"Well, I want to know what the hell you've been telling the cops about me. Some girl detective shows up at my work—at my *work*, Sophie!—asking all kinds of questions. I don't need that crap."

"For the record—" Sophie slapped a mosquito on her arm and wiped her hand on a paper napkin. "I did not tell the cops to talk to you. I didn't have to. Bonnie Hernandez is detecting. That's what detectives do. If you want to—" She raised her palm, traffic-cop style, when he tried to interrupt. "If you want to bitch at someone, go bitch at Teddy Waterfield. I'll bet she's chatting with Bonnie right this moment, telling her all about how you and I offed her son and threw his body in a hole."

"Huh. I wasn't even in the same state when her precious pansy got himself killed." He shifted on his feet, eyeing the half-full pitcher of mojitos. Sophie didn't offer him a drink, nor did she invite him to sit. He said, "Same song, second verse. The old broad's still alive, eh?"

"And as sweet-natured as ever, from what I hear. Why don't you pay her a visit, tell her exactly what you think of this vendetta of hers?"

Dean grunted. His gaze flicked around the huge backyard. "I just might do that."

Yeah, right, I thought. The onetime bad boy was afraid of the little old lady on Wallings Drive.

He tried to cover his trepidation by standing over his ex-wife and jabbing his cigarette at her. "You're the damn mayor," he barked. "Do something about that nosy bitch."

"I have no control over what my former mother-in-law says or does."

"I'm not talking about the Waterfield woman and you know it." Red patches mottled his face. "That detective will back off if you order her to."

"You know it doesn't work like that, Dean," Sophie said. "For crying out loud, she considers me a suspect too. Get a grip."

"It's the same old story." He got in her face. A speck of foamy spittle decorated the corner of his mouth. "You were never willing to help me when we were married. Why start now?"

I said, "I need a car."

They turned to me in unison. Dean blinked. "What?"

"Sophie says you sell used cars. I need a car."

I watched outrage war with greed beneath the cultivated calamity that was his scalp. Guess which instinct won out.

Dean smiled. "I sell pre-owned cars, yes." He straightened both his spine and his grease-spotted necktie while his ex-wife settled back on her chaise with a knowing grin. She lifted my glass, raised a toast to me behind his back, and polished off my mojito. "What are you driving now?" He started to flick his cigarette butt into the grass until Sophie barked, "Nope!" and pointed to the big ashtray.

"Eleven-year-old Civic," I answered. With a worn timing belt and an unnerving tendency to sob and shudder when I pushed it past thirty. So no lie, I really was in the market.

"Well, not to worry, Jane, I'll put you in something real nice," he said. "We have a one-year-old Lexus convertible on the lot. A hair over six thousand miles on her. Loaded. She's a beaut."

And no doubt out of my price range, but there would be plenty of time for him to learn that although, by a fluke of fortune, I lived in Crystal Harbor, I wasn't *from* Crystal Harbor.

I stood and extended my hand. "Sounds great, Dean. I'll come by the lot tomorrow. Let me walk you back to your car and we can talk about it."

4

Back to the Stone Age

I SHOVED A fat straw through a plastic cup lid and sucked in a mouthful of cold papaya-ginger smoothie. My eyes drifted shut as I savored the sweet, creamy, pale orange concoction. When I opened them, Cheyenne O'Rourke was holding out my change, her plain adolescent face fixed in its customary bored stare.

The girl was on probation for second-degree assault related to an incident last spring. That meant she had to hold down a job, but no one said she had to like working at Janey's Place, Dom's health-food joint. Sometimes when my biological clock howled like a rabid werewolf, I'd think of Cheyenne and feel a little better at not having added another sullen Long Island youth to the world.

Yet. I was thirty-nine. Theoretically there was still time.

I gave Cheyenne the cheeriest smile and thank-you I could muster, out of scientific curiosity to see if any degree of friendly human interaction would get through to her. Sexy Beast, getting a free ride in the straw bucket tote hanging on my shoulder, yipped merrily, tail wagging. (Yeah, I know, but he stayed in the basket and the store's owner wanted to remarry me, so I wasn't worried about getting tossed out of the place.)

The girl slammed the money drawer shut and went back to picking at her neon blue nail polish. Experiment concluded.

I wandered outside and took a seat on the pretty, apple green bench parked in front of the store, flanked by flowering shrubs in big planters. It was about ten in the morning and pleasantly mild for mid-July, with low humidity and a light breeze. I let SB out of the basket but kept him on the leash. He investigated his surroundings, nose twitching, then jumped onto my lap to gaze longingly at my smoothie. Passersby paused to pet him and coo baby talk. SB has no idea why total strangers behave this way, but he accepts the fawning attention as his due.

This papaya-ginger smoothie was the only thing I ever ordered from Janey's Place, not being a health-food person myself. I'm more of a convenience-food person. My customary breakfast is Fruity Pebbles, and my favorite lunch is pizza and orange soda. Dinner is McWhatever or Chinese takeout. So you might be wondering about the smoothie, which is purported to soothe cranky bellies. I'd been introduced somewhat accidentally to this particular libation several months earlier, and dang if I hadn't fallen in love with it. It's like a milkshake without the guilt.

Okay, you got me. I don't feel guilty for my junk-food habit. Life's too short.

Janey's Place was tucked between a pottery gallery on one side and UnderStatements, Lacey Vargas's lingerie boutique, on the other. The bench I sat on happened to be positioned next to the boutique. I couldn't resist peeking through the display window to see if I could spot Lacey. My curiosity was piqued now that I knew she'd been the girlfriend of Tim Whatshisname, the man whose death had been caused by

Sophie's late husband, Ernie.

I detected movement in the store and squinted to see past the window glare. Lacey was ringing up a purchase for Maia Armstrong, a popular local caterer. I knew Maia well. She and I routinely referred customers to each other.

As I stared through the window, I felt a tugging on my cup. I looked down to see Sexy Beast licking my smoothie straw. I actually considered wiping off the straw and continuing to use it—for about a nanosecond until I recalled the last thing I'd seen him lick. My love for my pet only goes so far. I yanked out the straw and lobbed it toward the trash bin near the curb. It bounced off the lip of the bin and onto the sidewalk.

Crystal Harbor isn't the kind of town where you want to be seen littering. I'd go from Jane Delaney the local Death Diva to Jane Delaney the local Litterer. So I got up and did the right thing as Maia exited the shop, toting a pale yellow shopping bag stamped with the elegant UnderStatements logo in gold. Maia was a pretty woman in her mid-thirties. Today her froth of Afro coils was held off her face with a narrow silver headband.

We exchanged cheek pecks and Maia sat on the bench to lift SB onto her lap. She bestowed scritches galore and unashamedly cooed baby talk until he rolled onto his back in adoring surrender. The caterer was one of SB's favorite people, and not just because of her sweet nature.

"I know what you're waiting for." Maia reached into her purse for a small plastic bag, from which she extracted one of her homemade doggie biscuits. She baked them for her schnauzers, Bruno and Margaret, but carried around a supply to woo the local canine populace. She set SB on the sidewalk and made him earn his treat by sitting and shaking hands.

He attacked the biscuit with zeal, holding it down with his front paws and biting off portions. The thing looked a little like an oatmeal cookie, and probably tasted pretty darn good.

Maia put her hand on my arm, her expression caring. "I understand you found him. That couldn't have been easy."

"What? Oh, you mean Ernie Waterfield?"

She nodded and squeezed my arm.

"Well, really, we're talking about bones. It was startling but not…" *disgusting? gross?* "It wasn't so bad."

"Poor Sophie. How's she holding up?" She knew the mayor and I were pals.

I didn't want to say too much. Maia was no gossip, but Sophie was a public figure, after all, and the rumor mill in this town, once it was fed a kernel or two, tended to grind away unmercifully at people and their reputations.

I offered Sophie's own words. "It happened a long time ago. She's doing fine."

"I'm glad to hear it." Maia smiled with genuine relief. She noticed me peeking into UnderStatements. "You should go in. Lacey's having a sale. Twenty-five percent off—even things that were already reduced." She pawed through the white and gold tissue paper in her shopping bag, glanced around to guard against prying eyes, and showed me a plum-colored silk nightgown and matching robe. "I got these for half the original price."

I agreed the set was gorgeous and gave her a conspiratorial smile. "Do you have anyone special in mind to wear this for?" Maia was unattached.

"Not really," she said, but her shy grin told a different story. "Maybe. We'll see."

I couldn't help it. "Anyone I know?"

"I'll tell if you will."

"Who, me?" I asked. "Sadly, there's nothing to tell."

"That's not what I hear." Maia leaned closer and lowered her voice as a trio of teenage girls strolled past, each glued to a phone. "Russell Appel says Dom's been buying up every tulip in the store for months." Russell was the local florist.

Tulips are my favorite flower, which Maia well knew. "I made him stop," I said. "My house was beginning to look like a funeral parlor."

"It's so romantic, though." Maia's expression was downright gooey.

"Been there, done that. Dom and I have too much history."

"But he's so obviously in love. It's adorable." She seemed almost embarrassed to add, "And he's rich. I mean, crazy rich. Not that that's important."

"No, of course not," I said, and we giggled like schoolgirls.

"Well, I have to go." Maia stood and checked her antique pendant watch. "I'm meeting with the Bergmans in ten minutes."

"What are they having catered?" I asked, then answered myself. "Not Jenny's bat mitzvah. Wasn't she a toddler, like, last week?"

Maia smiled. "Time flies. Jenny wants a *Doctor Who* theme for the reception."

"Good luck with that." A final round of cheek pecks and scritches, and she was on her way.

I sucked down the last of my smoothie, let SB lick the cup, then tossed it and tucked the little dog into my tote.

What the heck. There was a sale, after all. I entered the

comfortably cool, potpourri-scented lingerie shop, an oasis of silk, lace, and chiffon in hues from virginal white to surprise-him-at-the-door black and everything in between.

Lacey (her real name, no lie) was returning tried-on items to their proper racks. She gave me a bright smile and we exchanged greetings. She was in her early fifties and, to put it kindly, plain, from the homely face to the soft, well-nourished figure—not as plump as Sophie by a long shot, just your basic middle-aged spread. Her best feature was her dark blue eyes, which she played up with a tad too much makeup behind fashionably retro black eyeglass frames. Her wavy, brown hair fell just past her shoulders. She must get it dyed, but I'd never detected gray roots. Lacey Vargas was no beauty and doubtless never had been, but she did her best with what she had.

"Is it okay?" I indicated Sexy Beast in his straw-tote chariot.

Her smile froze in place. "Well, sure, as long as she stays where she is. We have a lot of delicate things here."

I didn't correct her on SB's gender. I just thanked her and asked about the sale.

"It's all reduced." She swept her arm. "Everything in the store, and the best stuff is going fast, so you came just in time."

Sophie had told me that Lacey and her late fiancé, Tim, came from working-class stock in New Jersey. That explained Lacey's slightly nasal pronunciations, which turned *all* into *awl* and *fast* into *fee-ust*. Her obvious attempt to tamp down her native accent only drew more attention to it, like raising a pinky while sipping from a teacup. I had little doubt she was aware of the snide comments some of the highborn locals made about her.

They were the same comments they made about me, the

lower-middle-class Death Diva weirdo transplanted almost by divine decree from a basement hovel on the South Shore to a Nimitz-class home right here in Crystal Harbor. The house I inherited has six and a half bathrooms, for crying out loud. There are a couple I haven't even enthroned myself in yet.

Lacey and I were fish out of water in this rarefied burg, and the privileged locals made darn sure we never forgot it.

"What are you looking for today?" she asked.

"Um…" *Any info that might shed light on Ernie Waterfield's death and help get Sophie off the hot seat.* "I'm not sure. Maybe a nice pair of panties?" I was aiming for the cheapest thing I could think of. UnderStatements was no bargain outlet, sale or no sale.

Lacey led the way to a rack filled with frilly dainties on tiny plastic hangers. "With this discount, if you're getting the panties, you may as well go for the matching bra. Color?"

"I, uh, hadn't thought that far."

She winked. "Is it for someone special?"

I wished people would stop asking me that. "Maybe." There was the sender of the tulips, of course. But he wasn't the man who popped into my mind in that instant. Instead I pictured myself wearing nothing but a skimpy bra and panties, sitting on the back of a black Harley and hugging a lean, muscular—

"No," I hastily said. "No one special."

Sexy Beast gave a single bark. It sounded like, *Liar.*

Mind you, there hadn't been an iota of hanky-panky between me and the padre, if you didn't count what went on in my overactive imagination.

"No one special, huh?" She gave another wink. "That's not what I hear."

Oh brother. Did Dom have everyone in town on his payroll, pushing me into marrying him again?

"How about pink?" I said.

"Pink it is." Instead of asking my sizes, she gave me a professional once-over and started flipping through items on the rack. I expected her to choose something in soft baby pink. Instead she held up a sheer, hot pink push-up bra and matching thong for my examination.

"Wow," I said, then looked at the price tag. "Yikes."

"Twenty-five off, remember." Lacey steered me toward the fitting rooms.

Yikes minus twenty-five percent was still *yikes*, to my slender wallet at least. Unlike yours truly, most of the women who bought their frillies at UnderStatements did so because they could afford to live and shop in Crystal Harbor, not because a generous bequest had plucked them out of one of the poorest towns on the Island and deposited them in one of the wealthiest towns on the Island.

I found myself in the fanciest fitting room I'd ever been in, complete with silk wall covering, a brocade-upholstered bench, antique sconces, and a carpeted mini stage set in front of three-way mirrors. She hung the undies on a hook as I set my tote on the carpet, admonishing Sexy Beast to stay put. He yawned and curled up in the bottom of the tote, which was comfortably padded with a sweater that had belonged to his first mommy, Irene McAuliffe.

"What about, you know…" I indicated the thong. I was accustomed to buying my underpants in plastic-wrapped three-packs.

"Just try it on over your panties," she said, closing the door. "Let me see when you have them on."

I began shucking out of my denim crop pants and T-shirt. On the other side of the door I heard the slide of hangers as Lacey rearranged items on racks. Who knew how long I had her to myself? Another customer could come in at any moment. "So that's really something, huh?" I called. "About Ernie Waterfield?"

The *zing* of the hangers abruptly stopped. Lacey sounded more Jersey than ever as she said, "I never did think that murdering scum killed himself out of guilt. That woulda meant he had a conscience."

The victim of "that murdering scum" was, of course, Lacey's long-ago boyfriend Tim. I dropped my serviceable white bra on the bench and released the electric pink one from its hanger. "The whole thing is a tragedy all around."

Lacey's voice was tight as she said, "Look, no offense, Jane. I know you're friends with the mayor and she was married to the guy back then, but if you ask me, that bastard got what he deserved."

"I guess I can't blame you for feeling that way," I said. "You must have been devastated when Tim died. I know I would have been. Such a senseless death."

"If it wasn't for Colin, I think I would've gone totally off the rails."

"Colin?" I said.

"Our son—I was pregnant when Tim died. Colin's the image of his dad. When I look at him now, I think that's how Tim Holbrook would've looked at thirty-four if he'd never met Ernie Waterfield. How're you doing in there?"

Tim Holbrook. Why did I know that name? "Oh, fine, I'm just… um… just getting this thing on."

The door opened, making me jump. Lacey's gaze landed

approvingly on my chest, which no longer looked like my chest. More to the point, it looked like my chest times two. My cups runneth over and then some. Then she looked down at the thong and almost managed to maintain a neutral expression. Almost.

"I need to do laundry," I said by way of explanation. I'd kept my own underpants on as instructed—my old, white granny panties whose stretched-out elastic waistband covered my navel. Lacey's gaze flicked to the mirror behind me, and quickly away. I possessed an okay rear end, but the sight of it encased in threadbare white cotton which was itself wedgied by a delicate pink silk thong? Not so okay.

Lacey placed more items on the hooks and set a pair of fuchsia high-heeled mules on the carpet. "These will complete the look."

Before she could beat a retreat, I said, "I have to ask you something, Lacey. You said Tim's last name was Holbrook?"

She nodded, a quizzical look on her face.

"I hope you don't mind my asking, but... well, I've been performing a particular assignment annually for twenty years. Almost as long as I've had my business."

"Your Death Diva business," she said.

"If you want to call it that, yes." I should just give up and make it my official title. It was how everyone knew me, and it was kind of catchy. "An anonymous client has paid me to deliver flowers—a big, expensive arrangement—to Timothy Joseph Holbrook's grave in New Jersey every year on September twenty-fifth."

Lacey went still, her sapphire eyes wide. "That's my Tim. That's the day he died."

"I had no idea who he was," I said, "only that someone

wanted to pay his, or her, respects without being identified. So it wasn't you who hired me?"

"No," she breathed, and I believed her. She seemed genuinely surprised and perplexed. "I don't know anyone who would've done that."

"His parents?" I asked.

Lacey shook her head. "They never could've afforded it, and they died years ago. Never got over losing Tim," she added bitterly. "It took years off their lives, I know it did."

"What about you?" I asked gently, feeling ridiculous having this conversation in my current getup but determined to find out what I could, for Sophie's sake. "You don't get over a tragedy like that overnight."

"What do you mean?" She looked wary, making me wonder whether Detective Hernandez had paid her a visit.

"Nothing, I just… I'm glad you found happiness with someone else," I said, recalling what Sophie had told me about Lacey's hasty marriage to Porter Vargas.

A lilting chime from the store's entrance announced an incoming customer.

"I concentrated on raising my son, that's how I got over it." Lacey's tone was all business. "Let me know if I can bring you anything else."

And she was gone. I heard muted conversation as she greeted the newcomer.

So. Who'd been shelling out big bucks every September to have me deliver those elaborate arrangements to Tim's grave all these years? I pondered that as I struggled into the forest green garter belt and matching fishnet stockings. I slipped my feet into the stiletto-heeled mules.

Holy cow. I pivoted to regard my image in the three-way

mirrors, trying to ignore the granny panties—which wasn't too difficult considering the show going on up top. I owned a handful of thongs and push-up bras acquired over the years, but they couldn't hold a candle to the elegantly slutty ensemble I found myself in. The colors Lacey had chosen actually complemented each other. I could imagine Dom's enthusiastic reaction, though he and I hadn't been intimate since our divorce seventeen years earlier.

And yes, I was pretty certain how the padre would react too. Martin appreciated sexy outfits. Hadn't he once declared a particular dress of mine "totally hot"?

Lacey had brought a shortie kimono into the fitting room, a deliciously delicate confection made of the thinnest forest green silk. Against my better judgment, I looked at the price tag. Ah, only $890—after the discount. I should buy two, they're small, yok yok.

I pushed my arms through the sleeves, letting the robe slip off one shoulder and striking a variety of pinup poses in front of the mirrors.

The conversation outside cranked up in volume. I emitted a groan as I recognized Nina Wallace's voice.

"Four and a half months," Nina said. "My due date is Thanksgiving, isn't that just perfect? I threw away all my old nursing bras years ago, thought I was done with all that." Her tinkling laugh carried clearly.

Yeah, go ahead and laugh, lady, I thought. The whole town knew her husband was not the father of her unborn child. Her husband knew it too, but he was standing by his wife for the sake of their two teenage daughters.

The door chime trilled again and another female voice joined the mix. Lacey's sale was pulling in the customers, all right. I'd been lucky to grab a little private time with her. A few moments of muted conversation followed and then Nina's voice rang out loud and clear—as long as I kept my ear plastered to the door.

Oh, please. Tell me you wouldn't have done the same thing.

"I was only eight years old when Ernie Waterfield supposedly killed himself," Nina declared, "but even then I knew there was something fishy about it."

Sure you did, I thought. *A regular little savant.*

"And how could Sophie not have known about him before they got married?" she continued. "Unless she didn't *want* a normal, hetero man for a husband. There are women like that, you know. I'm not saying the mayor's one of them necessarily, but you have to wonder."

I had it on good authority that Nina, currently the president of the Crystal Harbor Historical Society, intended to unseat Sophie during the next mayoral election. Clearly she meant to take advantage of any opportunity to sully her opponent's name—a venerable Crystal Harbor tradition.

The newcomer spoke. Her voice sounded familiar, but I couldn't place it. "Do you have any theories about who might have killed him?"

I almost guffawed when Nina said, "I hate to speak ill of anyone, particularly an elected official, but I feel a responsibility in this case to share my misgivings. I personally would not be surprised if it turns out Mayor Halperin did away with her husband."

"What do you base your suspicions on?" the woman asked.

"I don't know if you're aware, but Ernie's mother bribed Sophie—thirty million is the figure I heard—not to divorce her son once she realized he was a homosexual. And she got remarried shortly after his supposed suicide, so who knows? Maybe she got tired of keeping up appearances with her gay husband and decided she wanted a real marriage plus the money. It's a credible scenario, is all I'm saying."

I pulled the robe closed, tied the sash belt, and yanked open the door. Who the heck did Nina Wallace think she was, spreading a rumor like that around town? Had she no shame?

As if I hadn't learned the answer to that one long ago.

I stalked right over to her, teetering on the four-inch stilettos and weaving around a rack of shapers (your grandma's girdle by another name), ignoring everything and everyone else in my determination to shut down her rumor-mongering ASAP.

Nina looked as ladylike and put together as always, in a sleeveless floral maternity tunic and white capri leggings. If anything, her baby bump only emphasized her otherwise trim figure. She sported a glowing midsummer tan and a new, short hairdo, her dark hair sleek and feathery around her pretty face.

I got right in that pretty face, my finger wagging. "You have no right to spread vicious rumors like that, Nina. It's irresponsible and self-serving. First you paint a picture of a happily married fruit fly, then in the next breath Sophie Halperin is a greedy, scheming murderer. Well, which is it? You can't have it both ways."

I towered over petite Nina in my ridiculous shoes. I was surprised to see her rear back, her silver-gray eyes wide in alarm. The Nina Wallace I knew was ballsier than that.

"And who are you?" the new customer asked.

I wheeled on the woman and spat out my name, about to admonish her for stoking the gossip mill. Only then did it begin to dawn on me what was going on here. My gaze flitted from the familiar-looking woman, who held a microphone, to her companion, a sturdy young man hoisting a big camera on his shoulder.

I found that camera and its bright light aimed at me as I tugged my robe tighter, belatedly recognizing Miranda Daniels, a TV reporter with the popular cable show *Ramrod News*. Hers is the kind of shrill "investigative reporting" that seeks out the most lurid angle of every story, inventing one when necessary. The show is not my preferred viewing. Okay, maybe once in a while if there's nothing better on.

This, I realized, was why Nina had pretended to be terrified of me. She'd been playing to the camera.

Miranda perked up at the mention of my name. "You must be the Jane Delaney who found Ernest Waterfield's skeleton."

"Talk to Jane," Lacey murmured as she slunk through the doorway to the back room. "She knows a lot more about all this than I do." Clearly she wanted no public association with a sordid story like this, particularly on a sensationalist show like *Ramrod News*.

Nor did I, especially in my current state of dishabille. Granted, the naughty undies were concealed by the robe, but still. I cast a longing look at the door to the fitting room, but Miranda and the cameraman had deftly shifted position to block that particular escape route.

Miranda shoved the mic in my face. "Tell us how you discovered the skeleton, Jane."

My heart tried to crawl up my throat. "I, uh, I just looked under the tree and there it was." My chuckle sounded like an asthmatic chicken.

"What were you doing in the cemetery immediately after a major storm?" she asked.

I glanced at Nina, silently praying for help. Yeah, right. She looked like a cat teasing a trapped chipmunk. "I… can't reveal what I was doing there that afternoon." Miranda's eyebrows lifted toward her bleached roots. I swallowed hard. "I mean, it's… it's classified information."

"Classified?" A mean little smile. "Sounds mysterious."

"It has to do with my business," I said. "I respect my clients' privacy." As the reporter opened her mouth to pursue this line of questioning, I tried in vain to scoot around her. "You know what? I really don't think I want to say any more."

"What kind of business brings you to cemeteries at all hours?" she persisted.

There was that hateful mic again, inches from my nose. An angry flush stung my face. "I'm the Death Diva, okay? I'm the damn Death Diva. I do stuff to dead people, and I have no intention of talking about it." And yeah, maybe I could have worded that better.

Miranda plowed ahead. "You seem pretty certain Mayor Halperin had nothing to do with her first husband's murder. What about the bribe she accepted from Ernie's mother?"

"It wasn't a bribe, for crying out loud, it was a gift."

"Thirty million?" Miranda showed me her sharp little teeth again. "That's some generous mother-in-law."

"It was three million bucks," I said. "I don't know where Nina got that thirty million figure. Now, could I please—"

"You seem to know quite a lot about this strange case, Jane." Miranda edged closer as I tried to melt into a rack of lace negligees. "Have you shared your insights with the Crystal Harbor Police Department?"

Nina cocked her head as if to say, *Good question, Jane. Have you?*

"All right, I've had enough." I shoved the mic, and Miranda Daniels, with just enough force to make her back off. In that instant Sexy Beast appeared, barking like a, well, like a real dog. He attacked Miranda's leg, sinking his little fangs into her slacks and hanging on for dear life, snarling and scrabbling for purchase. Protecting me again, the sweet, deluded little furball.

"Get this thing off me!" Miranda shrieked, trying to shake off the tiny poodle, who clung to her slacks with... *rabid?* can I say *rabid?* not in the, you know, diseased sense... Okay, whatever, with rabid canine determination.

"Don't you dare hurt my dog!" I yelled, while attempting to grab SB, no small feat as he was jerked this way and that, firmly attached to the hem of Miranda's no doubt very expensive ivory silk slacks. "If anything happens to Sexy Beast, I will sue you and your horrible show back to the Stone Age!"

The cameraman took his eye off the viewfinder just long enough to quirk a questioning eyebrow at me. Yeah, so I'm metaphor-challenged, what of it?

Finally I managed to catch SB on the upswing and pry his jaws from the reporter's pants. I tucked him under my arm and, sweaty and thoroughly disheveled, sprinted back to the fitting room.

5

Graphic and Disturbing

SIX HOURS LATER, I parked my crappy old Civic in the circular cobblestone courtyard in front of my big brick-and-stone house. I carried my shopping bag up the steps of the covered portico flanked by white double columns, fished my keys from my purse, and let myself in through the massive double doors. The sack I carried through the foyer and dining room to the butler's pantry was not, alas, pale yellow printed with the gold UnderStatements logo. It was a plastic sack from the supermarket.

I unpacked the contents: Fruity Pebbles, two-percent milk, frozen fried chicken, and orange soda for me; Vienna sausages and cheddar for Sexy Beast, who'd come running in from the living room to greet me. I gave him a sausage and put away the rest of the food in the adjacent kitchen, pulling a cold orange soda from the fridge and tearing open the box of cereal.

I sauntered into the sunken game room, a sunlit space separated from the breakfast room by a low wall. I still thought of it as the game room, though one of my first acts as the new owner had been to give Irene's fancy poker table to her lawyer and longtime friend Sten Jakobsen. I didn't play poker, and I couldn't look at the well-used table without missing Irene terribly.

And yes, technically *Sexy Beast* is the property's owner, but if I left decorating decisions up to him, the house would be filled with tennis balls, shoes, dog-biscuit dispensers, fire hydrants, and random garments that smell like me and/or his dearly departed Irene.

I flopped onto the ivory leather sofa, really an enormous horseshoe-shaped seating area strewn with squishy pillows and throws in shades of rose, slate, and pale green. It was my favorite spot in the house. Well, next to the whirlpool tub in the master bath.

Instead of curling up next to me, Sexy Beast trotted up the two steps into the living room and gave a couple of imperious barks. I froze in the act of picking up the TV remote. That was his herding bark. Not that poodles are herding dogs, they're in fact water retrievers, but SB liked to gather his humans into one spot, the better to watch over them and keep an eye out for the random suburban grizzly bear.

Only, who was he herding? No one else was in the house. It was just me and—

"I hope that's not your dinner."

—Martin McAuliffe. The padre sauntered down the two steps from the living room, looking like he owned the place. Which wasn't far from the truth since not even the most high-tech locks and security system seemed capable of keeping him out. Not that he let himself in on a regular basis. It had been months since he'd done so—to my knowledge at least. For all I knew, he could be sneaking in every night and standing over my sleeping form with a chainsaw and a machete, trying to decide. Lord knew Sexy Beast would do nothing to stop him, the padre being one of his favorite bipeds.

I swigged from the bottle of soda. "As a matter of fact, no.

I have a date later." So there. It was a little before six now. At eight I was scheduled to meet a man I'd corresponded with on dog-loving-singles.com for dinner at the Harbor Room. The waterfront restaurant was a local historical landmark thanks to its venerable age and connection with Prohibition rum-running.

Martin toted a black plastic liquor-store sack. He set it on the carpet and settled on the sofa right next to me, ignoring the leather acreage extending in either direction practically to the adjoining towns. In return, I ignored the bare feet he propped on Irene's six-thousand-dollar coffee table. I still thought of the house and its furnishings as Irene's, a habit hard to break. SB jumped onto Martin's lap, nudging his hand every time the padre stopped rubbing him.

"Fine by me," he said, meaning my date. "SB and I will order in. It's a junk-food paradise in there." He tipped his head toward the kitchen. "Don't you ever eat anything without two dozen ingredients?"

"Who said you could stay here while I'm gone? When I leave, you leave. In fact, I don't recall inviting you in. The door is right through there." I pointed.

"Did I forget to mention?" He reached into the cereal box and grabbed a handful of Fruity Pebbles. "We're roomies now. I'm going to live here."

I sat speechless, staring at him. "You didn't just say—"

"We'll have pillow fights, do each other's hair. I'll be fun. Not to fret, I took the maid's room." He jerked his thumb in the direction of the laundry room, next to which was a modest-sized bedroom with en-suite bathroom. "Miles away from your palatial suite upstairs. You'll never even know whether I'm in the house."

"How reassuring." I turned to face him directly. "Listen to me, Padre. You are not moving in with me."

"Already did. Borrowed Mom's car and got it done in one trip. This room is just crying out for a state-of-the-art video-game system," he said, indicating the three-thousand-inch flat-screen TV mounted on the opposite wall. Okay, I don't know how many inches it really is, all I know is it rivals the big movie screen in the home theater downstairs.

"Not in this house, no way," I said. "And I still didn't say you could stay here. Your stuff is being hauled to the town dump the next time you walk out of here."

"Crystal Harbor has a town dump?"

"You know what I mean. This is my house and I get to say who stays here."

"I believe it's his house." The padre stroked Sexy Beast, who promptly rolled over and presented his downy stomach for stroking. "And he seems to want me around, don't you, boy?"

SB made that satisfied, guttural rolling-*R* sound I thought of as his doggie purr. *Et tu, Sexy Beast?*

"I brought you a present to say thanks." Martin reached down to the bag he'd brought and presented me with a bottle of my favorite añejo tequila. He smiled, watching my face. This was pricey stuff, and the last bottle I'd owned had been a birthday present from Irene three years earlier. I'd made it last, but it had been months since I'd had a sip of this nectar of the gods.

I dragged my gaze from the gorgeous bottle to the padre's face. "Yeah, right. You brought it to bribe me."

He shrugged and set the bottle on the coffee table. "Semantics."

Speaking of bribery and accusations of such…

"What do you think of this whole business with Ernie Waterfield?" I tucked the box of cereal between us. Sexy Beast licked his lips and I fed him one piece. A blue one.

"I think Sophie better have a good criminal lawyer."

I sighed. "Sten hooked her up with someone, a big name from the city. It's so unfair. She couldn't possibly have committed murder."

He was silent for a long moment. "You can never say for sure what a person is capable of when push comes to shove."

I shifted in my seat to face him. "We're talking about Sophie here. She's… she's one of the best people I know."

He raised his hands. "I'm not arguing that, but people do things under duress, that's all I'm saying."

I thought about that, and about the man sitting next to me. Martin McAuliffe's background was a mystery, but I had my suspicions. I'd already decided I'd rather not know.

"I visited Sophie today in her office at Town Hall." I told him about my anonymous client and my annual trip to place flowers at a cemetery in New Jersey. "I thought maybe she'd hired me in secret to pay her respects to the man her late husband had accidentally killed. She denies it was her and I believe her. And Lacey Vargas doesn't know who it could be. She was Tim's girlfriend. Then I thought, well, maybe it was someone else who was close to Ernie."

"Such as…?" he asked.

"His mom."

"That doesn't sound like the Teddy Waterfield I've heard about," he said. "Making a coat out of Dalmatian puppies, maybe. Memorializing the victim of her son's boneheaded prank? Not so much."

"I know, but I'm at a dead end here."

"Why don't you hire Ben to look into it for you?" Martin asked.

"I can't afford a private detective." Ben Ralston was a local PI and a friend of Martin's.

"A thing like that'll take him no time. I bet he'd do it as a favor if Mom asks him nicely." He grinned. "Why do you think I'm bunking with you? Ben is moving in with her. I like Ben, but that's one small house, and when a mouse sneezes in the attic, you hear it in the basement. Plus that cat of hers creeps me out."

I'd met the cat, an ill-tempered Siamese named Miss Persephone. I'd met his mother, Stevie, too. She was a youthful sixty-one, having had Martin at age nineteen. He had no contact with his father, a married deacon and the son of Irene's late husband.

Yeah, don't even try to figure out the family tree, you'll get a headache.

Bottom line: I liked Stevie and I liked Ben. I was glad those two had found each other.

"You really think Ben would do it for free?" I asked.

"Buy him a bottle. I'm told it works wonders." There was that devilish grin again.

"Then sure, let's see what he can dig up," I said. "If I can discover who's behind my trips to Tim's gravesite, it could shed some light on all this. Such as, is my client a local? Why would someone in New Jersey hire someone on Long Island to schlepp flowers to a Jersey grave?"

"Because you're the only one who does this sort of thing?" he asked. "Aside from me, that is."

Martin had recently launched a competing Death Diva—

Death Divo?—business, specifically by raiding my clients. That had been a few months earlier when he was miffed at me. I don't think he'd done any Death Divo'ing lately. He made his living bartending and… well, like I said. I'd rather not know.

"Hey," I said, "aren't you supposed to be at Tierney's now?" Tierney's Publick House was the Southampton watering hole where he worked, and summer was high tourist season. Martin must make a bundle in tips this time of year.

"A buddy's covering for me."

"Wait, what time is it?" I snatched up the TV remote.

"A few minutes past six. When's your date?"

"It's not that. I'm missing *Ramrod News*."

"What, I'm not sleazy enough?" Martin asked. "I wouldn't have pegged you as a *Ramrod* viewer."

I gave him a brief recap of that morning's catastrophe as I switched channels. Within moments I was staring at Miranda Daniels's hateful face, larger than life and in high definition. I could count her false eyelashes. Her frown of concern almost looked sincere.

"I must warn you," she gravely intoned, "the footage you are about to view is graphic and disturbing. If you have young children, you might want to send them out of the room."

Thank goodness. She must be featuring a different story. Maybe our sensational three-decades-old murder wasn't sensational enough. My relief was short-lived as an image of my own slutty-looking self filled the enormous screen.

"Yowza," was all Martin said.

"Shut up." I raised the volume.

The lady on the screen—that couldn't really be me, could it?—had long, disheveled, strawberry blond hair and wore a dark green kimono that revealed pillowy, hoisted-to-there cleavage and the lacy top of a hot pink bra. Fishnet stockings and do-me mules completed the fetching ensemble. The best part? Under the camera's bright light, the robe was sheer.

Yeah, that's right. You could see straight through it to everything underneath. The push-up bra. The garter belt. The thong. The granny panties under the thong.

Martin leaned forward and squinted. "What's that you've got on under the—?"

I smacked him with the cereal box. Multicolored pebbles flew in all directions, much to Sexy Beast's delight.

The camera homed in on my angry face as I said, "Sophie Halperin is a greedy, scheming murderer."

I bolted upright. "What?"

"You said that?" Martin asked.

"No! I mean yes, I said that, but I didn't say *that*. They took my words out of context."

Miranda again. "That was Jane Delaney, one of Mayor Halperin's closest friends and the person who actually discovered the skeleton of Ernest Waterfield. The mayor is the widow of Mr. Waterfield and the prime suspect in his murder. If you're wondering what kind of people she calls friend, keep watching."

Another shot of my furious face. "I'm the Death Diva, okay? I'm the damn Death Diva. I do stuff to dead people, and I have no intention of talking about it."

"Wow," Martin said, and snatched the cereal box away from me before I could smack him again.

The TV screen was now split between Miranda's talking head and a bespectacled older man wearing a tie and tweed sport coat against a backdrop of shelved books. Miranda introduced him as Dr. Charles Amos, professor of religious studies at Peconic University.

Miranda's frown did not extend to her Botoxed forehead. "Dr. Amos, you've studied the footage we shot earlier today. What can you tell us about this self-described Death Diva, based on your expert knowledge of satanic cults?"

The professor straightened his eyeglasses. "The history of sexual deviancy in such cults is well documented. Wild orgies, black masses, tales of sexual slavery... This so-called Death Diva, with her salacious garments and shocking lack of modesty, fits right in with what we know of modern devil worship. As for the unusual garment she's wearing under her, um, underpants, that no doubt has ritual significance and demands further study."

My jaw hung open. The padre placed a Fruity Pebble on my tongue and made the sign of the cross. "Exorcisms are my specialty. For you, no charge."

"Can you explain the significance," Miranda asked the prof, "of this vicious dog? For the benefit of those just joining us, the animal belongs to Jane Delaney, known in satanic circles as the Death Diva." Cut to video of Sexy Beast attacking the hem of Miranda's pants as she screams and flails her leg. From his spot on the couch, SB growled at his own image on the screen. But then, he growls at anything with four legs.

"This animal is what's known as a 'familiar,'" Dr. Amos said. "The purpose of a familiar is to assist its master in various malevolent acts and to offer protection."

I turned to Martin. "Familiars—aren't they for witches? Is he saying I'm a witch now?"

He shrugged, staring at the screen. "All right! Was that a nip-slip?"

I gasped. "No!" I was once more onscreen, shot from above

as I attempted to disengage SB's teeth from the reporter's pants. My robe was in disarray, the sash undone, my "salacious garments" on full display. I didn't see an errant nipple, but I did see the ritual white granny panties in all their baggy, saggy glory as I snarled at the reporter, "If anything happens to Sexy Beast, I will sue you and your horrible show back to the Stone Age!"

Cut to a perplexed Miranda, grinning, shaking her head. "Professor? Can you enlighten us? Who or what is 'Sexy Beast'?" She dodged an imaginary lightning bolt. "Should I be afraid to say the words out loud?"

Dr. Amos chuckled. "Satan is known by many names, as I'm sure you're aware. Lucifer, Beelzebub, the Prince of Darkness, and of course Beast as in six-six-six, the mark of the Beast. 'Sexy Beast' is obviously how this oversexed devil worshiper and her cohort refer to Satan."

"Isn't there a movie by that name?" Miranda asked.

"Yeah," I hollered at the screen, "the movie my dog was named after, you dumb—"

"Is there?" Dr. Amos asked. "It has nothing to do with this animal. Have you had your rabies shots?"

"He never even broke skin!" I yelled at the TV. "I hate you. I hate you both."

Martin patted my arm. "They can't hear you."

Miranda thanked Dr. Amos for his contribution, but she wasn't finished yet. "Let's hear from another Crystal Harbor resident, one who's a bit more—" she tittered "—normal."

Here was Nina Wallace, with her tasteful grooming and adorable baby bump, looking and sounding like everyone's favorite Sunday-school teacher. "I hate to speak ill of anyone, particularly an elected official, but I feel a responsibility in this case to share my misgivings. I personally would not be surprised if it turns out Mayor Halperin did away with her husband."

I groaned, my face in my hands. "Sophie will never speak to me again."

"I wouldn't be so sure." Martin rubbed the back of my neck. It felt like heaven and was almost worth what I'd just gone through. "She knows how these vultures operate."

I switched off the TV as Miranda wrapped up her commentary and moved on to another hard-hitting news story, this one about taxidermy classes aimed at preschoolers. "Well, my business is in the crapper for sure. Who'd hire me now?" I made air quotes. "An 'oversexed devil worshiper' who turns on her best friends." I was perilously close to tears. SB did his doggie hug, sitting up with his belly and front legs pressed against me. He licked my chin.

The padre stripped the seal on the tequila, eased out the cork, and handed the bottle over. When I just looked at it, fighting back sniffles, he tipped it to my mouth. The pale golden liquid slid over my tongue and warmed my insides. Tequila like this has more in common with a fine cognac than with the stuff Martin dumps into the blender at Tierney's with margarita ingredients.

"Don't stop," I murmured, as his strong fingers kneaded the tight muscles of my neck and shoulders.

"Wouldn't dream of it," he whispered, his breath warm on my ear. He urged me to take another sip, then commandeered the bottle and took one himself before handing it back.

We stayed like that for several minutes, passing the bottle back and forth as he continued to massage away my tension. A heady intimacy suffused me, one I was loath to end. I could have stayed like that all evening, being comforted by a sexy man of mystery, my dog, and a bottle of the best booze on the planet. I felt Martin shift closer and wondered distractedly if he was going to kiss me.

The doorbell rang. Sexy Beast leapt off the couch and ran barking through the living room and into the foyer. I sighed.

Martin patted my back. "Stay. I'll get it." He followed SB. I heard the front door open, then a male voice.

"What are you doing here?" Dom. SB yelped in excitement, greeting him.

"I live here," Martin said. "What are you doing here?"

"That better be a joke. Where's Janey?" Dom stalked into the game room and took in the sight of his ex-wife drinking straight from a bottle of high-end tequila.

"Did you see?" I asked miserably.

"Why do you think I'm here?" He sat next to me, in the spot recently vacated by Martin, who sat on the steps to the living room, giving SB scritches. "I heard about what happened at Lacey's store this morning," Dom said, "so I tuned in to the show."

"Oh God, it must be all over town. Everyone saw me make an ass of myself on that awful program."

"For the record, you didn't make an ass of yourself," he said. "That Miranda person did it for you."

"Gee, thanks," I groaned.

"No, I mean…" Dom started rubbing my neck, taking over where Martin had left off, which felt a little surreal. Also flattering. I wasn't accustomed to that much physical masculine attention in one day, if you took a certain seven-pound canine out of the equation.

Dom said, "What I mean is, she obviously manipulated

your words. Anyone who knows you will see that."

I looked into his kind, dark eyes. "You think so?"

He nodded.

"But there's all the rest of it, that satanic business." I started to lift the bottle to my lips. Dom gently took it from me and inspected the level of liquid in it.

"Did you drink all this?" He set the bottle on the coffee table.

"I had help." The fact is, I was a little tipsy and liking it.

Dom looked at Martin, still perched on the steps. "He says he's living here now. A joke, I assume?"

I sighed.

"Janey?" He tipped my head to look at him. "You're not shacking up with this guy, are you? I've told you before, he's bad news."

"I'm right here," Martin said pleasantly. "I can hear you."

"Of course I'm not shacking up with him," I said. "He needs a place to stay, is all."

"That's what hotels are for," Dom said.

"It's *temporary.*" I gave Martin a pointed look. "Only until he can find permanent accommodations."

"No, Janey." Dom shook his head. "I'm sorry, I don't like it."

Yeah, well, I didn't like divorcing you and watching you rack up two more marriages, a fiancée, and three kids—kids the two of us should have had together—but I don't recall having had a say in any of it.

Except the divorcing part. I'd spent the past seventeen years regretting that one monumental mistake. Now that Dom was eager to remarry me, however, I found that thirty-nine-year-old Jane Delaney, after everything she'd endured and accomplished on her own, just might not need him anymore.

"No one's asking you to like it," I said. "I'm capable of choosing my own houseguests."

Dom opened his mouth to say something, then closed it. He looked at Martin, then at me. "If he stays here, then so do I."

"Oh, for heaven's sake."

"I don't trust this guy, Janey, and neither should you."

A memory flashed then from three months earlier, of Martin shouting at me to run and save myself. To leave him in what had become a death trap when it looked like there was no way to save us both.

Before I could shake off my reverie and formulate a response, Martin spoke up. "Look, man, you don't even know me, and the way I see it, you don't get a vote."

The two men stared each other down while I choked on testosterone fumes.

"I'm moving into your room, Janey," Dom said at last. "To keep you safe. I won't take no for an answer."

"No," I said. "There's your answer."

Abruptly Dom rose and strode into the kitchen. I craned my neck to watch as he located my purse, pulled out my wallet, and extracted the spare house keys he knew I always carried in the change compartment. He returned, pocketing the keys.

"Good grief," I said, "Martin isn't even sleeping upstairs. He's staying in the maid's room, back there." I pointed toward the far back corner of the house.

Dom thought about that. "Then I'll take the room across from yours."

"No, you won't," I said. "The upstairs is mine alone. If you insist on staying here, Dom, you'll have to sleep down here on the couch or something. *And...*" I raised a finger. "You both pay rent."

"I thought I was a houseguest," Martin said.

"If you stay free, there's no incentive to find your own place," I said, and tossed out the first figure that leapt into my cranium. "A hundred bucks a night. Nonnegotiable."

"Deal," they said in unison.

"Paid weekly in advance. And I'm not feeding you." Considering the effect that humiliating *Ramrod News* broadcast would no doubt have on my Death Diva business, I'd probably need the guys' rent money just to keep myself in Fruity Pebbles and orange soda.

I stood. "I'm going to go call Sophie. Then I'm going to get ready for my date."

"Oh, you have a date?" Dom made a conspicuous effort to look okay with that. "Anyone I know?"

"No," I said.

"It's someone she met on Dog Loving Singles dot com," Martin informed my ex.

"How do you know that?" I demanded. "You know what? Don't answer that." Martin had a history of sneaking into my house to snoop around, starting when Irene was alive and its sole resident. He and his step-grandmother hadn't exactly been best buds.

"And one more thing." I picked up Sexy Beast and headed for the curved staircase in the foyer. "If you boys decide to kill each other, do it outside."

6

Such a Coy Wench

"IT'S A LOT peppier than what I'm driving now." I was behind the wheel of a nice-looking three-year-old red Mazda 6, negotiating lane changes on a six-lane highway. Sophie's ex-husband, Dean Phillips, sat in the front passenger seat.

"A rickshaw would be peppier than what you're driving now," he said. "How long did you say you had it? Eleven years?"

"Well, it's eleven years old, but I've had it for seven. Bought it used."

"You're smart to stick to pre-owned." He ran his fingers through those unfortunate hair plugs. "New cars lose half their value, eh, the moment you drive off the lot."

"So you said." If he wanted to pretend I was looking for a used ride because I was a savvy shopper, and not because it was the only thing I could afford, I'd play along. The first car he'd tried to get me into had indeed been the nearly new Lexus convertible he'd mentioned at Sophie's house. It was, as he'd said, a beaut, and I'd allowed myself one lingering, wishful gaze as I took in its gleaming sex appeal. An experienced salesman, he'd managed to conceal his disappointment when I'd confessed that my car budget would maybe cover the Lexus's leather upholstery and one of its fancy wheels.

Which is how I'd ended up test-driving the Mazda. It was late afternoon on a brutally hot Saturday, a good test of the car's air conditioning, which performed like a champ. The flip side of using AC was the closed windows, which resulted in a concentrated, eye-watering miasma composed of Dean's spicy cologne, his liberally applied hairspray, and his stale smoker's breath. If I did take the car, I'd probably need to fumigate it.

Dean had yet to mention my television debut on *Ramrod News* the previous evening. Either he was exercising discretion in the interest of making a sale or he simply hadn't seen the show. My money was on that first thing. It seemed the entire town of Crystal Harbor had watched the show.

As much as I needed a car, I could have shopped a lot closer to home or scoured the used-car ads. The fact is, I felt kind of sorry for Dean, a hapless nobody who'd never managed to find a stable career, much less joy in what he did for a living. If I was going to spend money on new wheels, he might as well be the one getting the commission.

But I had another reason for seeking out Sophie's ex.

He said, "Have you thought about buying a hearse?" His Canadian accent turned *about* into something closer to *aboot*.

"Uh, can't say that I have," I admitted.

"Think about it. It'd be great for business," he said. "You can leave it plain or put a fancy 'Death Diva' design on it. Maybe a cartoon of you wearing sexy underwear."

So much for discretion. "Well, that's an interesting idea, Dean. Maybe for a second vehicle down the road. Right now I need something a bit more sedate, for when my job is kind of, you know, undercover."

"Oh, sure, sure. Just say the word, eh, I'll put out feelers for the right hearse. Think about the cargo space."

That was about as good a segue as I was going to get. "So," I said. "How long were you and Sophie married?"

"Huh? Oh, just ten months." I felt his eyes on me as I steered into the left-turn lane to make a U-turn and head back to the dealership. "Listen," he said, "I know I came off as kind of, uh… worked up at her place a couple of days ago. Well, I was worked up. It's not every day the cops question you about some murdered guy."

"At your place of work, no less." I tried to sound sympathetic. "You're allowed a normal human reaction. I know something like that would've freaked me out for sure." As indeed it had a few months earlier when Bonnie had considered me a suspect in Irene's murder, but that didn't bear mentioning at the moment.

I'd been nervous about calling Sophie the evening before, to apologize for unwittingly calling her a greedy murderer on national TV. She'd dismissed my concerns, claiming to have been amused by the absurd coverage. She'd even recorded it for posterity. That's the kind of friend she was, and why I felt obligated to help clear her name.

The sad fact was, even the legitimate press had turned Sophie into a punching bag. Even if she was proved innocent—I mean, *when* she was proved innocent—it would probably be too late to salvage her local political career. Nina Wallace might very well be our next mayor. The thought made me want to follow Teddy Waterfield's example and become a well-heeled hermit.

I said, "You mentioned you were out of state when Ernie was killed?"

"Boston. Flew there for an info seminar about a franchise

opportunity," he said. "One of those drive-through convenience-store chains. Didn't work out."

What a shock.

"You know this crap I'm going through now, with that girl detective?" he said. "It's all Teddy Waterfield's fault. That crazy old bat convinced herself that Sophie and I killed her son for the money. This was back when everyone else thought he offed himself. I figured that nonsense was ancient history, but whaddaya know? Turns out the guy really was murdered."

I played dumb. "What money?"

"Sophie didn't tell you about that, eh? Better get over." An emergency vehicle was coming up fast behind us, whooping and hollering. I moved to the right lane and we watched it race past. He continued, "So Sophie marries the love of her life only to find out he's a f—he's gay. I mean, how dense do you have to be not to figure that one out before you start choosing china patterns, am I right?"

"I wouldn't say 'dense.' Maybe too innocent for her own good." I honked at a driver who'd never heard of checking his blind spot before changing lanes, forcing me to swerve and tap the brakes. This car was responsive, another plus.

"Okay, whatever," he said. "I know you two are tight. You gotta stand up for her."

Dean fell silent and I gave myself a mental kick in the pants for defending his ex when I'd had him talking. "I love this car, by the way," I chirped. "You've made a sale, Dean."

"Now, that's what I like." He thumped the dash. "A girl that knows her mind. I can't tell you how many female customers bust my chops over colors and cup holders."

Now that he knew the sale was in the bag, I said, "So if there was money involved like you said, where did it come from? I thought Ernie and Sophie were just scraping by."

"The Wicked Witch of Crystal Harbor."

"Teddy?" I asked.

He nodded. "You know she's loaded, right? I guess you never met her?"

"Yes and no."

"Yeah, she's not what you might call a social butterfly, eh, not since her precious boy died. Consider yourself lucky your paths never crossed. That's one serious ball-buster. 'Scuse my language."

I waved off his apology. "Why mince words? If she's a ball-buster, she's a ball-buster." *That's me, Jane Delaney, your friendly, foulmouthed Death Diva.* Anything to keep him talking.

He chortled. "Ain't that the truth. You know what, Jane? You're okay."

"Thanks. You're not bad yourself, Dean. So. Ernie's mom gave the newlyweds money to live on. Not exactly the actions of a ball-buster."

"Wait, I didn't get to the good part. Mama Waterfield is thrilled that her son the, uh, the gay guy is married. Her cute new daughter-in-law will turn him around, she thinks—Sophie was hot stuff back then, believe it or not." He made a hot-stuff gesture, and I held my breath against the chemical onslaught of the cologne he'd splashed on with such enthusiastic abandon.

Dean went on. "Everything's gonna be okay, Teddy thinks. She'll get the grandkids she's always wanted and all will be right with the world. Only problem, the new Mrs. Waterfield isn't getting any from her bridegroom, eh, and when he finally admits the reason, she's ready to give him the old heave-ho. Are you with me?"

I let out the breath I'd been holding. "Like a tick."

"Teddy isn't about to stand for that. She just knows that a little hetero whoopee will cure her boy. So she makes Sophie an offer she can't refuse." A pause for dramatic effect, then: "Three. Million. Dollars. That's how much Teddy paid Sophie to stay married to her homo son. Three million smackers."

"Wow. That's a lot of money," I said.

"She couldn't divorce him, is all. Otherwise the dough was hers to keep."

And Dean's, too, I thought, if he somehow ended up married to her. Which could happen only if her first husband kicked the bucket. Technically the money would be Sophie's, not his, but as her husband, he'd benefit from her windfall.

I said, "Were you and Sophie, um… No, I shouldn't ask." Oh, that Jane Delaney, such a coy wench.

"Were we getting it on when she was married to Ernie?" He grinned. "Is that what you're too polite to ask?"

"It's none of my business."

"Nah, she kept it under lock and key," he said. "Wouldn't cheat on him, even though nothing was happening between the sheets."

"That must have been frustrating for you." I passed the dealership on the left and got ready to make another U-turn.

His bark of laughter reverberated inside the close confines of the Mazda. "You're telling me. I was a horny young buck back then, eh, used to getting what I wanted—not bragging, just telling it like it was—and she was, well, she was hot stuff like I said. Tell me I can't have it, I want it all the more. Sexy *and* rich, an irresistible combo, you know what I mean?"

"I've always thought so." He was describing Dom.

His arm snaked over the seatback behind my head. "So

why aren't you married, Jane? I don't see a ring."

No no no, we're almost at the dealership. Don't get sidetracked now. "I was. Didn't suit me. So nothing happened between you and Sophie until Ernie died?"

"I moved in fast then, I don't mind telling you."

"Who could blame you?" I said. "If you hadn't acted on your genuine love for Sophie, someone else might have grabbed her on the rebound and married her for the wrong reason."

"Wrong reason?"

"Her money?" I said.

"Oh, right. Turn here," he said, unnecessarily.

I got into the turning lane and waited at the blessedly red light. "I'm sorry things didn't work out for you and Sophie," I said.

"Yeah, me too, but what are you gonna do? Marriage means mutual support, you know? Like doing for each other."

You were never willing to help me when we were married, Dean had said that day at Sophie's house. *Why start now?* The house she'd bought for him to live in wasn't enough?

"She didn't support you?" I asked. "You mean emotionally?"

"In all ways. When it came to groceries and whatnot, I mean sure, we both pitched in. But I had a dream, you know? A no-lose business idea. All I needed was capital. Woulda barely made a dent in her bank account."

"What was this idea?"

"Okay." He ran his palm across an imaginary sign. "Robot vacuum cleaner."

"Wow."

"Incredible, right? And remember, eh, this was thirty-something years ago. Was I ahead of my time or what? Would've made millions. Only, *my* robot vacuum cleaner's nothing like that dopey little round thing that cats ride on. Mine looks like a…" He made a va-va-va-voom gesture in the vicinity of his chest. "Like a sexy girl, you know? Dressed in a little apron. High heels."

"Wow." Words, as they say, eluded me.

"Well, that's what she *would've* looked like if I had the dough to get a prototype made up. But Her Highness wouldn't part with a nickel." His wary gaze flicked to me. "Don't mean to be running her down." Suddenly worried about his sale.

"Forget about it." I executed my U-turn. "Listen, I've been friends with Sophie forever. There's nothing you can tell me about her faults that I don't already know." I gave Sophie's ex a conspiratorial wink, feeling like the worst friend in the world.

Get over it, I admonished myself. *You're doing this for her.*

"I've done the math," he griped. "How much money I would've made if she'd just loosened the purse strings a little. Like, seventy million, that's how much her pathological stinginess cost me. And after everything I did for her."

Like what? I wondered. "Maybe she thought your idea wouldn't work," I suggested, "and she'd lose her investment."

"Yeah, she made all those noises, but bottom line, she sabotaged my dream. Which should've been her dream too, eh, if she was a normal, loving wife."

I'd told Sophie I didn't know anyone who didn't like her. I supposed I could no longer make that claim.

I turned off the highway and into the dealership's lot. After I parked, Dean insisted on demonstrating, in exhaustive detail, the climate-control system, sound system, seat adjustment, wipers, lights, console storage, fold-down backseats, how to access the spare, etcetera, etcetera, ad nauseam. No feature was too inconsequential to rate mention. Did you know you can change the taillight bulbs from inside the trunk? Well, okay, you probably knew that, but it was a revelation to me. Not that I'd stop paying my mechanic to perform the task. I mean it's, you know, car stuff.

I followed Dean to his desk on the sales floor, where we haggled over the price and I eventually prevailed. If there's one thing I know how to do, it's drive a hard bargain. We talked about the warranty and all that boring grownup stuff. I stood to leave. Dean stood too, glancing at his fake Rolex.

"Listen, it's quitting time," he said. "There's a nice bar down the road. Fifty-two beers on tap. Great fried mozzarella. Feel like getting a drink?"

That was just what I needed, two shoot-me-now dates in less than twenty-four hours. Last night's dinner had been memorable, to put it politely. My date, Ralph, not only loved dogs, he bred them. Wait, that didn't come out right. You know what I mean. My date hauled a fat grandma's brag book out of his man-purse and proudly displayed dozens of photos of golden retrievers—thirteen at last count—of all ages and in various stages of sleep and activity throughout his house.

All floor space not strewn with well-used newspapers was thickly carpeted in dog hair, as was the furniture, including the kitchen table and counters. It drifted in corners and collected into balls like golden tumbleweeds. I'd assumed my itchy nose was psychosomatic until I noted that Ralph's clothing bore a liberal coating of the same yellow hairs. He even, yes, smelled like a golden retriever. After dinner, he invited me back to his place for dessert.

Okay, that gagging sound you just made? I'd manfully

refrained from making that same sound while I'd graciously declined his offer.

I smiled at Dean. "Sounds like fun, but I have an important assignment." The important assignment was to pick up some General Tso's and fried dumplings, park my carcass in front of my gargantuan TV, and channel-surf until I inevitably stumbled across an episode of *Law & Order*. "Give me a call when the car's ready."

7

Freezer-burned Giant Tortoise

THE TANTALIZING AROMA of grilled food made my stomach squeal as Sexy Beast and I joined the happy swarm of humanity at the annual Crystal Harbor street fair. A large section of Main Street had been closed to traffic. Booths lined the roadway, offering everything from cups of beer and lemonade to food of every type to children's games and local information booths.

The first of these we passed was sponsored by a no-kill animal shelter. Three young people from the shelter had brought a few dogs and cats needing a good home. I was proud of SB. Not the most well socialized animal—one of the many things Irene didn't believe in was exposing her precious pooch to other dogs—he'd been making progress during the spring and summer, thanks to regular trips to the town dog park. Thus he now did more friendly butt-sniffing than growling.

In particular he hit it off with the sweetest white pit bull mix named Showgirl. They made quite the striking couple, as you can imagine. I was so tempted to take her home and love her forever, and don't think her handlers didn't try to make that happen, but I knew my limits. For one thing, I didn't see how I could fit sixty-pound Showgirl in my tote bag as I went about my busy day. Regretfully, we bade the menagerie farewell and moved on.

It was midafternoon on Sunday, and I was thankful we weren't being treated to yesterday's brutal heat. The temperature hovered in the low eighties, the sky slightly overcast, which was okay as it enhanced the comfort level. SB and I strolled among the throngs of locals and day-trippers, exchanging greetings and following our noses to the nearest ginormous grill, set in front of a Thai restaurant. The grill was manned by the restaurateur and his family. I treated myself to marinated chicken skewers, and then to a big plastic cup of beer at the next booth, operated by a local brewery. I looped the handle of SB's leash on my wrist to perform the all-important food-beer-and-dog juggling act.

Sexy Beast coveted the Thai chicken in his polite way, licking his lips while making tiny sounds deep in his throat. I gave him a couple of bites from the inside part of the meat, which I'd determined bland enough for him. Then he heard, "All gone" in that distinctive singsong tone that informed him that even though he saw more chicken on the skewer, it wasn't for him. He happily, or at least obediently, gave up begging and trotted alongside me.

I recognized the tall, white-haired man examining a striking cobalt blue vase at a booth featuring pottery made by the young couple who owned the gallery next to Janey's Place. Sten Jakobsen had been Irene's lawyer and close friend, and it was his responsibility to see that her bequest of the house and maintenance funds, as well as my guardianship of her darling Sexy Beast, were being properly managed. We shared a clumsy hug as I tried to keep every precious drop of India pale ale in my cup. I wondered what he'd say if I told him the house Irene had bequeathed to me—or rather, bequeathed to Sexy Beast, but let's be real—had been turned into a kind of bachelor's boardinghouse. I decided to keep that bit of news to myself.

I'd always had a great deal of admiration and affection for Sten. I'd bet serious bread he wasn't a *Ramrod News* viewer, but he had to have at least heard of my disastrous appearance on the show. Perhaps he'd even made a point of catching a rerun or recording of it, considering the position of responsibility I held in caring for his late client's estate and pet.

The thought of proper, upright Sten Jakobsen seeing me in that sexed-up lingerie—and those granny panties!—made me want to step on a landmine.

My expression might have given me away. In lieu of a simple good-bye, Sten placed his big hand on my shoulder and gently smiled down at me. In his signature leisurely, basso profundo way, he said, "Remember, Jane, we have no control over the bottom-feeders. All we can do is be our best selves."

My eyes misted. I placed my beer on the pavement, balanced the chicken skewer on the cup's rim (with a firm command to SB to "leave it"), and gave my friend Sten a proper hug.

"Get a room, you two." The voice and pugnacious attitude belonged to none other than Mayor Sophie Halperin. I turned with more than a little trepidation, even though I'd spoken with her on the phone just after the show aired. She'd had approximately thirty hours to ponder my performance and realize why she should be good and mad at me.

Indeed, Sophie wore a scowl, as well as a colorful, strawberry-dotted sundress and, for some reason known only to her, a gigantic sombrero, complete with dangling pompoms. She pushed the sombrero back on its lanyard and propped her fists on her wide hips as the hubbub of activity around us stilled. Our friends and neighbors stared, eager for a show.

If they were looking for a catfight, they were to be disappointed. Sophie opened her stubby arms wide and said, "What, no hug for your mayor?" I fell into her arms, squeezing my eyes against the stinging tears and hugging her for all I was worth. SB barked madly, standing up against my legs and demanding to be let in on the love-fest. Sophie made it a good, long bear hug, ensuring that everyone in the vicinity got an eyeful, then stood with her arm around my waist and commanded our stunned audience to stop by the high school's booth and donate to the seniors' upcoming trip to Europe.

"Go on now, get over there," she barked, and they meekly obeyed.

I felt like disgraced Scarlett O'Hara being publicly embraced by the wronged Melanie Wilkes in *Gone With the Wind*. What good deeds had I performed in some past life to deserve a friend like Sophie Halperin?

I thanked her again for being such a stand-up pal and moved on before I could start blubbering in earnest.

SB and I passed a pocket park where a couple of dozen youngsters congregated. There was the requisite bouncy castle, and next to that a fenced-in pig race. The things an otherwise self-respecting hog will do for an Oreo! On the other side of the castle was a pony ride. Sexy Beast couldn't seem to decide whether to growl at the big, ugly dog with the toddler on its back or to grovel in submission, so he did both. Talk about mixed messages. The pony just clopped on by, unimpressed.

I tossed my empty cup and skewer in a trash barrel and we continued on, SB having himself a sniffing extravaganza, me greeting friends and acquaintances and trying to ignore the occasional smirk or speculative glance. We passed a baked-goods booth manned by Nina Wallace, the profits to benefit the town Historical Society, according to the sign. I looked the other way, pretending not to see Nina as she, believe it or not, waved cheerily and tried to beckon me over. Yeah, that would happen.

Dom manned a food booth in front of Janey's Place, accompanied by an excessively bored looking Cheyenne O'Rourke, both of them wearing apple green Janey's Place T-shirts. I led SB over so he could greet his beloved Dom as if it had been years since he'd last seen him. Dom offered him a small piece of some vegetarian crap meant to resemble meat. You'd think it was the real thing the way SB scarfed it up.

Dom turned to me. "I know what you want." His smile was a tad suggestive, or maybe that was my imagination. He started tossing ingredients into a blender. Okay, it was my imagination. "One papaya-ginger smoothie coming up. On the house."

On top of the beer and chicken? Well, why not? I tried chatting with Cheyenne as the blender did its thing. You'd think I was conversing with an overly made-up tree stump for all the response I got.

Detective Bonnie Hernandez strolled by with her gorgeous, perfectly groomed, perfectly behaved red standard poodle, Frederick. She pointedly ignored Dom, who noticed her but quickly redirected his gaze to the creamy orange smoothie he was pouring for me.

For the record, Frederick wasn't the only well-groomed poodle in attendance. Yesterday I'd brought Sexy Beast to Rocky, the best groomer in these here parts, so my pet would look his best strutting around the street fair. Rocky (no last name, so Hollywood) had actually gotten me to laugh at the *Ramrod News* segment by dressing Sexy Beast in a little red-satin devil's outfit, complete with satanic horns.

It helped that he was flamboyantly gay—Rocky, that is, not Sexy Beast. He hadn't known I had such an impressive *rack*, darling, it was one of those *sneaky* ones, and why on earth had I left the house wearing those *hideous* white *briefs* and was it true I'd found Ernie Waterfield's *skeleton*?

Rocky, as it turned out, had known Ernie, which surprised me. He didn't strike me as being of Ernie's and Sophie's generation, but that was probably because he was slim and fit, with short, neatly trimmed salt-and-pepper hair and good skin.

Rocky had told me that Ernie had confided in him that he was in love—not with his fiancée, Sophie, but with another man. Rocky, who'd apparently always been open about his sexual orientation, had urged Ernie to call off the engagement, for his sake and Sophie's, and to come out of the closet. But his friend had been under the thumb of his domineering mother and it was not meant to be.

I led my elegantly coiffed Sexy Beast to the high school's senior-trip booth, which was manned by a tall, blond man in his mid-thirties and a couple of high school kids, a boy and a girl. The students lavished attention on SB as I dug through my purse for my checkbook. When I handed the man a check for twenty bucks, he thanked me and asked if I had a student in the school. I was taken aback until I thought about it a second and was forced to acknowledge I was old enough to be the mother of a high schooler.

"Nope, I just want the kids to have a good trip." I switched my smoothie cup to my left hand and reached across the folding table that constituted the school's booth. "I'm Jane Delaney."

"I know." Grinning, he shook my hand, and I realized this handsome guy with warm hazel eyes and a pleasantly craggy face had seen The Show.

My face flamed. The curse of the naturally strawberry blond—a mood-ring complexion that conceals nothing. "My reputation precedes me," I mumbled.

"I'm Colin Vargas." He reached down to pet Sexy Beast, who'd gone under the table to check him out. "I teach advanced-placement American history."

"Oh. You must be Lacey and Porter's son."

"I'm Lacey's son." He straightened. "Porter is my stepfather."

Hmm… Most people wouldn't feel the need to make the distinction. Colin had never even met his biological father; his stepfather had raised him from birth. I recalled Lacey telling me her son was the image of Tim Holbrook, the man who'd sired him. He certainly looked nothing like swarthy, black-haired Porter Vargas.

I said, "Somehow I wouldn't expect an AP history teacher to be a fan of a show like *Ramrod News*."

"My mom told me about it and I caught the segment on YouTube."

His words whacked me in the solar plexus. "It's on YouTube?" I croaked.

His genial smile faded. "You didn't know." A woman with a couple of small children in tow approached the booth. Colin gestured to the students to attend to her.

"Oh God," I groaned. "I'll never live this down."

"I wouldn't worry," he said. "This sort of thing has a limited shelf life on the web. Just be grateful you're not a litter of puppies or a grumpy cat."

"How many hits did the video have? Did you notice?"

He hesitated. "A little over a million at that point."

I clapped a hand over my mouth and froze in that position. SB whined and pawed at my legs.

"Jane?" Colin took hold of my arm. "You okay? Maybe you should sit down."

I dropped my hand. "Over a million people have seen me wearing that—that—and saying those things…"

He tried to steer me to the curb, presumably so I could sit with my head between my knees, the better to remain fully conscious and aware of the depth of my humiliation, as well as to draw even more attention to myself. I was the subject of enough gossip as it was.

"It's okay, Colin." I set the smoothie cup on the table, produced my smartphone, and brought up YouTube. "I'm not a fainter." I was, however, a pretty spectacular upchucker under the right circumstances. Such as discovering that the video titled "Sexy Satanic Death Diva" had racked up 2,374,917 views. Plus, of course, thousands of comments.

I placed a hand on my roiling stomach. Whose idea had that Thai chicken and India pale ale been anyway? And what had possessed me to pour a smoothie on top of it?

That's when I recalled that this particular smoothie was supposed to be good for stomachaches. I sucked on the straw and coaxed SB away from a half-eaten ear of grilled corn that lay in the gutter. I think I said the usual nice-to-meet-you stuff as I took my leave of Colin, but I can't be sure.

Two point three million views and climbing. My accidental appearance on *Ramrod News* was the gift that kept on giving. What had been a perfectly lovely street fair now felt like a horror-movie fun house as I negotiated my way through the chattering, fun-loving crowd. Eventually it dawned on me that someone was calling my name.

"Earth to Death Diva!" The man was in his late twenties, of medium build, with short red hair, a short red beard, and the kind of peeling, sun-scalded complexion only a redhead could manage. I recognized him as the owner of the Harbor Room, where I'd had dinner with the breeder of golden retrievers and his pelt. I'd met this guy once or twice before and now scoured my memory for his name as he beckoned me to the restaurant's booth.

Kevin… Keith… Ken… something K.

Every year the Harbor Room sponsored the largest, fanciest booth, with a festive tent, nautical decorations, and an entire outdoor kitchen. Next to the booth sat an authentic rum-runner boat that had been used in the 1920s to ferry smuggled booze from offshore vessels to the restaurant.

I approached the booth, lifting Sexy Beast to keep him from scavenging the assorted edible tidbits that littered the pavement. The owner (Karl? Kasey?) grinned and left the booth, where several workers served fairgoers such popular delicacies as shrimp skewers, lobster rolls, and the aforementioned grilled corn. The mingled aromas drew in crowds from up and down the street.

Keenan… Kiefer… Keanu… My mind had gone Hollywood in search of this guy's name. Unnecessarily as it turned out.

"Kyle Kenneally. Remember me?" He chucked SB under the chin. SB seemed not to know what to do with that.

"Of course," I said. "How are you, Kyle? Looks like your booth is pretty popular there."

He glanced back at it. "I'm giving every customer that

signs up for our email newsletter a coupon for a free appetizer. Want to see them in the restaurant."

"Smart."

"Listen, Janet, I have a… well, a job I want to hire you for."

"I always like to hear that." Kyle had never hired me before, but I welcomed new clients, now more than ever since I expected to lose a bunch over the *Ramrod* fiasco. Maybe he hadn't caught the show. "And it's Jane, by the way."

"Huh? Oh. Right. Anyway…" He led me behind the booth where we'd have something approaching privacy. I set down Sexy Beast but kept a good grip on the leash.

"Wait here." Kyle ducked into the booth and emerged with a lobster roll in a paper boat, along with a handful of napkins. I gratefully accepted it, my nausea forgotten. I mean, lobster.

SB sat his little butt on the ground, his dark eyes locked on the hot-dog roll overflowing with gooey lobster salad as I took the first bite and bit back a groan of ecstasy. I looked directly at SB and he swiftly averted his gaze. This is his way, and we can play the game for as long as it takes me to eat something. He covets my exotic human food but tries to be subtle about it. If he gets frustrated enough, he'll emit a faint whimper, just to remind the alpha female that she's responsible for sharing with the omega member of our two-animal pack.

I plucked a mayonnaise-slathered chunk of lobster and offered it to him. He gave it a delicate sniff, then gulped it down and licked his snout to get every last speck of lobstery deliciousness.

Meanwhile Kyle looked at me with an expression not unlike Sexy Beast's, but less subtle. Hmm…

"So what do you need done?" I wiped my mouth and took another bite.

"I need you to dig up my mama and put something in her coffin."

I managed not to spew lobster all over him, but it was a close thing. I squeaked the food down my gullet and cleared my throat. "Excuse me?"

"She's buried in Whispering Willows Cemetery," he said. "You know that place pretty well, right? And you know how and when to sneak in so no one'll see you." His leering grin spoke volumes on the subject of whether he'd caught the show. I'd bet real money he was wondering if I was wearing those naughty undies, not to mention the ritual granny panties, under my T-shirt and shorts.

"Kyle, let me be clear." SB scooted a little closer and licked his lips. With an exasperated sigh I offered him another bite. "I do not exhume dead people. Never have, never will."

He laughed, glancing around and lowering his voice. "You don't have to pretend with me, Janet. I know all about your, uh, religious practices. Don't tell me something like this isn't right up your alley."

Good grief. "My religious practices?"

He spread his hands. "Hey, I make no judgments. You can worship any way and any *thing* you want, as long as no one gets hurt. Much," he snickered.

"Kyle, I—"

"I'll pay you five thousand bucks."

I was struck momentarily speechless while an unruly corner of my brain calculated what it would take to quickly unearth a casket, mess around with it, and cover it up again. The sod would need to be carefully replaced—

I gave myself a vigorous mental shake. "I don't know what gave you the idea that I would… well, I know what gave you that idea, but let me assure you, it's not going to happen."

"Six thousand."

"What do you want to put in her casket anyway?" I asked.

"Her pet giant tortoise, Romeo."

I had to ask. "Dead or alive?"

He looked aghast. "Dead, of course. What kind of sicko do you take me for?"

The world was full of sickos. I was just aiming to narrow it down.

"Romeo died last week," Kyle continued. "He was over a hundred eighty years old. I've got him in the walk-in freezer at work."

Remind me not to order… well, anything at the Harbor Room ever again.

"I'm sorry, Kyle, I'm not doing it. It's illegal for one thing. I don't do illegal things." Much. I mean, there's a fine line on which I've found myself teetering on more than one occasion, but for purposes of this discussion, it was best to keep things black and white.

"Hear me out, Janet. Mama was devoted to Romeo. She grew up with him. So did I. He's been in our family for generations—they think he might've been one of those Darwin tortoises. I know she'd want to be buried with him."

"A giant tortoise that old must be a big fellow."

"Oh, man." Kyle beamed, holding his arms wide to indicate circumference. "I used to ride on him when I was little."

When all else fails, try reason. "Did you even stop to think he can't possibly fit in your mother's casket?"

"I did think of that, sure, but Mama was tiny and she's been gone eight years. I don't see how she can take up that much room at this point, and if you were to saw Romeo in half—"

"All right, we're going to stop right here." I didn't think anything or anyone could put me off a good lobster roll, but Kyle's latest conversational salvo had done the trick. I placed the little paper boat with about a quarter of the sandwich untouched at SB's feet. You'd think food was a new and glorious concept for him, the way he went after it.

"If you want to bury Romeo with Mama, you're more than welcome to try. Only, don't call me to bail you out." An idea leapt up and whacked me on the noggin. "You know, an animal with a pedigree like that shouldn't be thrown in a hole in the ground. I'll bet there's a natural-history museum somewhere that would be happy to take a donation like that. Maybe stuff him and put him on display in one of those dioramas."

He pondered that. "You think so?"

"With your name as donor right there on a brass plaque."

"Huh. Imagine that." He imagined it, then grimaced and shook his head. "Forget it, I don't have time to look into all that."

"Why should you?" I made a here-I-am gesture. "That's the kind of thing I do for people."

He looked dubious. "Donations to museums?"

"Anything to do with dead folks." Granted, most of those folks were of the Homo sapiens variety, but I was no stranger to the Best Friend Pet Cemetery. And granted, I'd never arranged the donation of an animal specimen, but I've handled many other kinds of donations on behalf of survivors. Why not an older-than-dirt giant tortoise named Romeo?

"What's this going to cost me?" he asked.

"Five thousand bucks."

His look said, *Nice try.* "One thousand."

"An assignment like this promises to be very time-consuming, Kyle. Five thousand if I can get him into the American Museum of Natural History in Manhattan—"

"With a plaque!"

"With a plaque," I agreed. "Thirty-five hundred without the plaque. Same deal for the Smithsonian."

"The Smithsonian!" His look was rapturous. I almost expected to hear angels singing.

"Two thousand bucks if I get him into another legitimate museum." There must be scores if not hundreds of such institutions all over the world. A few hours with a search engine, a few emails and phone calls. Easy money.

"Deal," Kyle said, visions of a brass plaque in the Smithsonian dancing in his head.

"You're responsible for my expenses, if any, and for the cost of transporting Romeo to whatever institution accepts him, in whatever manner they require." Which could cost more, I guesstimated, than my fee, unless the museum paid the freight. I'd have to look into all that.

"No problem."

"I'll draw up the work order and swing by the restaurant this evening so you can sign it and I can get moving on it." I didn't want to give him too much time to mull it over and strike out on his own in the dead of night with a shovel and a half-thawed big-ass reptile. "I'll need a five-hundred-dollar down payment in cash, refundable if I don't succeed. And I, uh, will need to see Romeo. So I can assure the recipient that he's well preserved and all that." No one wants a freezer-burned tortoise.

"Great." There was that skeevy look again. He moved a little closer and seemed not to hear the low groan emanating from SB's throat. "There's a cozy private room where we can have a surf-and-turf dinner and toast our venture with a bottle of Cristal."

Another icky man angling for a date. And I was waffling about Dom why?

"Sounds lovely." I shortened the leash and made SB heel. He wasn't a biter, but every animal has its limits, and as much as we both disliked Kyle, the prospect of a four-digit fee with minimal work made me all warm and squishy inside. I'd drink his champagne (don't judge me, it's Cristal!), but I'd keep the door open and ask one of my new roomies to phone me with an "emergency" twenty minutes after my arrival at the Harbor Room. Yeah, I'm sure Kyle knew that old trick and I didn't care. I'd be a blur before he could draw in a breath to gripe about it.

We agreed on seven p.m. and I took Sexy Beast on a detour to a side street so he could do his business far from the crowded fair. After we returned to Main Street, I noticed some kind of hubbub about a half block ahead, with a crowd and intermittent cheering. Being a fan of hubbubs, I quickened my pace and spied a long line of females of all ages waiting their turn at a dunking booth. The object was to throw a ball—you got three tries—at a round red target on a big yellow board and cause some poor sap to fall into a huge vat of water.

The poor sap sat on a perch above the water and behind a cage so he wouldn't get beaned by an ill-aimed ball. The vat itself had a big window in front so everyone could watch him flail around underwater before hauling himself up for another dunking.

Oh, did I mention? The poor sap in question was Martin McAuliffe. And the padre didn't appear at all unhappy to be the center of all this female attention. He wore Hawaiian-patterned board shorts and nothing else, and he was wet and tasty-looking. He sat on that perch and called out encouragement to the pretty young thing preparing to try to dunk him. Sadly for her, she threw like a girl and the padre kept his seat. He blew her a kiss and the next woman stepped up.

No way was I going to squander an opportunity like this. SB and I took up position at the end of the line, in back of Rocky, the lone male in the queue.

"I hate to break it to you, Rocky," I said, "but Martin's straight."

"A boy can *dream*, can't he?" Sexy Beast's groomer lifted him for a cuddle.

The line moved fast and the padre kept his perch. The ladies tended to become a tad flustered when confronted with his blue-eyed charm up close and it affected their aim. When it was Rocky's turn, he morphed into Nolan Ryan and aced it on the first try. Martin went down with a thunderous splash and remained underwater for a good long while, mugging for the crowd. Sexy Beast barked with delighted abandon, excited by the ruckus. Rocky stepped up to the window and gave it a big, smacking kiss, much to the amusement of the ladies and Martin, who spewed bubbles laughing underwater and blew him a return kiss.

Then it was my turn. I handed Rocky the leash and weighed the ball in my hand. The padre, seated once more, commenced to hurling jolly invective, insulting my aim, my throwing power, and my overall athletic prowess before I'd even tossed the first ball. I ignored him and quietly assumed my pitching stance, focusing laserlike on the target.

The other women observed the proceedings with interest, whispering among themselves and no doubt wondering about the relationship between the wet and wild padre and the Sexy Satanic Death Diva.

Martin thought he knew everything about me, having sneaked into my home who knew how many times and pawed through my stuff. What he couldn't know is that I'd left my high school softball trophies in my proud parents' den, so take *this*, Padre.

I wound up my underhand pitch, hurling the ball faster and straighter and with more power than any of my predecessors, including Rocky. The bell rang and Martin went down mid-insult. Through the window he gave me a surprised, impressed look. I responded with a jaunty salute, took the leash back from Rocky, and went off in search of cotton candy.

8

It's That Nympho Death Diva from TV

I RECOGNIZED LACEY VARGAS by the back of her well-coiffed head. Also by the presence of her husband, Porter, as the two engaged in an argument near the cotton-candy machine. I didn't know Porter well, but he was easy to recognize with his coal black hair—dusted with silver in all the right places—athletic physique, and patrician air. Porter glanced around and, apparently anxious to avoid a scene, pulled his wife off the street and into the nearest shadowed store doorway to continue their heated conversation.

I watched them out of the corner of my eye as I bought a blue cotton candy and took a lazy stroll. Sexy Beast liked cotton candy, as it turned out. The tacky spun sugar proved an elusive treat, dissolving on his tongue in seconds. But his disappointment was short-lived as he then got to lick and lick and lick his sticky-sweet snout.

Lacey seemed to be giving as good as she got with her husband, getting in his face and stabbing a finger at his chest. I wished I could hear what they were saying, but the fair was noisy and I couldn't get closer to them without being obvious.

Lacey swung her arm in a swift, angry gesture. My imagination filled in the blanks. *Get away from me, I don't ever want to see that smug face of yours again.* Or: *I'm going to throw all your stuff on the front lawn, so don't bother coming home.* Or less drastic: *If your mother's pot roast is so much better than mine, go have Sunday dinner with her.*

On the other hand, what did I know about the Vargases' relationship? I could be witnessing one of the minor tiffs all married couples experience. *So go buy the damn burger and fries already. If you don't care about your cholesterol, why should I?*

Whatever she'd said, Porter's response was to turn away and eat up the sidewalk with brisk strides while Lacey stalked back to the fair. Porter turned at the first corner and I kind of, well, followed him. Visually at first, just keeping him in my sights, before stepping onto the curb and trailing him at a distance. Anyone who noticed would no doubt assume I was simply taking my dog for another potty break.

The sidewalks were deserted. Most of the locals were at the fair. Sexy Beast lifted his leg and marked everything vertical between Main Street and Murray's Pub a block and a half away, which is where Porter ended up.

I followed him inside a few minutes later. Murray's was a small, pleasantly dark, unpretentious pub that had existed in this spot in Crystal Harbor since the end of the nineteenth century when the townsfolk made their living mainly in fishing and farming. The pub had survived Prohibition by serving something called "near beer," a supposedly nonalcoholic libation that would have proved anything but, had the authorities not been bribed to look the other way.

As my eyes adjusted to the dim, beer-scented interior, I scanned the empty tables and booths before spying Porter sitting at the center of the bar. He nursed a neat double whiskey and watched silent baseball on the television. Closed captioning took the place of sound because the bartender, Maxine Baumgartner, preferred listening to bluegrass. Thankfully, she kept the volume low enough for customers to converse.

Which is what I intended to do with Porter Vargas. I passed him and took a stool at the far end. We exchanged polite nods and he went back to the game. "I have the dog with me, Max." I directed Maxine's attention to my canine companion, who turned a few circles and curled up on the scarred plank floor near my barstool. Our busy afternoon walking and eating had tuckered him. "Is that okay?"

"Let me check with the boss. Yeah, she says TV stars get to bring their little purse dogs into the joint." Maxine owned the place. She was fifty-something, with a blond ponytail and a rusty smoker's voice. "Beer?"

"I had beer at the fair. *That* looks good." I indicated Porter's drink. He glanced my way and this time his gaze lingered. I tracked the path of recognition in his eyes from *I think I've met this woman* to *What do you know, it's that nympho Death Diva from TV.*

"Hi, Porter, we've met," I told him. "Jane Delaney."

"Right, I remember. How are you, Jane?"

"I'm okay, but SB and I have both had enough of that fair."

"Tell me about it." He gestured to Maxine to pour me the same thing he was having. "Put it on my tab."

"Well, thank you." I smiled and he left his barstool to take the one next to mine. Silently I pleaded with him not to come on to me. Not that Porter was of the same icky ilk as Kyle,

Dean, and Ralph, but he was a married man, and that was pretty icky in itself. Not the being-married part but the cheating-on-your-spouse part.

"And some of those crinkle fries," he added, then turned to me. "You like regular or spicy?"

"I'm a spicy girl." Argh, did I just say that?

His chuckle sounded more agreeable than lecherous. "Good to know."

Maxine placed my drink in front of me. "The fries'll be a couple of minutes. Just me here today—I wasn't expecting customers 'cause of the fair."

She disappeared through a door and I took a tentative sip of the whiskey. It was good. Smooth. I hadn't paid attention when she'd poured it. "What is it?" I asked Porter. "Not bourbon."

"Rye." He pointed to an attractive bottle on the shelves behind the bar. "A small-batch distillery." And probably über-expensive, but the owner of Vargas Sporting Goods could afford it.

"It's so peaceful and quiet in here," I said, and meant it.

Porter lifted his glass. "Silence is the mother of truth."

"Who said that?" I asked. "And don't say, 'I just did.'"

He smiled and drained his glass. "Benjamin Disraeli."

Rich, handsome, and educated. If he'd possessed his stepson Colin's six-three or so height, we would have been talking masculine perfection, but Porter was of average height. I couldn't help contrasting him with his wife. Lacey wasn't much in the looks department and she certainly didn't come from money. I'm guessing she'd never gone to college, or if she did, her education had been interrupted when she got pregnant by Tim Holbrook, lost him due to Ernie's horrible prank, and married Porter Vargas shortly afterward.

Porter got up and went behind the bar. He plucked the bottle of rye off the shelf, refilled his glass, and resumed his seat, leaving the bottle on the bar. "So just to get it out of the way," he said, "I saw you on that show. I mean, it happened in my wife's shop. I figured I had to check it out."

"You don't need to make excuses," I said. "Everyone in town has seen it, if the whispers and leers mean anything."

"Your best bet?" He looked me in the eye. "Make it work to your advantage. Figure out how to spin it."

"Spin it? Like turn it into a positive?" Right, like that could happen. "Your stepson Colin told me not to worry, that it would blow over."

"Colin's not a businessman. He chose to *teach* instead." His tone was derisive.

"Instead of what?"

"Instead of working with me. Joining the family business and someday taking over as CEO." He tossed back a healthy gulp of whiskey.

"He must be really devoted to teaching."

Porter stared at his glass, at the play of light through the amber liquid as he turned it in his hand. "What he's devoted to is the memory of his sainted father." His speech wasn't what I'd call slurred, but it was getting there. I assumed the booze had loosened his tongue. I wasn't above taking advantage of his impaired state if it meant I could glean even a micron of information that could help Sophie become Suspect Numero Zero.

"His biological father, you mean?" I asked. "Tim Holbrook?"

His smile was not pleasant. "Of course you know his

name. Everyone knows his name. My wife makes sure of that. Did she show you Tim's picture on her phone? Before cell phones, she carried his snapshot around. You think she ever carried a picture of me?"

Colin had made it clear Porter was not his father. The animosity seemed to go both ways. "Was Tim a teacher?"

"He was going to be a teacher once he graduated. High school history, of course."

"Were you and Colin ever close?" I asked.

"I tried, but Lacey never gave us a chance," he said. "I wanted to raise him as my own and not tell him about Tim. You can imagine how that went over. From the moment he was born she was showing him photos and videos of his 'real' father, taking him to see Tim's parents every weekend—his 'real' grandparents."

"That couldn't have been easy for you," I said.

"All those things normal families do together? It was just the two of them. They took vacations, played tennis, went skiing, took *my* forty-foot yacht out for days at a time, all that family stuff. She cut me out of everything. Oh." He raised a finger. "Not everything. I did get to pay for it all. The tennis lessons, Ivy League tuition, even the damn therapist she insisted he needed because he'd never gotten to know his real father." He tossed back the rest of his drink and poured himself another. "And that lingerie store of hers. Who do you think bankrolled that?"

Talk about a cheap date. I couldn't imagine a sober Porter Vargas sharing his personal problems with a near stranger. He wasn't finished.

"I tried to get Colin interested in ocean kayaking," he said. "That's something Ernie and I used to do. Lacey was never into it and I thought, I don't know, I thought maybe it was something special Colin and I could do together. Like a real father and son. I bought him the top-of-the-line ocean kayak, one Vargas Sporting Goods doesn't even sell."

Something in my chest squeezed. "He wasn't interested?"

He shook his head and tried to top off my drink. I placed my palm over the rim of my glass. "Driving," I said. He shrugged. His eyes looked a little glazed. I hoped for his sake he wasn't planning to get behind the wheel. If Lacey didn't track him down and drive him home, I could always offer him a lift.

"Colin got married last year," Porter said. "I barely know his wife, Samantha. I mean, they sometimes come for Sunday dinner, but she's like this polite stranger. God knows what he's told her about me."

"I heard how you and Lacey met," I said. "It sounds romantic."

"Meeting at a funeral? You have a funny definition of romantic."

"No, it's that you were, well, you were doing a favor for a friend, right? Ernie? He couldn't very well attend Tim's funeral himself, no matter how guilty he felt. So you went in his place." That's what Sophie had implied.

"Yeah," he said flatly. "I was doing a favor for a friend."

"And Lacey was there, of course."

His expression softened. "She was… she was heartbroken. Like her whole world just crashed in on her. Just this sweet, vulnerable girl."

"Did you know she was pregnant when you met her? I mean, was she showing?"

He shook his head. "She was only a couple of months along, but she confided in me that very day. Her family didn't know, of course. Very strict Italian Catholics. I mean, they figured it out later when she delivered this big, strapping baby five months after the wedding. And he didn't look anything like me, that's for sure. One look at that kid and there could be no doubt who the father was."

"But by then she was a married woman, so…"

"Right. I'd made an honest woman of her, so there was a minimum of drama from her folks. They were thrilled to have a grandson. All they cared about was when we'd have more."

"You didn't have more children, though, did you?"

His bitterness was palpable. "Her choice, not mine."

"It was… what's the right word?" I said. "Noble of you. To marry this girl you barely knew who was carrying another man's child."

"Noble?" He chuckled. "Lacey's family, once they realized she'd hidden a baby bump under her wedding gown, assumed she'd tricked me into marrying her—you know, that she'd kept the pregnancy from me and all that. When I set them straight, they called me a saint. Completely undeserved. The fact is, I was head over heels for her and still am. Tim's baby wasn't a deal-breaker by any means."

"Tell me something," I said. "Did you know Ernie was gay?"

"Honestly? No. And we'd known each other forever. Since kindergarten. But he didn't give off those vibes."

"So he was in the closet." That's how Rocky had described it.

Porter nodded. "I began to suspect, though. Until he took up with Sophie. But even then they weren't, you know, all over each other the way some couples are. I just thought it was the way he was."

Maxine returned with a gigundo pile of spicy crinkle fries, apologizing for the delay. Her sharp gaze moved from the half-empty bottle of rye to Porter's bleary gaze. He tapped his empty glass, silently requesting a refill.

"No." She recorked the bottle and replaced it on the shelf behind the bar.

He pulled himself up to object, and I got a peek at the powerful CEO unaccustomed to being told no. Maxine's implacable expression said he'd be wasting his time. After a moment, Porter backed down.

"How many have you had?" she asked.

He held up three fingers, then hauled out his wallet. To me he said, "Sure you won't have another?"

"I'm sure." I picked up a hot crinkle fry. I'd pay for my overeating later, but it sure tasted good now. "Thanks, Porter."

"Max lays in that rye just for me," he said. "Isn't that right, Max?"

"That's how it started, but people see it up there, they want it." She shoved the fries under his nose. "Eat. It'll help soak up the booze."

"I never understood that," he said. "Even if the booze gets 'soaked up' by food, it's still in your stomach. It's still going to get into your system."

"You've been making that same dumb observation for thirty-something years." Maxine started cutting up limes. "Get some new material."

"You two have known each other that long?" I said. "I thought you bought this place only about ten years ago, Max."

"Yeah, but I managed the student-union coffeehouse at Peconic U," she said, "when I was a senior. Porter worked the grill—whenever he decided to show up. You'll never know how close I came to canning your ass," she told him.

"My folks made me take an on-campus job senior year." Porter leaned on his elbows, spinning his empty glass and not eating enough fries to soak up anything. "Thought it would aid my character development or something. Help prepare me for my future running the family business." His expression told me what he thought of that high-minded idea.

"Ernie Waterfield worked the same shift." Maxine scooped lime wedges into a bowl and started in on the lemons. "Eight p.m. to closing at midnight, Mondays, Wednesdays, and Fridays."

Porter looked up at her. "How do you remember all that?"

"I'll tell you how I remember." She wagged the paring knife at him. "When you have one short-order cook who shows up for every single one of his shifts, without fail and on time— that would be your pal Ernie—and one who shows up only when he feels like it—"

"When did I ever feel like it?" he asked.

"—and it's your first job with any authority," she continued, "and it's your responsibility to schedule workers, and you find yourself scrambling for a last-minute replacement and more often than not can't find one, you tend to remember the particulars. Like poor Ernie working twice as hard because his buddy decided to blow off work. He's the only reason I kept you on. He kept persuading me to give you one more chance. And trust me, Porter." Maxine offered a wicked grin. "You don't want to know everything I remember from back then."

9

#MagicalGrannyPanties

I HAD NO need of a GPS as I drove from Crystal Harbor to a working-class town on the South Shore not far from where I grew up. Dog-loving-singles.com had connected me with a nice-sounding guy named Roger, an electrical engineer with a wire-haired dachshund. He was nice-looking too. His photo almost looked like Daniel Craig. Yum.

In our email exchanges we decided to leave the pups at home and meet at Jimmy's Sweet Shop, a charmingly old-fashioned soda fountain that had been serving up homemade ice cream and sundaes for the past century. It was a good choice for a first blind date, and one that held special significance for me. Dom and I had our first date at Jimmy's when we were in the eighth grade. I took that as a good omen.

Thus it was with optimism and pleasant anticipation that I parked my new—well, not *new* new, but new to me—red Mazda, listened to the bells tinkle as I pushed through the old wood-and-glass door, and took a journey back in time.

Jimmy's still smelled like Jimmy's, a dairy-sweet perfume overlaid with the scents of hot fudge, caramel, and warm, freshly rolled waffle cones. The Formica-topped counter and vinyl-padded barstools stretched from front to back. Add tiny black and white tiles underfoot, a whitewashed tin ceiling overhead, and the same lazy ceiling fan I remembered from a quarter century before, and I was once again that nervous thirteen-year-old with her first major crush.

Any other eatery would be begging for business on a Tuesday evening, but this was Jimmy's and it was high summer. The place wasn't jam-packed, but it was busy. I scanned the folks sitting at the counter for Daniel Craig—I mean Roger, without success. He must not have arrived yet. I started moving toward the counter. Maybe I could grab a couple of empty barstools, or persuade someone to move over so I could get two seats—

Just then a dark-haired man turned toward the door and spotted me. He smiled. I stopped in my tracks.

What was Dom doing here? Well, this was going to be awkward, me with a date while my ex…

No. No, he didn't. He couldn't have.

Dom waved me over. He patted the empty barstool next to him, still grinning.

I made my way to him but refrained from hoisting my heinie onto the stool. "Explain."

"Sit first, Janey." He patted the seat again. "You don't want to know what I had to go through to save you a seat in this place. It's dog eat dog."

I sighed. I sat. "Speaking of dogs, a wire-haired dachshund, Dom? Where'd you come up with that?"

"I'm actually thinking of getting one. Jumbo hot fudge sundae," he instructed the young fellow behind the counter. "Butter pecan, mint chocolate chip, and coffee, with three cherries and cookie crumbs and coconut instead of nuts."

"You got it." The server grabbed a jumbo sundae dish and

started scooping. Meanwhile Dom sat nursing a single scoop of mango sorbet.

So he remembered my favorite sundae combo. So what.

Okay, it was sweet. This whole stupid charade was sweet, but I wasn't letting him off that easy. "If you tell me that was an actual picture of Daniel Craig," I said, "I will hate you forever."

"Of course it was Daniel Craig. That was the weak link in my cunning plan, but knowing how hot you are for him—"

"It's just *Casino Royale*," I objected. "It—it's a very good film."

"That you've seen at least ten times," he said. "It's not that good. If it makes you feel better, I chose a picture that's not so instantly recognizable. It has the essence of Daniel Craig without the immediate aha factor of: Hey! That there's Daniel Craig."

"I still can't figure out how you engineered this thing," I said, watching carefully as the young man behind the counter added dollops of genuine whipped cream—as in not the spray variety—to my concoction in progress.

"You don't think I'm capable of orchestrating something like this?" he asked.

"I think you're capable of *thinking up* something like this." My mouth was watering. I dragged my gaze from the three cherries being lovingly positioned. "I *know* you don't have the computer skills to pull it off."

"Ah. Well." He took a bite of mango sorbet. "Maybe you underestimate me."

"And maybe you had help."

"All right, Martin helped me with the technical details— with the dog-loving web site and all, and creating a false persona."

Wait a minute. Martin was helping Dom woo me? I didn't know how I felt about that.

Oh, who am I kidding? I knew darn well how I felt about it. "Well, wasn't that nice of him," I managed to say. "I thought you two despised each other."

"I wouldn't put it like that," Dom said as the server set the embarrassingly large and elaborately festooned sundae in front of me. "We've been getting to know each other better these past few days. He's not all bad."

It had been five days since Martin and Dom had moved into my house. While Martin slept in the maid's room on the first floor, Dom had positioned an air mattress at the foot of my circular staircase. The idea was that if the padre ever got it into his depraved head to try to skulk upstairs to the sanctum sanctorum—otherwise known as my bedroom—in the middle of the night, Dom would leap up and protect my honor.

I thought it unlikely that a guy who could sleep through a twenty-one-gun salute thought this particular strategy had a prayer of working. Every morning I padded barefoot with SB down the thickly carpeted stairs in my sleep shirt and boxers, tromped across Dom's air mattress as he limply rolled this way and that, and shuffled to the kitchen, where the padre had, by all indications, been up since dawn, doing the *Times* crossword and working his way through a second pot of java.

After having, you know, not even attempted any middle-of-the-night skulking. Just imagine my relief after having lain awake most of the night with minty breath and freshly shaved legs, listening intently, just to make sure he didn't try any funny business.

He did, however, cut a swath through my precious stash of Fruity Pebbles. He'd purchased his own groceries, as ordered, but couldn't keep his mitts out of my gaily multicolored breakfast cereal. He yammered on about the importance of protein for breakfast, but did he crack one egg? I rest my case.

Dom, naturally, wouldn't swallow a Fruity Pebble if it sprouted wings and flew straight into his cake-hole. Too much sugar and artificial color for him. A committed vegetarian, he'd laid in steel-cut oatmeal, tofu, and other so-called healthful foodstuffs too hideous to recount.

I had to get on their cases to fill and empty the dishwasher, pick up after themselves, and do their own darn laundry, but otherwise they weren't bad houseguests. I mean boarders.

The night before, I'd come home after a job at Ahearn's Funeral Home—videotaping a wake for some reason known only to my client—and found Dom and Martin in the kitchen cooking dinner together. I repeat, they were cooking together. As in collaborating on preparing a meal in a friendly and cooperative manner.

I promptly shoved the pizza I'd picked up into the fridge, poured myself a beer, and watched Dom prepare a delicious spinach salad with oranges, candied walnuts, and goat cheese while the padre seared a pair of porterhouse steaks on the indoor grill, an activity Sexy Beast observed with lip-licking fascination. Fresh farm-stand corn boiled away in a pot, and one of them had swung by Patisserie Susanne for assorted pastries.

So yeah, I guess they were getting along a little better than before. It had all been too strange. Not being one to turn up my nose at a free porterhouse and chocolate croissant, however, I'd shut up and eaten.

I swallowed the first orgasmic spoonful of ice cream and hot fudge. "So now that you and the padre are such good pals, you'll be happy to know I've started throwing some jobs his way."

"I know," Dom said. "He told me. Seems you have more new clients than you can handle. Eleanor Storch is bragging to anyone who'll listen that she hired you to plan her memorial service."

"Meanwhile she's the healthiest eighty-year-old I ever met," I said, "but if it makes her happy, who am I to turn down her cash deposit?"

I'd been so busy with work that Dom and I hadn't had a chance to chat much lately, even though we were, for the first time in seventeen years, living in the same house. "For the first time ever, I'm turning away jobs," I said. "Who knew that gaining a reputation as a devil-worshipping sexpot would have people clamoring to hire me?" Well, Porter Vargas had known—a savvy businessman through and through.

"Those are sound qualifications in someone's book, I guess," he said.

"Yeah, well, some of the jobs, I'd never consider taking." I told him about Kyle Kenneally and his ex-tortoise, Romeo.

My meeting with sleazy Kyle at the Harbor Room Sunday evening had been blessedly short, but that wasn't due to the timeworn ploy of a faux emergency call. Oh, Martin had made a phone call, all right, but rather than dialing my cell as requested, he'd called in a bomb threat to the restaurant. Claimed the Harbor Room had poisoned him with an off mussel and he'd rigged the place to blow in five minutes. Which had not only me and Kyle but about two hundred paying customers and staff practically trampling one another to escape the place.

At least I'd had time to check in on Romeo, get Kyle's

signature and deposit, and toss back a couple of glasses of Cristal, so no complaints on my end.

"I heard a rumor," Dom said, "that there's now a Death Diva fan club."

I nodded, wiping my mouth. "They have a web site and Facebook page. I'm trending on Twitter. Never thought I'd say those words. Naturally, my devoted followers have concluded that Ernie was one of my ritual satanic sacrifices. Forget that I was, what, seven when he died."

"But a precocious seven," he said.

"Thank goodness my phone and address are unlisted. But that doesn't stop them. They address the letters to 'Death Diva, Crystal Harbor, New York,' and sure enough, they get to me."

"I know, I've seen the envelopes at the house," Dom said. "Plus a few packages. Dare I ask what's in those?"

"Gifts. Let me ask you. What am I supposed to do with a table runner hand-embroidered with pentagrams and horned devils?" More accurately, horny devils. Use your imagination.

"For when you serve devil's food cake?" he suggested.

"Har."

"Deviled eggs? That's all I got. What else did they send you?"

I groaned. "Do I have to say?"

Dom removed the sundae from in front of me. I was left holding an empty spoon.

"All right, all right," I said. "Panties."

He replaced the sundae. "This is getting interesting. What kind of panties?"

"What kind do you think?" I said. "Granny panties."

"What are granny…? Oh."

"My devoted fans have decided that big, white, full-coverage briefs do indeed have special magical powers," I said.

"Yeah, the power to wilt a guy's… interest."

"They're already coming up with Halloween costumes, not so loosely based on that getup I'm wearing in the *Ramrod News* segment. Oh, and? You'll like this. There's a Death Diva video game in the works."

"Yes!" Dom shot his fist. "Now I'll get to see how you look with triple-D boobs."

"Paired with an eighteen-inch waist, no doubt. And sexy lingerie."

There was that irresistible grin of his, like a caress, those dark espresso eyes crinkling at the corners. In that charmed moment, the divorce never happened. The past seventeen years never happened. We were just Dominic Peter Faso and Jane Angela Delaney, two kids from Mr. Bender's eighth-grade Spanish class hoping not to embarrass themselves on their first date ever.

Dom leaned in to me, and he smelled even better than the ice cream tasted. His breath felt like sun-warmed silk as he murmured, "It's been an awful long time since I've seen you in any kind of lingerie, Janey."

My face heated as memories crowded in on me. Those first tentative gropings in my parents' finished basement. Our active sex life as young marrieds. We couldn't get enough of each other. His hands, his mouth, the weight of him…

I looked away to compose myself. The teenage girl on my other side chatted animatedly with her friend. Our server scooped cones for the large family that had just come in.

I turned back to Dom and affected a lighthearted tone. "Not true. I know you saw me in that lovely outfit on TV."

His half smile told me he wasn't falling for the diversion tactic. "I've missed you, Janey," he said with heartbreaking sincerity. "I miss you every day. Let's undo our mistake."

He wanted to marry me again, to have the family we should have had all those years ago when he'd said no to kids— and then proceeded to father three of them with two subsequent wives. While each month my aging ovaries said to the departing egg, *Maybe you'll meet a nice sperm, you'll bring him home, yes? And would it kill you to wear a little lipstick?*

"Dom, I—"

"I know what you said. You've changed. So have I," he said. "Maybe we needed this time apart to find out what's really important. To mature."

"Seventeen years?" I couldn't conceal my hurt.

He took my hand in both of his. It felt so perfect, so natural, my eyes stung and I had to look away again.

I'm not going to give up, Janey, he'd said back in April. *Somehow I'm going to prove to you that we belong together.*

"It was my fault," he said. "I accept full responsibility for our breakup. I didn't know my own mind. I didn't appreciate what we had, the once-in-a-lifetime bond."

My phone trilled. And yeah, my ring tone's still "Tequila." Why mess with a good thing? But talk about lousy timing. I gave Dom an apologetic look and pulled the phone out of my purse, prepared to dump the call. Until I saw who it was.

"Sorry, Dom, I have to take this." I greeted Ben Ralston, the private investigator who was now living with Martin's mother, and whom she'd sweet-talked into doing a free favor for yours truly.

"Is Martin behaving himself over at your place?" Ben asked.

"He's been a regular gentleman," I said, and watched Dom go on the alert. "Puts the seat down and everything."

"Maybe we're talking about different guys. So." I heard him thump his desk, his way of announcing an end to small talk. "You want to know the identity of the anonymous client who's been hiring you every year to place flowers on Timothy Holbrook's grave."

"That's about the size of it," I said. "Were you able to find out?"

His rude *pffft!* was answer enough. "You owe me a free Death Diva job, Jane. I've got one in mind. You ever see *Weekend at Bernie's?*"

"Ben, cut the crap and tell me who it is already!"

10

The Ballad of Tim Holbrook

PORTER WAS SWIMMING laps in his backyard pool. Lacey had answered the door and, when I told her Dom and I were there to speak with her husband, directed us through the ultramodern house and out the sliding doors to the multi-tiered deck and the big, rectangular pool beyond. Someone in one of the nearby McMansions was grilling chicken. The smoky aroma mingled with the scents of cut grass and a garden full of blooming roses. Lacey's project, I assumed. I couldn't imagine Porter Vargas on his knees trimming rosebushes.

It was a balmy night and fully dark by then, but the subtle outdoor lighting combined with the underwater lights lent a warm elegance to the space. Chaises and umbrella tables dotted the teak pool deck. I remember thinking they must have some kick-ass parties back there.

We stood at the head of the pool and watched Porter execute a neat swimmer's turn at the far end and perform a graceful, flawless crawl, eating up the distance between us in seconds. "Hey, guys," he said as he hoisted himself out of the pool with the agility of a monkey. Porter was in exceptional shape for his age, kind of what you'd expect from the CEO of a multinational sporting-goods empire.

He dried his face and hair with a yellow towel, slung it over his neck, and lifted a water bottle for a long swig. "Did Lacey offer you something to drink?"

"Yeah, thanks, we're fine," Dom said. The two of them knew each other from business and social functions.

I decided to launch right in to it. "I need to talk to you about Tim Holbrook."

Porter's eyebrows rose in mild surprise. "All right, though I don't know what I can tell you that's not a matter of public record at this point." He gestured to a cluster of cushioned teak chairs surrounding a small table, and we all sat. "Why are you interested in Tim?"

Dom had insisted on accompanying me, against my strident objections. I have to admit, at that moment I was grateful for the silent strength of his presence, not knowing what direction this conversation would take.

Does that make me a helpless little female, looking to the big, strong man to keep her safe?

Thanks a lot. The correct answer was *no*.

I said, "I want to know why you've been hiring me anonymously for the past twenty years to deliver flowers to Tim's grave on the anniversary of his death."

Porter stared at me for a moment, then gave a little shake of the head. He opened his mouth to object, but I cut him off.

"I know it was you, Porter," I said, "so let's skip the part where you pretend you don't know what I'm talking about."

He held my gaze for a long, charged moment, then slumped a bit. He gazed across the dark lawn beyond the pool. "Ernie felt terrible about what happened to Tim… about what he did to him. It would have looked kind of odd if I'd personally brought flowers to the grave of my wife's dead boyfriend, but I wanted to do it for Ernie. Because he wasn't around to do it himself." He shrugged. "So when I found out about the types of services you perform for people, I decided to hire you anonymously. That's all. No big mystery."

"It takes a good friend to do something like that for his dead buddy," I said.

"Yeah, well."

"The thing is, you didn't do it for Ernie."

His eyes narrowed. "What are you saying?"

"You're the one who felt guilty," I said, "because it was you, not Ernie, on the boat with Tim that night." Porter's incredulous gaze shifted between me and Dom, as if seeking an explanation for this madness. I continued, "You're the one who thought it would be great fun to leave Tim in the ocean and make him swim to shore."

"I don't know where you got a crazy idea like that." He slapped his towel angrily onto the deck, and I sensed Dom tensing, his protective instinct on high alert. It gave me the courage to plow ahead.

"I got it from Ernie himself," I said. "Sophie was looking through some of his old notebooks today, where he worked on songs he was writing. She found the draft of a ballad. It lays out the whole story. About how Tim died, and how Ernie took the blame so you wouldn't be kicked out of school." I ignored Dom's look of confusion.

"Bull," Porter said, but he looked uncertain.

"He named names in this song," I continued, "including yours. I don't think he ever intended for anyone else to see it. I think it was kind of a cathartic exercise. He was the true friend, the friend who was willing to risk expulsion and possibly prison to protect you."

Porter raked his fingers through his wet black hair. "I don't believe you. Why would this come out now?"

It was my turn to shrug. "Ernie's been on Sophie's mind lately. She was going through some of his stuff and there it was."

"I want to see this notebook."

"Maybe if you ask Sophie nicely, she'll show it to you. Or not," I said. "You're not her favorite person at the moment, as you can imagine."

I watched Porter digest this, watched as resignation replaced kneejerk denial. He leaned back wearily. "I was a kid. Kids do stupid things. No good can come of making this public now."

"You weren't a kid," I said, "you were a senior in college, a legal adult. Was it hard persuading Ernie to take the blame for Tim's death?"

Porter looked bleak. "Not really. You'd think it would have been, but he was a true friend, like you said."

"He was in love with you."

Porter jerked as if stung. "I'm not gay."

"I didn't say you are. It's not a tough leap to make," I said. "The sacrifice he made for you? The risk he took? He was in love with you, and you took advantage of that fact."

He sighed. "It wasn't that big a risk for him. We both knew his mother would make it all right, that there'd be no serious repercussions for him."

"By handing out payoffs, you mean. Buying the silence of everyone who knew what happened. Or thought they knew."

"My folks would never have done that for me," he sneered. "They were all about self-reliance. Taking responsibility for your own actions."

"Wow," Dom said, his tone flat. "What a concept."

"There's no ballad, by the way," I said. "Ernie never wrote about what really happened that night, as far as I know."

His expression was part outrage, part grudging respect for my successful ploy. "Then Sophie doesn't know."

"No. It's just us three," I said. "Why? Are you hoping we'll keep quiet about it?"

He leaned forward. "Lacey must never find out. It would kill her."

"To learn that the man she's been married to for thirty-five years is the same man who left her beloved Tim out there to drown?" I said. "The father of her child? Yeah, I can see how that wouldn't go over well."

"I'm serious," he said, with vehemence. "I'll do anything to keep her from finding out."

Dom leaned forward and folded his arms on the table, looking steadily at Porter. It was a subtle warning, but one not lost on the other man. Porter leaned back and took a deep breath.

"So what made you suspect it was me and not Ernie on his boat that night?" he asked.

"First of all, I discovered that you're my anonymous client," I said, "and don't ask how. Then I remembered something Maxine mentioned the other day at Murray's. She said Ernie always showed up for work at the campus coffeehouse senior year, without fail. He had the same shift as you, eight to midnight, Mondays, Wednesdays, and Fridays." I could tell by Porter's expression he'd figured out where I was heading with this. "September twenty-fifth, the night Tim died, was a Wednesday. A witness reported seeing Ernie's boat in the ocean off Montauk at around ten p.m."

"Only, Ernie was at work," Porter said. "Or so you assumed from a casual remark made decades later by a bartender."

"By the student manager of the coffeehouse," I reminded him. "And you often skipped work."

"Not much to base your assumption on." He folded his arms over his chest. "That it was me and not Ernie on that boat."

"Until you obligingly confirmed my suspicion," I gave him a frigid smile. "Thanks for that, by the way."

Dom nudged my foot under the table. Message received: I was coming on too strong. Porter was liable to shut down just when I needed him to open up. And okay, so Dom was right. About this. Not about the getting-remarried thing. Maybe. I sat back and took a silent, calming breath.

"Listen man, it's just us three here," Dom said. "We know you didn't intend for Tim to die. No one would think that. It was a horrible accident. And like you said, you were a dumb kid back then. Not exactly an exclusive club, by the way." He raised his hand as if to say, *I was a card-carrying member.* "Plus you were probably drunk as hell that night, am I right?"

Porter scrubbed his hands over his face. "Wasted. I'd liberated a bottle of twenty-five-year-old single-malt from my dad's liquor cabinet. Tim brought a case of beer. I think we went through most of it."

Dom grinned. "You don't fool around. Was it just you two on the boat?"

Porter nodded. "I wanted to scare up a couple of girls, make a real party of it, but Tim said he had this girlfriend back home in Jersey and he didn't cheat. It wasn't a party if we both weren't getting some, so that idea got canned."

"Did Ernie know you were borrowing his boat?" I asked.

"Sure." He frowned. "You think I'd take it out without asking him?" As if that were the serious ethical issue here, and leaving a drunk kid to fend for himself in the cold, dark ocean merely a sidenote.

Here came Dom's foot again, a preemptive strike. The guy had always been able to read my mind. I kicked him back.

"So you and Tim just, what, drank and fished?" Dom asked.

Porter snorted. "We were going to fish, we'd brought bait and tackle—I'd caught a twelve-pound bonito the week before. But we went through the first six-pack before we even set foot on the boat, so in the end, we never even dropped a line. Mostly we just talked. Drank and talked."

"About what?" I said.

Porter had that faraway look again. "He told me about his girlfriend."

"Lacey, right?" Dom said.

"Lacey Borelli." His expression softened. "I remember thinking what a musical name that was. They'd been going together four years. Imagine that. At the age we were then. He took out his wallet and showed me her picture. Sweet little dark-haired Lacey. No great beauty, but she had the smile of an angel. I think I fell for her right then, just looking at that smile."

I looked over his shoulder, past the pool and deck to the house. The object of Porter's adoration stood behind the sliding doors, a dark silhouette against the glowing backdrop of their family room. I couldn't tell whether the angelic smile was in place. Somehow I doubted it.

"Were you both drinking about the same amount?" Dom asked.

"Yep. Tim was bigger than me, this big, tall, blond kid, but he wasn't used to booze. I had a lot more tolerance, but I think it was a point of pride with him to match me shot for shot, beer for beer. He was… wow, he was polluted. I guess that's why he told me his secret. No one else knew."

Dom and I looked at each other. "What's that?" I asked.

"He told me Lacey was pregnant. Her family didn't know, no one knew but the two of them."

"And you," I said. "So when you told me that Lacey confided in you the day of Tim's funeral…"

Porter shrugged. "I already knew. I kind of worked my way around to the subject, let her know she could trust me."

He'd manipulated her, in other words.

"She must have been panicked," I said. "There she was, an unmarried pregnant girl from a religious family, like you said. And now the baby's father is dead."

"He was going to pick out a ring the next weekend." Porter looked solemn. "Have a quickie wedding before she started showing. That's what he told me."

"I'm surprised the police never made the connection," Dom said. "About Ernie being at work when this happened."

"Why would they?" Porter said. "Ernie confessed to it right away, so there was no need to investigate. I, um, I asked him for this favor the next morning, as soon as I realized what happened."

A favor. It was just a favor for a pal. Ernie seems to have done a lot of favors for Porter. Lending him his boat. Saving his job. And finally, this biggie. I had to wonder what, if anything, Porter had done for his friend in return, aside from capitalize on Ernie's doomed crush on him.

"One thing I don't get," Dom said. "Why did Tim go into

the water in the first place? As drunk as he was?"

"Why else? To sober up." Porter closed his eyes briefly. "Seemed like a sensible idea at the time. The guy was on the swim team. I must've figured… well, I didn't doubt he'd make it to shore okay. I remember laughing as I headed back to the marina, thinking how pissed he'd be the next day."

At last I allowed myself to look past Porter to the woman standing a few feet away. Lacey had padded out barefoot a couple of minutes earlier, wearing a chiffon swimsuit cover-up and carrying a tray laden with snack bowls, glasses, and a pitcher of iced tea. As she'd approached, the gist of what we were discussing had appeared to sink in. I was the only one who'd known she was there.

The men noted the direction of my gaze and turned to see her standing as if paralyzed, her face drained of color.

Porter leapt up and started toward her. "Lacey. Sweetheart, I—"

She jerked back, dropping the tray. Glassware shattered on the teak decking amid a shower of iced tea and lemon slices. Nuts and olives went flying. Porter seemed not to notice. He advanced, halting only when a large glass shard pierced his foot, causing him to stumble. Dom and I were on our feet now, grim witnesses to a domestic meltdown long in the making.

"Don't you come near me." Her voice was a near growl, her expression one of stunned horror.

"Please listen to me," he begged, balancing on one foot to yank out the glass. Blood ran from the cut, smearing his fingers and dripping onto the deck. "I love you, Lacey. I love you so much. You must know that."

"How could you?" It was a hoarse whisper, nearly

inaudible. "How could you do it? And then to keep it from me all these years?"

"I—I was afraid." He took a couple of bloody steps toward her. She shuffled backward. "Afraid of losing you. The instant I met you, I knew you were meant to be mine."

Fury transformed her plain features, now flooded with hot color. "How dare you! I was never meant to be yours. I was Tim's and he was mine and you destroyed that. You took him from me. You took him from Colin. Then you made your best friend take the blame. And you never owned up to any of it. Coward!"

"Lacey." Porter dropped to his knees in front of her, weeping openly. "Please understand. Please give me a chance to explain. I can't lose you."

She stared down at her husband in disgust, her own face wet with tears. "And all this time, I never told a soul what you did to Ernie. You did it for me, that's what I thought. You did it for Tim. To even the score. To give me peace. What a laugh. It was to keep him quiet about who really killed Tim, wasn't it? The only one you cared about was yourself."

Her husband shook his head, uncomprehendingly. "I don't—"

"He killed Ernie." She directed this statement to Dom and me.

It took me a moment to find my voice. "Are you saying that Porter—"

"I saw," she hissed. "He doesn't know I was there that afternoon, parked out of sight. I saw him put Ernie's body in the trunk of the car—Ernie's car—and drive away."

"Lacey." Porter groaned, stumbling to his feet. "Sweetheart, why are you doing this? Don't do this."

"You'll pay!" She launched herself at him, pounding his head with her fists while he just stood there and took it. I sprang at her, glass crunching under my sandals, and tried to pull her off him. She was surprisingly strong. I'd expected someone as well padded as Lacey to be weak and out of shape, but there was substantial muscle under the layer of flab. I recalled Porter telling me she used to play tennis and ski. Maybe she still did. Or maybe raw fury had lent her strength.

Dom stepped in then. Even he had to struggle to haul her off her husband, but he managed. Porter bled from his mouth and nose. I'd never seen anyone look so sad and forsaken.

"You'll pay for Tim," she screamed as Dom held her back. "If it's the last thing I do, I'll see that you pay."

11

The Quick Brown Fox Murdered the Lazy Yellow Dog

THEODORA AUGUSTA WATERFIELD answered the door promptly. The first thing I noticed about Ernie's mother was the bib apron that protected her khaki crop pants and short-sleeved, patterned blouse. The oft-mended apron was made of yellow and white gingham decorated with ruffles, faded red rickrack, and an appliquéd basket of red apples. It appeared to be from another century—the midpoint of the previous century, to be precise. Her hands were encased in yellow rubber cleaning gloves, her veiny feet in well-worn blue scuffs. Her thick, white hair was pulled back into a short ponytail. She wore no makeup.

"Why, it's Jane!" she said, in a resonant, authoritative voice that belied her eighty-something years. She stood aside to let me enter her single-story, cedar-shake ranch home. "Come in, come in, the air conditioning's on. I usually keep it off," she continued, striding away with the air of one who's confident she's being followed, "but it's beastly out today, don't you think? Don't you think it's beastly out?" When I didn't answer, she stopped and turned to peer at me from over her rimless reading glasses. I almost plowed into her.

"Um, yes, it's well over ninety," I said. Beastly indeed, and noon was more than two hours away. I had been unable to phone her in advance of my visit, not that my sudden presence at her door appeared to disturb her. Her number was unlisted and no one I asked could provide it. Some even speculated the reclusive old woman didn't possess a phone.

Not true, I discovered as she led the way through the labyrinthine house to the big country kitchen, which smelled faintly of pine cleaner. I spied an avocado-colored wall phone with its twisted curly cord. I almost expected to see a rotary dial, but it had buttons, the numbers all but worn away. The antique stove and refrigerator were also avocado. There was no dishwasher, I noticed.

This woman was reputed to be a multimillionaire. At the moment I saw no evidence of it—aside from the size of the old, sprawling house, tucked well off the beaten path on what had to be at least fifteen acres of wooded land.

"Excuse me, Mrs. Waterfield," I said, "but how do you know who I am?"

"Well, that's an inane question." Teddy stripped off the rubber gloves and draped them over the side of the sink, which bore the faintest residue of powdered cleanser. "I recognize you from that absurd television program, of course. You'll excuse my appearance. Wednesdays are cleaning days. It's awfully helpful to keep to a firm schedule, don't you think, dear? Lemonade?" She untied her apron and hung it on a hook next to a key ring and a wide-brimmed straw hat.

"I'd love some lemonade. So you saw the show?" I grimaced. "I'm embarrassed."

"Sit, sit." She tossed her hand toward the kitchen table,

covered in a floral-printed plastic tablecloth. I sat. "Good heavens, you certainly *ought* to be embarrassed. What a perfect ass you made of yourself. Cookies? They're chocolate chip."

Well, gee, lady, don't hold back. All my friends—and yeah, my mom and dad, too—had reassured me that my TV appearance hadn't been that bad and it wasn't my fault and all that. Deep down I knew that Teddy's ruthless assessment was closer to the truth.

I said yes to the cookies. The woman Sophie had referred to sarcastically as "mother of the freakin' year" produced two glasses and a can of powdered drink mix, which she dispensed with a generous hand. I guess I'd been expecting something made from, well, lemons. She ripped open a bag of hard little store-bought cookies and shook some onto a plate.

The first sip of the neon yellow liquid made my teeth ache. Sure, I enjoy my orange soda and sweet cereal, but holy sugar rush, Batman, this stuff was off the charts.

"So you watch *Ramrod News*?" I asked, trying to get a bead on this woman.

"Another inane question," Teddy said, in a perfectly agreeable tone that somehow stung more than if she'd spoken with icy derision. She joined me at the table and drank deeply from her glass. "Of course, there must be millions of nitwits who tune in to that foolishness or it wouldn't be on the air. No, I read about it on the *Times* and *Newsday* sites and caught the show on Hulu."

Okay, what? The woman with the antique appliances and fat-fruit wallpaper read her morning news—and watched TV shows—on a computer? In my head a mechanical voice chanted, *Does not compute.*

"First of all," I said, "I want to extend my sympathy. I

know it's been decades since you lost your son, but all this… the discovery of his, um, remains… I'm sure it's opened old wounds."

"I never did believe that suicide business." Teddy looked at me levelly. "It must have been quite a shock for you, finding his bones in the roots of that tree."

"To put it mildly," I said. "Do you have any idea who might have murdered Ernie?"

She gave me a canny look as she lifted a cookie. "You are no doubt well aware of whom I suspected at the time. I was quite vocal about it, and you are, after all, a close friend of my former daughter-in-law's. I cannot imagine she failed to mention it."

"I apologize. Yes, of course she did." This woman tolerated nothing less than what she herself offered: unsentimental honesty. "The police didn't take you seriously."

"No, they did not. And now, well, so much time has passed, I doubt the killer can be brought to justice."

"There's no statute of limitations on murder," I said, "and Detective Hernandez is actively investigating."

"Please don't misunderstand me," Teddy said. "I would like nothing more than to see Ernest's murderer behind bars. But I'm a realist. Even if a viable suspect emerges, any defense attorney worth his salt will cast doubt on witnesses' memories from so long ago, stale evidence…" She sighed deeply. "I suspect I shall not live to see justice for my son."

"It sounds like you no longer believe Sophie did it."

She stared out the window. Outside, multicolored finches flitted around a hanging bird feeder while a squirrel scavenged fallen seeds in the grass beneath it. "I was never entirely convinced, mind you, I simply thought it was an avenue that needed pursuing." She looked at me. "I didn't dislike Sophie, despite my allegations. If I'd disliked her, I never would have offered her remuneration to stay with Ernest." She assumed, correctly, that I knew about the three million. "On the contrary, she struck me as a bright, personable young woman. Full of life. And obviously she cared for Ernest."

"You were hoping she'd turn him into a heterosexual," I said.

Her mouth quirked in a half smile. "That goal sounds ludicrous in these socially progressive times, but back then it was mere common sense to most people of my generation. Do you have children, Jane?" When I shook my head, she continued, "Most parents will go to great lengths to see their children happy. Fulfilled. Do you have any idea how difficult life was for an avowed homosexual thirty-five, forty years ago?"

"I think I do," I said. "It's not always a bed of roses nowadays either."

"Who would wish that sort of misery on a child? So yes, I was beyond ecstatic when Ernest and Sophie decided to marry." Her expression turned sober. "I thought she knew about his inclinations and loved him despite them. I thought she and I were, well, on the same page."

"But you never discussed it with her?" I asked.

"No." She sighed again. "Later I wished I had."

"When Sophie decided to leave him, you mean."

Teddy nodded. "She was… terribly disappointed to discover this had been kept from her. She was determined to divorce him."

"So that's when you offered her three million dollars," I said.

"And sensible girl that she was, she took it."

"It didn't bother you that she was staying with him just for the money?"

"I knew she loved Ernest. I believed that, given time, he would come to love her in the same way." Teddy saw my dubious expression. "Yes, yes, the consensus now seems to be that such transformations are a pipe dream. That one is born that way."

"Whereas in your day," I said, "it was thought to be an acquired trait. Usually the mother's fault, of course."

"For your information, it is still my day." Teddy's imperious expression took me down a peg. "I'm not in the ground yet, dear."

I smiled. "Noted." What do you know? I was actually beginning to like "the Wicked Witch of Crystal Harbor."

"Ernest's father died when the boy was only two and a half," she said. "I did my best to fill the roles of both father and mother. When I started noticing that Ernest was more interested in boys than girls, naturally I did think it was my fault. I tried to be tougher with him, enroll him in sports and so forth. Well, he did enjoy sports and did quite well in them, but that, I learned, had little to do with sexual orientation."

"You were a product of your times," I said. "It must have been very difficult raising a gay son alone in that prejudiced atmosphere."

"I thought if I had unintentionally turned him into a homosexual, I could turn him back." Her smile was as close to self-deprecatory as I'd seen. "I'm still not one hundred percent convinced the effort would have failed if his life had not been cut short."

"Speaking of that, Mrs. Waterfield," I said, "there's been a development, well, a couple of developments, I don't think you're aware of. They haven't hit the news yet." And Teddy wasn't plugged in to the Crystal Harbor gossip circuit.

"Well, don't keep me in suspense, dear."

I hoped this octogenarian had a strong heart. "It turns out Ernie—I mean Ernest was not responsible for Tim Holbrook's death. He was never on the boat that night."

She leaned back, frowning. "That can't be. He never denied it. He… What do you base this statement on?"

"Porter Vargas confessed his role. He borrowed Ernest's boat, got drunk on it with Tim, and left him in the ocean as a prank. The next morning Ernest agreed to take the blame because they both knew you would, you know, make it right."

"By spreading money around." Her faded hazel eyes looked suddenly tired. "Oh, Ernest, how could you have been so foolish?"

"Love makes people do foolish things," I said.

She didn't ask who the object of Ernie's affections had been. She didn't need to. "He and Porter had been good friends since grade school. When I began to realize Ernest was a homosexual, I suspected, naturally enough, that the two of them were involved."

"Except Porter isn't gay," I said.

"A fact that became clear by the time he was twelve or so. That boy had an eye for the girls, and they for him. That's when I began to think their friendship might do Ernest good, that the example the other boy set might… I don't know, rub off on him."

"Instead, Ernest fell in love with Porter," I said.

Teddy's mouth thinned. "That smooth-talking young man took advantage of my son's feelings for him. I'm sorry to say, Ernest made it all too easy for him. For example, he had an on-campus job at the coffeehouse in the student union. Lord knows he didn't need the money. He took the job only so he could spend more time with Porter, who also worked there."

"Porter claims he didn't know Ernest was gay," I said. "Not for sure."

"Well, that's utter nonsense. How could he not have known, as close as they were? He manipulated Ernest into taking the blame for what happened to that poor Holbrook boy. I should have seen it at the time. I should have at least suspected."

"Don't be so hard on yourself," I said. "You couldn't have known."

She looked me in the eye. "I believe in being hard on oneself. In analyzing one's mistakes, holding oneself accountable. If more people did so, our society wouldn't have half the problems it does."

Hard to argue with logic like that.

"I taught Ernest to take responsibility for his own actions," she continued, "not others'. Certainly not Porter Vargas's."

"There's more." I took a deep breath. "Porter's wife, Lacey, has accused him of murdering Ernest."

Teddy stared wide-eyed at me. "Is this true?" she whispered.

"It's true that she accused him. He didn't confess. Well, he might have confessed to Detective Hernandez by now. She brought him in for questioning last night."

"Tell me what Lacey said." Her hands trembled. "You were there?"

"Yes, Dom and I—Dom is my ex-husband—we went to Porter's house to confront him about the incident with Tim."

"How on earth did you figure out it was Porter on that

boat?" she asked. "After so many years?"

I smiled. "It's a little complicated. Anyway, Lacey overheard him own up to it and she, uh, she didn't take it well. Lacey was Tim's—"

"Yes, I know. His girlfriend. She's one of those who accepted remuneration to keep silent about the Tim business."

"Didn't it bother you, paying off those people, donating that new library to Peconic U?" I asked. "You used wealth to keep your son from, well, quite frankly, from taking responsibility for his actions."

I'd hit my mark. Trapped by her own words, Teddy gave a grudging smile of acknowledgement. "With the potential repercussions that serious, I felt obligated to step in."

"As Ernest had known you would. And Porter too. He says his parents would never have bailed him out like that."

"How very true," she said. "Porter Vargas Senior is without a doubt spinning in his grave."

"Anyway," I continued, "Lacey claims she witnessed Porter putting, um, putting Ernest's body in the trunk of his, Ernest's, car, and then driving off."

Teddy was eerily still for a moment. "I see."

"She could have concocted the story," I added, "to pay him back for accidentally killing Tim and then failing to come clean all these years."

She nodded. "I suppose it's possible."

The doorbell rang and Teddy excused herself. I immediately jumped up and poured most of my lemonade down the drain. I was seated once more when Teddy reentered carrying two medium-sized cartons and one small one. They were from Amazon, an online drugstore, and a gardening-supply store. I jumped up again.

"I would have helped you with these." I tried in vain to take them from her.

"I'm not an invalid yet, dear." She set the boxes on the counter.

"I see you like to shop online," I said.

"Oh, good heavens, yes. What a convenience! With a few clicks I can order practically everything I need. And with weekly grocery deliveries, I'm set."

"No need to leave the house."

She refilled her glass, tried to offer me more—"I'm good, thanks!"—and leaned against the counter. "You should cultivate a healthy skepticism where gossip is concerned, Jane."

"Gossip? Oh, you mean what people say about you, um, keeping to yourself?"

"I know the words 'hermit' and 'recluse' have been bandied about."

"That doesn't appear to bother you," I said.

She gave a dismissive wave. "The fact is, I welcome it. People are less likely to bother one when they envision a crusty old eccentric shut up with her... cats? Am I not supposed to have cats?"

I grinned. "At least two dozen of them, living and breeding among your mountains of hoarded possessions."

"The gossips would be shocked to learn I have a handful of close friends and that I actually do leave the house to visit, travel, and so forth," Teddy said. "I've maintained a subscription to the Metropolitan Opera for more than forty years. It is true that I do not shop in town or take part in local activities. Very simply, I have not the slightest desire to interact with ninety-nine percent of the residents of Crystal Harbor. Too many nouveau riche showoffs for my taste."

I wish I could defend the local citizenry, but the sad truth was, she'd nailed it.

"Present company excepted," she added, and I felt ridiculously honored.

"You know," I said, "Sophie is not at all like that. Well, I can't argue with the nouveau riche part. She is that, thanks to you. But she's also a good person of high character. Aside from you, no one loved Ernest more. She still speaks fondly of him."

"Yes. Well."

The subject made Teddy uncomfortable, but I had to speak my mind. "The discovery of his remains hit Sophie hard," I said. "Think about it, Mrs. Waterfield. I'd be happy to get the two of you together. At my place maybe? Or here, or anywhere you'd like. Just say the word."

Teddy was silent a moment. She didn't say yes, but she didn't say no either, which I took as a minor victory. "Come, dear. I'd like to show you something."

She led me through a rabbit warren of rooms, finally stopping in a small, wood-paneled study. The scent of lemon oil failed to totally eradicate a slight mustiness. She pulled a book off a shelf. On second glance I saw it was an old photo album.

"Sit with me," she said, and we took seats on a venerable old sofa that had probably been reupholstered a dozen times. She opened the album's cover and I was greeted with the image of a youthful Teddy cradling a newborn infant. I watched Ernie grow up as her knobby fingers turned page after page. Taking his first steps. Up to bat in Little League. Playing guitar in his high school rock band. Graduating college.

My breath caught in my throat when the wedding picture came up. There was Sophie in her white wedding gown, young and slim, looking heartbreakingly beautiful and thrilled to be marrying her soul mate. Ernie looked just as happy.

Teddy touched the picture. "She always had a special quality about her. I thought, if anyone can make this marriage work, she can." She sighed.

"Do you happen to know how Sophie met her second husband?" I asked. "Dean Phillips?"

Her expression hardened. "She met him in this very house. That man worked for the company that sanded and refinished my oak floors. He and another fellow spent several days here. It was right before Easter."

"He would have been around Ernest's age, I suppose. Mid-twenties."

"Insolent young man," she said. "He had his eye on my daughter-in-law from the moment he met her. I knew nothing good could come of it, but Ernest wouldn't listen."

"And you were right. Dean went after her." Again I felt the need to defend Sophie's character. "But it was one-sided. Sophie told me there was nothing going on between her and Dean while Ernest was alive."

Teddy chose not to comment on that. "Porter was here too that first day. He and Ernest and Sophie were on their way somewhere—to a concert in Manhattan, I believe—and they stopped by the house for some reason. At one point I passed the door to the basement and smelled marijuana smoke."

I didn't ask how she recognized the scent. "Who was down there?"

"Porter and Dean, as it turned out. The other man from the flooring company was hard at work. Ernest and Sophie were in the kitchen having a snack. Later I overheard Porter ask Dean if he could supply him with more marijuana."

"What did Dean say?"

"What do you think?" Teddy sneered. "He said he'd have it for him later in the week and took Porter's phone number."

"So much for Porter being a good influence on Ernest," I said.

"I'd long ago abandoned that hope. In fact, Dean used Porter to insinuate himself into their little clique—to get close to Sophie, no doubt."

"He was that smitten?"

"With her or with the money I'd given her or both," Teddy said.

"This clique," I said. "It didn't include Porter's wife, Lacey, I take it."

"Oh, goodness, no. She had no idea her husband and Ernest were still friends. Apparently she'd made Porter promise, when they'd married, that he would cut off contact with the man responsible for Timothy Holbrook's death."

"Or so she thought at the time," I said. "Obviously Porter broke his promise."

"I'm sure he thought she'd never find out," she said.

"But she did?"

"Oh, yes indeed. She was positively hysterical, and I don't use that term lightly."

"How do you know?" I asked.

"Well, because she came here and demanded I intervene to end my son's friendship with her husband," she said.

"Wow. She really did that?"

"Why do people persist in asking for confirmation of a statement they have just heard?" And then, as if to drive home her point, she added, "Yes. She really did that."

Another inanity. I was really racking them up. "What did you say?"

"When I could calm her down enough to listen, I informed her that both my son and her husband were grown men and more than capable of choosing whom they associated with, and that even if I were inclined to destroy a lifelong friendship, Ernest might have something to say about it."

"I don't suppose you mentioned that Ernest was in love with Porter," I said.

"You suppose correctly. Lacey responded that if I wanted to keep them apart, I could make it happen. Apparently she saw me as some all-powerful being who can accomplish her wishes simply by snapping her fingers."

I chose not to remind Teddy that she'd essentially done just that when she'd paid off Lacey and her family to keep mum about how Tim had died. "I can understand Lacey's point of view," I said. "It must have been a shock to learn that her husband was still friendly with the man responsible—the man she *thought* was responsible for Tim's death."

"Well, yes, of course," she said, "and I did take that into consideration, but the young woman was simply out of control. Sobbing, screaming. I was tempted to try what they used to do in those old movies—slap her face to bring her out of it."

"Oh yeah," I said, imagining Lacey Vargas's response to being slapped. "I'm sure that would have made the whole situation much better."

I couldn't help wondering if Lacey had made another stop before returning home. After getting nowhere with Ernie's mom, had she then taken her sobbing, screaming "hysteria" to Ernie himself? On the very day of his death? It would have been the first meeting between Lacey Vargas and the man she believed killed the father of her child. I could imagine various ways such a meeting might have turned out. None of them ended with a hug and a vow to do lunch soon.

Teddy was no dummy. The possibility had to have occurred to her. She'd probably mentioned it to the lovely detective. I didn't think there was anything to be gained by my bringing it up at this point.

I was beginning to like Teddy, but I didn't like what she'd done back then, throwing around her money to swab up her son's mess, and playing god with people's lives in the process. Lacey Borelli would never have wed Porter Vargas if she'd known that he'd been at the helm of Ernie's boat that fateful night.

And what about Ernie? If Porter had indeed killed him to keep him from spilling the beans about his own involvement in Tim's death, as Lacey claimed, then Teddy's act of maternal protection had been the springboard for her son's eventual murder. It was too ugly to contemplate.

I glanced around the cozy room, with its overstuffed furniture and shelves of books. An antique walnut desk was positioned near the window. A neat stack of papers lay on top, as well as a pen cup and a loudly ticking clock. One corner of the desktop appeared conspicuously empty.

She noticed me noticing. "That's where Ernest's typewriter usually sits. Actually it was his father's before him, a large, black Royal from the fifties. I enjoy seeing it there. It makes me feel close to both of them."

"Didn't Sophie inherit it along with his other things?"

Teddy nodded. "Sophie gave it to me after Ernest died. She thought I should have it, along with his grandmother's diamond engagement ring." After a moment she added, "That's the last time I saw her."

"Where is the typewriter now?" I asked.

"Oh, Detective Hernandez had to borrow it. To run some tests."

"I thought they did that thirty-two years ago when the fake suicide note was found," I said. "They determined it was typed on Ernest's machine."

"They did, yes. This was for some other tests." Teddy looked away from the desk. She took a deep breath and let it out slowly. "They suspect it might be the murder weapon."

I found my fingers pressed to my mouth, and lowered them. "Is that what they said?"

"They didn't have to. What else could it be? The thing is certainly heavy enough, all iron and steel."

I recalled Sophie fretting that Ernie might have been murdered in the home they'd shared, the historic farmhouse she loved so much. "Did the police take anything else?"

"The suicide note," she said. "Which as everyone now knows was written not by my son but by the brute who killed him in cold blood. I used to… I must have read that note a thousand times during the past thirty-two years, trying to… trying to make sense of it. He was so creative, my Ernest, so bright and loving and full of life."

Gently I said, "I thought you never believed he took his own life."

"Sometimes I would wake in the middle of the night and my thoughts would go… to dark places, and I would tell myself…" Her jaw trembled. "I would tell myself, you old fool, when are you going to stop this nonsense and face the truth?"

Without thought I reached over and closed my hand over hers. She squeezed it back with surprising force. How horrible, how emotionally exhausting, to live with that kind of uncertainty for so long. The discovery of her son's remains couldn't have been easy for Teddy, but at least it answered the Big Question that had tormented her for three decades.

"However, when I considered it rationally, from all angles," she said, "I knew he never could have done such a thing. Not my Ernest. No one would listen." Her eyes were wet when she looked at me. "I know Sophie must despise me for accusing her back then. I just felt so… so helpless. No one would listen," she repeated.

I dared not speak, my own throat clogged with tears. At last I said, "You might be surprised. Sophie's a lot like you, Mrs. Waterfield. She doesn't tolerate fools and she calls 'em like she sees 'em."

Teddy greeted this description with a watery smile.

I continued, "You don't strike me as a woman who shies away from uncomfortable situations. I'm happy to arrange a little get-together anytime you're ready."

12

Human Turducken

I ARRIVED AT the Crystal Harbor Public Library a little late. The town meeting had already started in the big community room in the basement. All the folding chairs, two hundred or so, were filled, with about a hundred more people standing cheek to jowl along the sides and in back. I hadn't expected it to be so packed, though in retrospect I probably should have. I squeezed through the throng blocking the doorway, nodding to the folks I knew. Anyone who lived and/or worked in Crystal Harbor was welcome to attend a town meeting.

I greeted Susanne Travert, the Frenchwoman who owned Patisserie Susanne, with a three-pointed European cheek kiss. I said hi to the young couple who owned the pottery gallery next to Janey's Place—I never could remember their names. Dean Phillips was there, too, standing on the left side of the room. We exchanged waves.

His ex-wife Sophie was at the front of the room, where a lectern and microphone had been placed. A redheaded middle-aged woman I didn't recognize stood at her seat, complaining shrilly about some parking situation in front of her home, located near the middle school.

Sophie had called this meeting to discuss issues of general

interest to Crystal Harbor residents, but the record attendance told me my neighbors couldn't wait for the latest juicy tidbit about the murder case currently under investigation.

I was surprised to see Officers Geri Marvin and Howie Werker standing in back. There isn't normally a police presence at these meetings. I managed to make my way over to them. "Hey, guys, what are you doing here?"

"We're not at liberty—" Geri started, but Howie cut her off.

"Detective wants us to keep our eyes and ears open." He jerked his head, indicating the front of the room. I recognized the back of Bonnie Hernandez's sleek head. She sat in the front row. I also spied Lacey and her son, Colin, his arm protectively around her shoulder. I'd heard that Porter wasn't contesting his wife's accusation but was claiming self-defense in the killing of Ernie. He'd retained a big-name lawyer and was out on bail, though not present at the meeting. No surprise there.

Dom and Martin had snagged seats in the center of the room, their heads together at the moment, no doubt sharing rude comments about the proceedings. They had not, I noticed, saved me a seat. Well, I certainly wouldn't want to intrude on a budding bromance.

I never claimed to be the most mature person, so you can just keep it to yourself.

Crystal Harbor was your basic WASP enclave, so dark faces tended to stand out in the sea of white. Maia Armstrong, the caterer, possessed such a face, as did Ben Ralston. The private investigator appeared amused as the argument intensified between the redheaded woman and Nina Wallace, on her feet now and shouting from the other side of the room while her husband, Mal, sat quietly beside her.

Nina said, "There are no parking restrictions in front of your house or anywhere else on that block."

"It's a zoo every afternoon," the redhead yelled. "Homeowners have rights too. I pay my taxes."

Nina spread her arms. "Where are parents supposed to park to pick up their kids?"

"Not in front of my house, that's where!"

Sophie tried to intercede. "Ladies, let's keep it civil—"

"I've seen you." Nina stabbed her finger toward the other woman. "Out there with your video camera, recording people's license plates. What is that, intimidation? Sorry, lady, I'm a Hannigan." Nina was descended from the notorious Prohibition gangster Hank "Hokum" Hannigan, who'd smuggled booze through Crystal Harbor back in the day. "Hannigans don't intimidate."

Others in the room chimed in with shouted encouragement, on one side or the other of the debate.

Sophie raised her voice to be heard over the cacophony. "All right, settle down." She looked to the back of the room. "Officers, what is the law regarding parking on Argyle Place to pick up middle schoolers?"

Howie spoke up first. "Parking on Argyle is legal. Period."

This only ramped up the redhead's outrage. "It's my street! I have rights!"

"It's not your street," Nina cried. "It belongs to the town. Are you the one who put dog poop in the door handle of my new Lexus? You are, aren't you?"

She started toward the redhead before Mal could stop her. The redhead advanced, making bring-it-sister gestures.

Howie groaned. "I do not want to have to break up a brawl between a crazy lady and a pregnant crazy lady."

History had just been made. I agreed with Nina Wallace on something. As it turned out, Howie didn't need to get involved. Nina and the redhead had to pass Sten Jakobsen to get to each other. Sten stood, all six feet four of him, and the two women abruptly halted. The old lawyer had presence, and when he chose to, he positively oozed authority. He chose to do so now.

In his precise baritone, he intoned, "Ladies, please sit."

That's all. A simple request. The redhead opened her mouth to deliver a parting shot. Sten's expression shut it. Grumbling, the ladies returned to their seats.

Before anyone else could introduce another topic of earthshattering importance, Sophie spoke into the mic. "Let's move on to the reason we're all here so I can get to my trivia game on time." Murray's Pub featured a raucous trivia contest every Wednesday night. Sophie was a regular fixture and she played to win.

Rocky's voice rang out. "I've put together a crack team this week, Mayor. We're going to beat the *pants* off you."

"No one wants to see that, Rocky," she said, to general amusement. "Guess I'll have to keep wiping the floor with you."

Kyle Kenneally, owner of the Harbor Room and a frozen giant tortoise, called out, "Did Porter Vargas do it?"

I saw Lacey jerk, and Colin's arm tighten around her shoulders. He bent to whisper in her ear.

Sophie gestured toward Bonnie. "Detective Hernandez is here to shed some light on the investigation. So keep it down and let her speak."

Bonnie stepped up to the mic, looking as pretty and put together as always. "Thank you, Mayor. In the week that's elapsed since the discovery of Ernest Waterfield's remains, the police investigation has focused on several persons of interest." She didn't mention that the mayor herself had been the primary "person of interest," at least until Lacey Vargas had accused her husband. Someone else mentioned it for her.

"So Sophie's off the hook?" Barbara O'Rourke hollered. She sat with her husband, Patrick, in the last row of folding chairs.

Sophie borrowed the mic from Bonnie. "If I have to stop the car and come back there, you'll be sorry."

Everyone chuckled except Detective Hernandez, for whom murder clearly was no laughing matter. "Obviously I can't discuss specifics. Some details have been withheld from the public to aid the investigation. Suffice it to say that while we have acted on certain leads, the case is far from solved."

The room hummed with surprised whispers. Hadn't Porter confessed?

Bonnie continued, "I urge all of you who were living here in Crystal Harbor at the time of Ernest Waterfield's supposed suicide to dig into your memory banks for information that might help us identify his killer. If you remember anything at all from back then, call the Crystal Harbor Police Department and ask for me. Any bit of information is welcome, no matter how inconsequential."

An old man stood and waved his wooden walking cane for attention, causing those sitting nearby to duck. Even from the back I recognized Norman Butterwick, a neighbor of Sophie's. Norman's luxuriant thatch of thick white hair and bespoke, Sputnik-era tweed sport jacket gave him away. His family had lived for generations in the house across from hers on the far west end of Main Street. Norman had to be well into his nineties and had been eccentric and forgetful for as long as I'd known him, which was more than two decades. He did, however, possess a strong, refined voice that carried.

He said, "I remember something from back then."

Sophie took the mic again. "That's great, Norman. Detective Hernandez will speak with you after—"

"I remember that a gallon of gas cost a little over a dollar. Also, they messed around with the formula for Coca-Cola. Coca-Cola, of all darn things!"

"Thank you, Norman," Sophie said. "I'll make a note of that. So that's the story," she told the crowd. "Put on your thinking caps and see if you can't help out the police. Do it because it's your civic duty." Her gaze swept the room, landing on individual faces. "Or do it for me. And Ernie. Because he was a wonderful man and didn't deserve what happened to him."

The somber hush that greeted this statement was broken by Norman Butterwick, who said, "I remember more things from back then, Detective."

"If your recollections have anything to do with Ernest Waterfield's murder," she said, "then please phone the police department tomorrow."

Sophie spoke again. "Now I'm going to turn over the podium to a relatively new resident of Crystal Harbor, one who's found herself at the center of some unwanted attention this week. My pal Jane Delaney has a few words for her neighbors."

I plucked my notes from my purse as I started up the center aisle to the front of the room. I'd selected my most businesslike outfit, the one I wore for assignments at funeral homes: tailored gray skirt suit, snowy white blouse, black pumps with ladylike two-inch heels, and a string of faux pearls. I'd pulled my strawberry-blond hair into a neat French twist and kept the makeup to a minimum, hoping to banish all thoughts of hot pink push-'em-up bras and sex-obsessed satanic Death Divas. Sophie had offered me this forum so I could begin to rehabilitate my public image.

Me and Aretha. All we want is some R-E-S-P-E-C-T.

I managed to maintain my composure as an older female voice yelled, "How did you know to look for Ernie under that tree if you're not an agent of the devil?"

Then some creep in a bespoke suit and three-hundred-dollar haircut wondered aloud, in his overeducated Thurston Howell the Third lockjaw, what I was wearing under that prim outfit, prompting Dom to spring out of his seat and lunge over four rows of chairs to get at him. The padre yanked him back and forcibly shoved him into his seat. Dom fumed, giving the creep the evil death-laser stare. Martin said something in Dom's ear that managed not only to defuse him, but to prompt a burst of sputtering laughter.

Just a few more rows to go and I'd be through this mortifying gauntlet and—

Oh! I stumbled to a halt, my bottom stinging. Someone pinched me! I knew I had to ignore it and keep on moving, knew it would be a mistake to confront the pincher. And I was immensely grateful it had happened outside my ex-husband's line of sight. It would have taken ten Martins to hold Dom back if he'd seen some stranger put his hands on me.

I was about to resume the walk of shame when I heard the snickers. I couldn't help myself. I glanced back and recognized the smug young pincher, though I knew he wouldn't make a connection between the devil-worshipping sex addict whose person he'd just violated and the plain-Jane nobody he'd briefly met about five years earlier. He was the grandson of one of Irene's friends, now showing off for his buddies, all of them doubtless home from college for the summer.

I pasted on the sweetest smile in my arsenal and approached the lanky fellow, who was slumped lazily in his chair with one flip-flop-clad foot extending into the aisle. Yeah, that's right, he was one of those guys who can't sit without spreading his legs as wide as they'll go.

"Logan, hi!" I chirped. "I thought that was you." I watched his face register alarm at my use of his name and then I nonchalantly pressed the heel of one of my ladylike pumps into his instep. Hard. His mouth gaped open and he sucked air.

"How's your grandmother doing?" I asked in my most solicitous tone. "It's been ages since I've seen Edith. She's always been so proud of you."

His mouth worked silently, eyes bulging, as he tried in vain to reclaim his foot. Meanwhile his buddies had a guffaw at his expense, unable to see us playing footsie in the aisle and assuming his red-faced discomfort was due purely to embarrassment at being recognized.

"What's that, dear? I didn't catch what you said." I leaned in close.

"You crazy bitch," he wheezed. "Get the hell off my foot."

"Oh, I sure will, Logan," I cooed, pressing harder. "I'll call Edith tomorrow and let her know we ran into each other. I'll tell her *all* about it."

I turned and strode swiftly to the podium, thanked Sophie, and launched right into it. "I see a lot of familiar faces here. I've lived in town for just a few months, but I've known many of you for years or even decades. I started my unique service twenty-two years ago when I was still in high school, and most of my regular clients live here in Crystal Harbor." Over the years, Irene had actively solicited new clients for me from among her friends. I probably wouldn't have a business if it weren't for her.

"Those of you who know me probably had a good chuckle at my embarrassing television debut," I said. "Those who didn't know me probably thought, Who is this weird Death Diva person and what *does* she do with dead bodies?"

From his seat, Dom scanned the crowd, his scowl daring anyone to make another rude comment, much to the amusement of the padre.

"I'm grateful for all the offers of work I've received during the past week," I continued. "The list of what I do for clients is quite long, and getting longer all the time as people come up with unique and original ways to honor loved ones who've passed. Unfortunately my TV appearance has caused some confusion regarding the scope of my services. I'd like to take this opportunity to correct a few misapprehensions and list some of the things that I am not and never will be available to perform."

I cleared my throat. "I will not mix human ashes into anyone's food." Even a detested mother-in-law's oatmeal, as was recently requested. "I will not break into the morgue for any reason, including to procure an anatomical 'relic' from a recently deceased celebrity. I'm pretty sure that's still illegal."

From the back Howie called, "That would be correct, Jane."

"For that matter," I added, "I will not steal anything from a corpse, even if you claim it rightfully belongs to you." Not anymore, that is. In the not-so-distant past I possessed fewer scruples and a demanding client in the form of Irene McAuliffe. I avoided looking at the padre, whom I'd first met during my one and only attempt to pilfer from the dead.

"If your idea of honoring a deceased loved one involves cannibalism in any form," I said, "do not contact your friendly neighborhood Death Diva. It's not in my *menu* of services." Several groans greeted this comment, whether due to disappointment or the bad pun, I couldn't say. Martin called out, "Dang it all!"

"The same goes for feeding human body parts to animals," I went on. "Yes, I know you love your dog, but if you think it through to its logical conclusion, being one with Fido after your death isn't all it's cracked up to be. If your goal is to spend more time in your backyard, buy a hammock."

I continued, "On a related note, I will not create a human/pet turducken, I don't care how much your granny loved her beagle, her cat, her guinea pig, and her gerbil." If that means I don't have an open mind, as I was accused when I vetoed that one, then so be it.

"Also, I will not dig up a grave, whether to take something out or put something in." I sent Kyle Kenneally a pointed look.

On the plus side, I was in negotiations with the Smithsonian regarding Romeo. I'd feared the whole thing would fall through when they asked for documentation about the Darwin connection. Kyle didn't have official paperwork, but he did have an original letter one of his ancestors had written about Romeo in the eighteen fifties, which apparently is the next best thing. They must have liked what they'd read, because they were sending someone to inspect the frozen carcass.

"Do not contact me about mutilating a corpse, no matter

how free one's husband was in life with the body part in question. Haven't you people heard of Craigslist? And for you gardening buffs out there, yes, I am willing to fertilize your tomatoes and zucchini with your remains after you die, but only—*only!*—if you have chosen cremation."

I proceeded to the next item on my list. "News flash, folks: human taxidermy is illegal, even if you've planned the most awesome Halloween decoration ever. Ditto for any *Weekend at Bernie's* scenarios."

Ben Ralston called out, "Can't you take a joke?"

"You assume you're the only one who asked," I responded. "Also, don't contact me with any request involving *un*spontaneous human combustion that doesn't involve a cremation chamber. If you promised your pal he'd go out in a blaze of glory, stick a sparkler in his mouth." Or somewhere.

And now for the biggie. "Okay, I shouldn't even have to mention this one," I said, "but here it is. I will not be a party to murder, no matter how much you offer. So if you find yourself in need of—" air quotes here "—'a nice, reliable hit man,' do not come knocking on my door." As one of Crystal Harbor's most respectable matrons had done this past week. I'd shared that particular request with Detective Hernandez, who'd arranged a sting by an undercover cop. The hopeful client, whose eye had wandered in turns from her hot young diving instructor to hubby's life insurance, was now cooling her heels in the hoosegow.

The good news was, I had a waiting list of folks with legitimate assignments in mind. I'd increased my rates and they still kept coming. In the past few days, hiring the famous Death Diva had become something to brag about. I wondered how long my lucrative celebrity would last before the locals moved on to the Next Big Thing.

I ended my little presentation by stating how proud I was to be a small business owner in Crystal Harbor blah blah blah and setting a stack of my business cards on a nearby table. Sophie called the meeting to a close and the room was immediately alive with the sound of chairs scraping and scores of competing conversations.

Small groups lingered here and there, catching up with one another and gossiping—Crystal Harbor's official town hobby. Martin was nowhere to be seen, but Dom was across the room talking to Bonnie. She gave him a teasing smile. They shared a laugh and she playfully smacked his chest. He bent to murmur something in her ear.

When last I'd looked, this formerly betrothed couple had been cautiously skirting around each other. Now… Now I didn't know what I was seeing. I'd never known Dom to be a cheater, but in my book, messing around with your ex-fiancée while trying to convince your ex-wife to remarry you counts as cheating. Even if the ex-wife can't make up her mind whether to give you another chance. I think. Then again, to be fair, Dom was on excellent terms with all his ex-wives, so why shouldn't he be friendly with his ex-fiancée as well?

"There you are." Sophie grabbed my arm. "I'm drafting you for trivia. Let's get a move on."

13

Skeleton Crew

"IF YOU'RE SO intent on rehabilitating your image," Sophie said, "try not living in sin with a couple of hot single fellas."

I gave her a wry smile. She knew perfectly well how my ex and my… What was Martin to me? *Friend?* Does *friend* work? Anyway, how those two had ended up camped out at my place. Sophie and I were walking the half mile from the library to Murray's Pub.

"Three hot single fellas if you count Sexy Beast," I said. "Unfortunately, there's no sin going on. Except gluttony—I'm eating better than ever. Those two idiots are playing TV chef, trying to outdo each other in the feeding-Janey department."

"So they *do* have something in common," she said.

"Speaking of men and sin," I said, "where's Porter living while he's out on bail? I can't see Lacey letting him back into the house."

"His mom lives in town. He's staying with her." Sophie might appear out of shape, but I had to hustle to keep up with her. It was close to eight p.m. and still light out, this being one of the longest days of the year.

"I'd hate to see those slippery lawyers of his get him off on self-defense," I said.

A born politician, Sophie waved and offered greetings to everyone we passed on both sides of the street. "Don't be so fast to convict Porter. He's not a shoe-in by any means."

I looked at her. "He confessed."

"Yeah, I know."

"Okay, spill," I said. "What else do you know?"

Sophie glanced around to ensure no one was within earshot. "For one thing, I know that Bonnie kept making him repeat his story."

"Isn't that Interrogation One-oh-One?" I asked. "Trying to trip up the perp by making him repeat his story?" My knowledge of law and order came mainly from, well, *Law & Order*. Give me a rainy day, some Buffalo chicken pizza, and a *Law & Order* marathon, and I'm a happy girl.

She said, "My deep-throat source in the department says there are questions about the murder weapon."

"Oh yeah?" I said. "What else did Howie tell you?"

She gave me a sideways smirk, letting me know my guess was on the mark. I wasn't surprised to learn Howie had shared inside information with onetime suspect Sophie. He was an accomplished, seasoned cop with good instincts. I doubted he ever thought she was guilty. But if it turned out Porter didn't do it, then Sophie could find herself in the spotlight once more.

"Try this one on for size," she said. "Cops went over my property real thoroughly, looking for heavy objects that had been there back when Ernie died."

"Like what?" I asked, visions of baseball bats and cast-iron skillets dancing in my head.

"They took the rack from my brick barbecue. That thing was built sometime in the fifties, and the rack's never been replaced."

"Okay, that makes sense," I said. That barbecue rack was a ponderous cast-iron thing, more than capable of doing the job. I sincerely hoped it didn't turn out to be the murder weapon. Sophie's locally famous grilled pizza wouldn't be half as crusty and delicious made on a brand-spanking-new rack.

"And large rocks from the edge of the pond," she added.

"They took all those rocks?"

She shook her head. "Only the blocky ones with some kind of edge. Left the round ones alone." She gave me a significant look.

"Ah." I was beginning to get it. "Interesting."

"Went through all the old tools and gardening stuff. Same deal," she said. "Anything heavy with an angle or corner, they took for forensic analysis."

"So they're testing for…" I wished I hadn't begun that sentence, but Sophie had no problem finishing it for me.

"Blood, hair, and tissue. They can detect the presence of blood even after all these years, depending on how the item's been cleaned and stored—which as far as those old rocks go…" She gave a dubious wag of the hand. "But get this. Bonnie asked about my patio. Whether it's the same patio from back then."

"Is it?"

"Nope. It was brick back then," she said. "Had it changed to slate about twenty years back. Were there any loose bricks the day Ernie died, she wanted to know. Asked a lot of questions about the bricks."

"Were there?" I asked. "Loose bricks?"

"Nope. That patio was solid. Ernie kept the place up."

"Okay, so what are you thinking?" I asked. "That Porter's version of events involved slamming Ernie's head into the patio?"

Sophie nodded. "I think that's precisely what he told the cops. Only problem, they seem to think the murder weapon had some sort of edge or corner."

"Then the examination of Ernie's skull must have shown that kind of injury, which is not consistent with getting his head slammed on a flat patio." I remembered something. "Teddy told me the cops took Ernie's typewriter. To test it as the weapon, she thought. It has an edge, and a heavy old antique like that could do a lot of damage."

Sophie gave me an enigmatic look. "You spoke with Teddy?"

I told her about my dropping in on Ernie's mom that morning. I filled her in on Lacey's visit to her the day Ernie died and speculated that Lacey might have dropped in on Ernie after getting the brushoff from his mom.

Sophie exchanged greetings with an elderly couple out for their evening constitutional. When they were a half block away, she said, "Did you share this with Bonnie?"

"Yep," I said. "She requested that I stop interfering in the investigation."

"Well, I'm the damn mayor of this burg and I say that as a private citizen, you can talk to whoever the hell you want to."

"I'd keep snooping around with or without your official approval, Your Honor," I said, "but I do appreciate it."

"So," she said. "Porter's story is falling apart. A lot of time has passed. You think he forgot the details?"

"You mean could Porter remember slamming Ernie's head on the patio when in reality he clocked him with a two-by-four? I can tell you that if I bludgeoned a guy to death, the particulars would remain sharp and clear. I'm guessing that's not the kind of memory that fades with time."

"Good point," Sophie said. "I read somewhere that people tend to recall the minutest details about events that trigger a surge of adrenaline. Like when you're scared, excited, whatever."

"So let's say Porter didn't do it. Why would he try to take the blame?" I answered my own question. "To protect someone. Who's he trying to protect?"

"That's a no-brainer."

"He's deeply in love with Lacey," I said. "You should have seen him when she found out he was behind Tim's death. He was literally on his knees, begging for her forgiveness."

"Yet she turned around and accused him of killing Ernie," she said. "That loving feeling doesn't seem to go both ways."

"I don't think it ever did. He was smitten from day one, while she was still reeling from Tim's death when they met."

"But here's this handsome, wealthy young man who's eager to marry her and legitimize the child she's carrying," she said.

"Your basic White Knight," I said. "An irresistible offer no matter how much you're mourning the love of your life."

"So here's where it gets interesting," she said. "Porter might have been guessing about the murder weapon, *but* he accurately described what Ernie was wearing the day he died. Scraps of material found with the skeleton match up."

"Hmm…" I said.

"And get this." Sophie glanced around and lowered her voice. We were almost at Murray's. "So did Lacey."

"So did Lacey what? Oh! You mean she knew what Ernie was wearing too?"

"Yep. Bonnie asked for as much detail as she could recall. Shirt, pants, shoes. Lacey got it all right. Which means maybe she really did see Porter move Ernie's body, like she says. Either that or she killed him herself."

"Or," I countered, "she was nowhere near Ernie that day, but Porter told her all about it."

"What, like, honey, I'm home. I picked up eggs and bread and killed my old buddy Ernie. He was wearing a plaid sport shirt and gray high-tops."

"I'm just saying we can't assume—"

"Hold up!" a male voice called. We looked back to see Ben Ralston jogging to catch up with us. "Stevie and I want to team up with you for trivia." He addressed this comment to Sophie as he held open the door for us. Everyone wanted to be on her team.

"Fine with me," she said as she preceded me into the pub. "Let's see what you're made of."

All of the battered wooden tables and booths were occupied, as well as most of the barstools. I recognized many of the customers. I searched for, and did not see, Dom or Bonnie. I tried not to wonder what they were doing, whether they were doing it together, and if so, whether they were doing it horizontally.

Stevie Borden, Martin's mom, motioned to us from the booth she'd staked out. A pitcher of beer and four glasses already sat in front of her.

"Nachos are on the way," Stevie said. She was sixty-one but could pass for forty-five, thanks to an active lifestyle and good genes. She had long blond hair and, unlike yours truly, was expert at styling it and applying makeup.

It was hard to believe that not only was this attractive, energetic woman a grandmother, but her granddaughter—Martin's daughter, Lexie—was a married woman capable of turning her into a great-grandmother at any time. Which meant forty-two-year-old Martin could be a grandfather. That was definitely too bizarre to contemplate.

We exchanged air kisses all around as Ben filled our glasses. I spied plenty of people I knew in the crowded pub, some of whom I'd seen a few minutes earlier at the town meeting. The padre detached himself from his table-mates to give Stevie a hard time.

"What kind of mother are you?" he demanded, stealing a nacho as she tried to slap his hand away. "Your rightful place is on your son's team."

"I'm sure you and your little admirers will do fine without me," she said, nodding toward the gaggle of pretty young ladies sitting at his table and sipping an assortment of colorful frozen concoctions. She reached over and squeezed Ben's thigh. "Besides, I prefer to spend the evening with my sexy young lover." Ben was about six years older than the padre.

"*Mo-om...*" Martin mock-whined. "Don't say things like that. You'll warp me for life."

Sophie spoke up. "As if you could get more warped. Now, go back to your harem and prepare to be humiliated."

Martin looked me over, from the businesslike French twist to the sensible pumps, his gaze lingering here and there. "You were wearing that outfit when I first met you, Jane. I like it. You look like a very strict librarian." The way he said "very strict" let me know he wasn't talking about late fines. "Maybe undo one more button."

Stevie turned to me, her tone cheerful. "Just so you know, Jane, I've long ago stopped apologizing for my son's behavior."

Ben yanked the nacho plate out of reach as Martin tried to snag another. "Am I going to have to chase you away with a stick? Buy your own snacks."

"He can't afford to," I said. "He's already paying for all those girlie drinks."

"*They're* paying for *my* drinks," the padre said. "So there."

"You make me prouder every day," Stevie said. "Now, git."

Maxine circulated among the tables, handing out packets of stapled answer sheets and pencils as the young waitress who worked only on trivia Wednesdays took drink and food orders.

"We've got to name our team," Sophie said. "Put on your thinking caps, guys."

Team members generally chose a name drawn from current events. Ben threw out, *"Janey and the Divettes!"*

"Divettes?" Stevie wrinkled her nose. "Too furniture-sounding for me."

Nina Wallace also made the rounds of the tables, setting out paper plates laden with chocolate-coated sugar cookies decorated with little white-icing skeletons. She was an avid baker and never went anywhere without bringing home-baked yummies. The first time she'd played trivia, she'd set out a platter for her table only, prompting Maxine to set her straight. *I hope you brought enough for everyone, Nina.* From then on, all contestants could look forward to free dessert.

I thanked Nina, then glanced at Sophie to see how the skeleton cookies had gone over with her. It was, after all, a depiction in frosting of the remains of her much-loved late husband. She picked up a cookie, examined it, took a bite, and pronounced it delicious.

"Okay, this gives me an idea," she announced. "We're the *Skeleton Crew.*"

This was greeted with *oohs* of approval from our teammates. I gave Sophie a wink.

Maxine brought the festivities to order. A self-described

loudmouth, she eschewed a mic and hollered out the rules, reminding everyone that if she even glimpsed a cell phone, the offender would be barred from trivia Wednesdays for life. There would be four rounds of ten questions, each round based on a specific theme. Tonight the categories were foodie knowledge, classic movies, world geography, and local current events.

Hmm… local current events. Suddenly I wished I'd gone straight home from the town meeting.

As soon as Maxine was satisfied that all tables had ordered enough drinks and food, she commenced the game, lobbing a softball question. That is, it was a softball for anyone with an interest in the culinary arts, which did not include *moi*: "What year did Julia Child's cooking show *The French Chef* premier?"

Sophie and I blinked at each other while Ben and Stevie, both apparently card-carrying foodies, argued good-naturedly over the answer. It was either 1963 or 1964. Ben prevailed, and Sophie, our de facto leader, wrote *1963* on the first line of the answer sheet.

The questions kept coming, with teams huddling and whispering and drinking and laughing. After question ten, Maxine collected the answer sheets to score them, after which she announced the correct answers and the teams' rankings.

"Round One goes to *Skeleton in the Closet*, with all ten questions answered correctly." Nina Wallace and her gal pals hollered and clapped.

Meanwhile I cringed at the team's name, a not-so-subtle reference to Ernie's homosexuality. Scanning the players, I witnessed a few disapproving head-shakes and furtive glances toward Sophie, whose only response was to bestow on Nina the kind of stare usually associated with the word *withering*. For her part, Nina appeared oblivious, toasting her teammates with her fetus-friendly orange juice and whooping it up.

"*The Sexy Beasts* are in second place," Maxine continued. "They got eight questions right."

I look at the table in question. *The Sexy Beasts* consisted of Maia Armstrong, Rocky, and the pottery couple. I saluted them with my beer glass.

"*Skeleton Crew* is tied for third place with—" Maxine read the team name written on the answer sheet "—*Ramrod News: Like Real News, Only Not.* Both those teams got seven right." Sten Jakobsen was on the *Ramrod News* team, along with a few folks I recognized from his law practice.

"Not good enough, guys," Sophie told us. "Come on, we can beat these amateurs."

"*The Devilish Divas* are in fourth place with six correct answers," Maxine said. I looked toward the bar, where *The Devilish Divas* sat. Officers Howie Werker and Geri Marvin had teamed up with Kyle Kenneally and his unfortunate date for the evening, a prim-looking young woman who sipped a white-wine spritzer and appeared flummoxed by the rowdy goings-on. None of the team appeared diva-like to me, but then who was I to judge? I'm the one with "Diva" in her nickname, and to me, applying liquid eyeliner is a mystery on the order of Stonehenge.

"In fifth place with five correct answers," Maxine announced, "is, appropriately enough, *Pentagram Schmentagram.*" This team was populated by Patrick O'Rourke and his wife, Barbara, plus another couple I recognized from around town.

"Tied for last place with a whopping one, count 'em one, correct answer—" she held up a single digit "—are *Jane's*

Double Ds and *Thongs for the Granny Panties.*"

Jane's Double Ds also sat at the bar, sucking down the suds at an alarming rate. It was the loathsome pincher Logan and his snickering cohort, now snickering over their oh-so-clever team name. They shared last place with the padre's team, *Thongs for the Granny Panties.* Neither Martin nor any of his adorable teammates appeared at all perturbed that they'd come in last.

During the second round Maxine showed brief clips of old movies on the bar TV. Contestants had to name the film. *Skeleton Crew* moved up in the rankings to second place, thanks to Stevie's addiction to classic films. *Thongs for the Granny Panties* jumped from last place to third. Someone on Martin's team—perhaps the padre himself?—knew a lot about Bette Davis and Gary Cooper. It irked me to think of Martin and his giggling, jiggling, daiquiri-lapping cuties coming out ahead of us in this contest.

So I was pleased when Maxine introduced the third round, world geography, and I saw Sophie rub her palms together and growl, "Bring it." Startlingly, she knew all the answers, including the two capitals of Benin.

I can tell you're dying to know, so here they are: Porto-Novo and Cotonou. See? Hanging with me makes you smarter.

My team held its ranking. Meanwhile Martin's team moved up to tie us for second place. Nina's team went into the final round in first place. I didn't want Martin to win, but I *really* didn't want Nina to win.

Fortunately, the final category was local current events. *Skeleton Crew* had a ringer in the form of one Jane Delaney, Death Diva and discoverer of skeletons. Correction: We had two ringers. Not only was Sophie the town's mayor and therefore privy to inside info, she was intimately involved in the events of the past week.

Sophie read my mind. "If we don't win this one, I'm tossing in the trivia towel for good."

"It's no secret to anyone," Maxine began, "that Crystal Harbor has been prominent in the news this week. Our very own Jane Delaney started the ball rolling, so I think it only appropriate that the current-event questions in our final round test your knowledge of the life and times of our intrepid skeleton wrangler."

Huh?

"No fair!" Logan, well on his way to falling-down drunk, stabbed a finger in my direction, the movement causing him to practically tumble off his barstool. "She knows, like, a lot of stuff about herself. She'll cheat."

"For the record, I did not know Jane would be joining us tonight," Maxine said. "More of a challenge. So what? Man up, Logan. By the way, I'm cutting you off. Question one: Who first called Jane Delaney the Death Diva?"

My teammates looked at me expectantly. "How am I supposed to know that?" I said. "Everyone just started calling me that and it stuck."

Ben said, "Yeah, but who was the first one?"

"I don't know."

"Do you remember when you first heard it?" Stevie asked.

I shook my head. "It was so long ago."

"Irene." Sophie tapped the pencil on the answer sheet. "It was probably Irene."

"I don't think so," I said. "She thought the name was kind of dopey, so…"

"Who were your earliest clients?" Ben asked. "It was

probably one of them."

I groaned, dropping my head into my hands. How humiliating to make wild guesses about my own life. I looked around the room and saw the other teams huddled, wracking their brains for the correct answer. Not Martin, though. He lounged back in his seat, chatting and laughing with his bodacious babes. Almost as if he didn't care whether he won or lost.

Or as if he'd already written the correct answer.

"Question two," Maxine called out.

"Irene," I hurriedly said. "Put down Irene." Maxine was diligent about researching answers before her trivia contests. I hoped I'd guessed right.

"What is the original location of Janey's Place," Maxine said, "the Crystal Harbor health-food restaurant named for Jane Delaney?"

Sophie frowned. "Is this a trick question? It's the one right here on Main Street, no?"

"Yeah, of course." I took the pencil from her and wrote the answer. "Why did she ask such an easy one?"

And so it went for eight more baffling questions, ending with, "Jane Delaney's 'familiar' is a dog named Sexy Beast. What is the name of Sexy Beast's mother?"

I started writing my own name before it occurred to me Maxine was probably referring to a mom with fewer thumbs and more nipples. I slapped the pencil on the table and uttered a naughty word. "Before you ask," I informed my teammates, "no, I do not know the name of SB's biological mother."

"Think back," Sophie said. "Irene never mentioned it?"

"She probably never knew her name," I said. "I mean, how obscure is that?"

"Time's up." Maxine started collecting the answer sheets, starting with our table.

I scrawled *Dick Cheney* on the paper, shoved it at Maxine, and tossed the pencil onto the table. "How did you manage to find out such a thing?" I asked her.

She shrugged. "Irene got all her poodles from the same breeder. I gave him a call."

Maxine took her time scoring the answers, giving her customers ample opportunity to order more drinks. All except for Loathsome Logan, who was forced to make do with ginger ale. The first time he tried to sneak a gulp of a buddy's beer, Maxine informed his pals that if they let him imbibe, she'd kick them all out and ban them from Murray's for the rest of the summer. From that point forward, they did the policing for her.

Stevie and Ben excused themselves to cross the room and chat with Martin. Sophie asked about the car Dean had sold me. She smirked. "Is it still running?"

"It's a dream compared to my last ride," I said. "That's all that matters. You know, I thought about Dean when Max asked that geography question about Boston."

She frowned. "What connection does Dean have with Boston?"

"He told me he was there when Ernie was killed," I said. "He flew up there for a business seminar."

"Oh yeah, some franchise gimmick. Always had something cooking, always convinced *this* was the scheme that'd get him rich. Only, he never stuck with anything long enough, or worked hard enough, to make it pay. And of course, it was never his fault."

"So I was wondering—and I'm sure you've considered this

already," I said, "but how can you be sure Dean really was in Boston when he says he was? Couldn't he have just told you he was leaving and, well, you know…"

"Secretly stuck around and offed the husband of the woman whose pants he was trying to get into?" she asked. "I'll tell you the same thing I told Bonnie when she brought it up. I called Dean at his hotel in Boston. He was there. We spoke."

"And this was the day Ernie died?"

"Yep." Sophie took a deep pull on her beer. "If Lacey's to be believed, she saw Porter get in Ernie's car and drive away with the body on the afternoon of June fifteenth, not long after lunchtime—she estimates it was around two o'clock. Which is right about when I phoned Dean. I was at work, eating a late lunch at my desk."

"Had he left a number where you could reach him?" I asked.

Sophie's smile was knowing. "You've been thinking about this."

I shrugged, embarrassed. Clearly she didn't consider her ex a suspect. "I just figured if he left you a number to call—"

"I know, it could be the number to some pay phone somewhere and not necessarily the hotel," she said. "But no, he didn't leave a number, so I had to call information for it. Knew he was staying at the Sheraton where the seminar was being held. Operator put me through to his room. I called to tell him Porter couldn't pick him up from the airport when he came in the next evening, due to a last-minute business dinner, and that I'd do it. Chatted for a minute and then he had to get back to the seminar. Satisfied?"

I shrugged again. "I had to ask." I stayed Sophie's hand as she started to refill my beer glass. I might not have a long drive ahead of me that night, but Crystal Harbor squad cars had a spooky way of materializing out of nowhere.

She said, "Did you forget that whoever murdered Ernie had to know the story of how Ernie supposedly killed Tim? That fake suicide note shortens the list of suspects. And if *I* didn't know about it back then, Dean sure as hell didn't."

"True." If not for that note, I might have suggested that Dean could have hired out the murder while he was hundreds of miles away establishing his alibi. "I just feel compelled to, I don't know, tie up loose ends."

"Can't blame you for that," she said. "But face it, Porter and Lacey have *something* to do with the murder, even if their stories have holes. The truth is in there somewhere."

My brain kicked the facts around. "So you didn't go home for lunch the day Ernie died."

"Almost never did," she said. "Too much work."

"I assume you mentioned that to Bonnie. I mean, you can't be in two places at once—slaving away at your place of business at the same time that you're clobbering your husband at home." I thought about Sten's law firm, where she'd been employed at the time. "Do paralegals have to account for every minute of their time like lawyers, for billing purposes?"

Sophie sat up straight. I could tell she hadn't thought of that. "Yeah. And Sten holds on to every piece of paper in perpetuity. He must have a warehouse full of old records at this point."

"So your time sheet for that day probably still exists."

"Not that our dear friend the detective will care. She'll just say I faked it to account for my whereabouts." She sighed. "Just wish I trusted Bonnie to get it right. Keep waiting for her to show up with handcuffs."

She went still, listening intently in the noisy bar. "Is that my phone?" She pulled it out of her purse and answered it, covering her other ear. I watched her expression tense. "No way, it's late and I've had a couple. Whatever it is can wait till morning. I'll be there at nine." She hung up, muttering curses under her breath.

"Please tell me that wasn't her nibs," I said.

Sophie grimaced. "New information has come to light, Bonnie says." She tapped the phone's screen and put it to her ear again.

"Who are you calling?"

"That lawyer Sten hooked me up with," she said. "No way I'm talking to the cops alone."

14

Johnny Appleseed

AS IT TURNED out, Sexy Beast's mother had two names. Either would have counted as a correct answer. Her registered name was Champion Monkeysee Monkeydo. Yeah, that's right, my neurotic little poodle shares the genes of a certifiable champion. Do they give blue ribbons for dribbling pee while prostrating oneself in fawning submission? Her "call name"—what her humans called her, in other words—was Bananas.

The padre knew this. He wrote it all out on his answer sheet. He also knew that I have sober, dignified Sten Jakobsen, of all people, to thank for my decidedly undignified, impossible-to-shake nickname, Death Diva. I must remember to thank him.

Oh, and the original location of Janey's Place? Not Main Street, thank you very much, but a big, apple green food truck, a kind of health-food roach coach that used to make the rounds of businesses too small to have their own cafeterias.

And yeah, it's understandable that this "original location" slipped my mind, considering I spent about a million hours behind the wheel of that thing way back when, serving up smoked-portobello club sandwiches and creamy carrot-coconut soup to hardworking vegetarians all over western Nassau County.

It's not my fault, it was a trick question!

Guess who got it right.

And guess whose team won the damn trivia contest. The padre and his nubile cheering section celebrated their triumph with little glasses of sherry and a sedate toast in honor of their worthy adversaries.

Just kidding. They screamed and pounded the table and knocked back booze and hugged and kissed and groped one another so thoroughly I began to suspect Martin didn't go there for the trivia.

Sophie was less vexed than I'd expected at our loss, distracted as she was by her upcoming meeting with Detective Hernandez. At least she'd lawyered up. Ben and Stevie gave her a lift back to the library, where her car was parked.

As was mine. They offered me a ride, but it was a gorgeous night and I opted to hoof it. I hadn't gone half a block when Martin jogged up behind me.

"I turned around and you were gone," he said. His breath was beer-scented, but he was by no means drunk.

I tried not to read too much into that simple statement. Such as: *I've been watching you all evening and when I saw you were gone, I thought my heart would break in two.*

"Where's your motorcycle?" I asked. "Library?"

He shook his head. "I walked."

"From the house?" I looked at him. "It's about two miles from there to the library."

"I like running into your neighbors and telling them I'm living with you."

I rolled my eyes, deciding not to let him bait me. It was too lovely a night for even a halfhearted squabble. "Do you tell them Dom's bunking there too?"

"Nah. He won't last."

"Oh, and you will?"

Instead of answering, he nodded toward the corner restaurant we were approaching. "Want to get a table?"

"I already had dinner," I said.

The restaurant, called Dewatre after its executive chef and owner, Pierre "Swing" Dewatre, featured outdoor seating in the summer. Swing had earned notoriety for serving exotic and endangered animals. Well, that was the rumor anyway, one the animal-rights groups had gotten all worked up over. For what it's worth, I never noticed any sketchy items on the menu. All I knew was, Swing made a sweet-and-sour brisket that was the most delicious thing I'd ever put in my mouth. If it was in reality sweet-and-sour panda, I didn't want to know.

"I ate too," he said, "but you can never have too much dessert. Swing makes a killer tiramisu."

"Some other time."

"I'll hold you to that."

I looked at him and then quickly away, shoring up my defenses against those crystal blue eyes and that deliciously predatory smile. The fact that the padre clearly knew how sexy he was should have been a major turn-off for a mature, sensible woman like me, but what can I tell you? Something about this guy turned me into a dopey, weak-kneed teenager.

"So what makes you think Dom's going to move out soon?" I asked. "Didn't he say he'd stay as long as you did?"

"He has a lot on his plate," Martin said.

"What, like running the Janey's Place intergalactic empire?"

"He has two families to take care of."

Right. Dom's two exes and their children. *His* children.

What's that you say? That you've had enough of me whining about how my biological clock is swiftly running down and it might already be too late? Okay, I won't bring it up again if you don't.

Unless I, you know, forget.

Martin continued, "And by 'take care of'—"

"I know." I held up my hand to silence him. "Dom gives his exes more than the agreed-upon financial support and has joint custody of all the kids and he fixes stuff around their houses and they let him pop in all the time without calling and they all get along *so* splendidly it makes me want to puke."

Martin answered this little tirade with silence as we crossed the street and turned another corner. When I could no longer stand it, I barked, "What?"

"I didn't say anything."

"Don't make me hurt you, Padre."

"It doesn't take a shrink to see you're still hung up on your ex," he said. "Is that what a guy has to do to ensure your everlasting devotion? Turn himself into Johnny Appleseed and turn all his exes into BFFs?"

I walked faster. Martin kept pace. "You make it sound all sister-wife. It's nothing like that. And Johnny Appleseed? The guy has three kids, not thirty."

"That you know of."

"You can shut up now."

He did, much to my annoyance. When we reached the library, he walked me to my car in the dark parking lot.

"I suppose you're expecting a ride home?" I said.

He slipped past me and got in behind the wheel. "I'll drive. You've been drinking."

"I had one beer!"

"Me too, but I weigh more. Higher tolerance."

I doubted that. Not that he had a higher tolerance, but that he'd stopped at one. But I was in no mood to argue. I slid into the passenger side of my new/old Mazda. He lowered the windows, turned off the A/C, and headed for Main Street.

After a few blocks, he took the opposite turn from the one that would take us to my house. Why was I not surprised? "Okay, where are we going?" I asked.

"It's early. You don't really want to go home, do you?"

"It's nearly midnight," I said. "And yeah, I'm a boring old broad and I want to go home to my little dog and my ugly old bathrobe."

"And Dom."

"You think you know everything about me," I said. "You think you know what makes me tick. You are so arrogant." So much for not arguing.

"Your bathrobe isn't ugly," he said. "Well, yeah, it's ugly, but in a sexy way."

"Oh, here we go. How on earth could my ratty, worn-out—No, don't answer that. I don't want to know—"

"You're incapable of thinking like a guy." He stopped for a red light and looked at me. "Which is actually kind of charming."

The light changed and we were off again. Had the big bad black sheep of Clan McAuliffe actually said that something about me was charming? I wouldn't have thought he knew the word. The air turned crisp and briny as we headed north toward the water.

I couldn't leave it alone. "So you like me in the ugly bathrobe more than the sexy lingerie from *Ramrod News*?"

"Why does it have to be one or the other?" He took the

turnoff for the town beach. "Variety is good for the soul."

Not to mention the libido. At this time of night, Martin had his pick of parking spots. He left the car at the edge of the beach and we wordlessly took off across the sand. The moon hung low on the horizon, half-full. Or half-empty, if you prefer. We saw few stars due to light pollution from this built-up area of Long Island, not to mention nearby New York City. The brisk breeze freed strands of hair from my French twist.

I'd left my shoes in the car, and the padre was barefoot too. The beach facing Crystal Harbor—the bay after which the town was named—was studded with rocks and pebbles, which felt cool and invigorating under my feet as we ambled toward the shoreline. North Shore beaches such as this, which are on Long Island Sound across from Connecticut, have little in common with the world-renowned South Shore ocean-facing beaches such as Jones Beach, with their vast stretches of pristine white sand.

Why's that, you ask? During the last Ice Age, glaciers advanced partway down Long Island, in the process carving out assorted land forms, bays, and waterways on the North Shore and leaving that coastline full of rubble. The South Shore is flatter, with mile after mile of lovely Hamptons-worthy beaches. Maxine hadn't asked about this during the geography portion of the trivia contest, but if she had, I would have been ready.

I wouldn't admit it to Martin, but I was glad he'd brought me to the beach. The sights, the smells, the rough sand underfoot—they were simultaneously stimulating and soothing. I had a feeling I'd sleep well that night. "For the record," I said, "I'm not still hung up on Dom."

"You're making progress, I'll give you that," he said. "You

changed your computer password from your anniversary to Sexy Beast's birthday."

I gaped at him. "When are you going to stop messing with my stuff? We had an unspoken pact. I let you live in my house and you leave my things alone."

"Okay, the thing about unspoken pacts?" he said. "The details can get a bit fuzzy. And for what it's worth, a pet's birthday is absolute amateur hour. I reset it with a stronger password this afternoon."

I stopped walking. "You gave my computer a new password? When were you going to share this with me?"

He shrugged. I forced myself to focus on his face and not on the way the breeze molded his gray T-shirt to his torso. In moonlight no less. "I'm telling you now," he said. "It's 'dollar sign ampersand I wear granny panties twelve twenty-nine.'"

"Not 'I wear granny panties twenty-four seven'?"

That impish grin. "Do you?"

You'll never find out. The words were perched on the tip of my tongue, ready to spring, but I restrained myself. After all, who knew? Instead I said, "That's a stupid password."

"The Y in 'granny' is capitalized, and the number is for December twenty-ninth, my birthday."

"Right, *your* birthday." I shook my head.

"It's a lot stronger than your pet's birthday. It'd be tough for a bad guy to guess."

Good thing I had a bad guy living in my maid's room to help me figure all this out.

"Dom wants to get married again," I blurted, and resumed walking.

"I know." The padre picked up a rock, weighed it in his palm, and hurled it far over the water. "He seems to think it's a done deal."

"Huh. Really?"

He shrugged. "It's no secret you've spent the past twenty years waiting for your soul mate to come around."

"Seventeen years," I said. "Don't make me older than I am. And I have not spent..." I sighed. "Okay, but that's all over, like you said. I've moved on. New password, new home, new..."

I hesitated. And no, I wasn't going to say, "new man." Shows what you know.

"New, um, friends," I finished.

"Plus," he said, "I noticed you moved your Dom shrine to the attic."

"My what?"

"Your wedding album and that box with all those pictures of him and his erotic love letters and all that. It's like a little shrine to—"

"You're not supposed to be upstairs!" I stopped and faced him, flapping my arms in frustration. "You're definitely not supposed to be snooping in my stuff."

Martin shoved his hands in his pockets, unfazed. "You've made progress, is my point. You used to keep that stuff in your bedroom closet."

"Only because basements don't have attics," I said. The last time he'd gone through my stuff—or the last time I'd known about it—I was living in Mr. Franckowiak's sad little one-room basement apartment in Sandy Cove. I didn't waste my breath telling him to respect my privacy. It was a lost cause.

The tide was coming in and cold water surged over my bare feet, getting them moving again. "Does Dom really think it's inevitable that we'll get back together?" I asked as we strolled along the wet sand. "What did he say?"

"It's less what he says and more his general attitude. He's looking at your house like he's trying to decide how much of his furniture will fit."

"He knows I couldn't move to his place. I can't move out of my house while Sexy Beast is still alive," I said, "according to the terms of Irene's bequest."

"I know," the padre said. "Because the house belongs to the dog."

If he was still bitter about that fact, he concealed it well. I wouldn't blame him if he was, considering that Irene McAuliffe had broken up his grandparents' marriage and ended up owning his beloved grandmother's dream house—which she'd then left to a seven-pound poodle.

I said, "So Dom thinks he's moving in? For real?"

Martin shrugged. "Yesterday I found him measuring the rooms."

"Pretty darn confident," I grumbled.

"A gung-ho business tycoon like him? Can't expect him to sit around twiddling his thumbs while the woman he wants gets over him and moves on to a more appreciative guy."

"More appreciative, huh?" *Got anyone in mind?* A small, round stone winked at me in the moonlight. I bent to pick it up, warmed its burnished perfection in my hand as we walked.

"I wouldn't be surprised if Dom pulls out the stops and makes your basic grand gesture." He illustrated this by making, well, a grand gesture. "Something that'll knock your socks off. Not to mention your granny panties."

"That was one day," I said. "My laundry had piled up." Jeez, would I ever live those things down?

"So go commando," he said. "It's what I do."

My gaze flicked to the back of his snug jeans.

Oh, please. Don't tell me that if you heard a guy this hot utter the *C*-word—in this case, "commando"—you wouldn't have yourself a little peek.

It was definitely time to change the subject. I said, "Detective Hernandez called Sophie at the bar tonight."

"Yeah, she looked like someone spat in her beer," he said. "What did Bonnie want?"

"To interview her again. Interrogate her, whatever. I have a feeling there's been a new development. Sophie called her lawyer."

"Smart woman."

15

Window of Opportunity

I AMBLED DOWNSTAIRS the next morning and marched across Dom's air mattress, accidentally kicking him in the head when he flopped into my foot.

Nothing. Not so much as an eye quiver. He was, as always, blissfully comatose. Sexy Beast paused, as always, to sniff his beloved Dom and make sure he was still breathing as I shambled into the kitchen. Martin was, as always, on his tenth or twelfth mug of high-test and working his way through most of a newly opened box of Fruity Pebbles.

He turned the *Times* crossword puzzle in my direction, as always, so I could admire the fact that every last one of the little boxes was filled in, and in ink, while I grunted something meant to sound encouraging and made tracks for the coffee carafe.

By now we had our routine down, like an old married couple whose special-needs but somehow high-achieving adult son would remain unconscious until precisely 7:38 a.m., when he'd suddenly bound out of bed, eerily alert and ready to tear another huge bite out of the natural, organic, and sustainably produced foodservice industry.

Dom had always been that way. Made no difference when

he hit the hay or where he laid his head. It was one of those quirks I used to consider lovable.

I'd made it through one and a half mugs of black coffee and was lingering over the *Times* Style section ($179.99 isn't too much for a designer salt-and-pepper set, is it?) when my cell rang. I didn't recognize the number.

"Jane, it's Porter Vargas." His voice sounded strained.

I checked the wall clock. Barely eight o'clock. Dom was getting ready for work, which is what I assumed my caller should be doing at this hour of the morning. "What's up, Porter?"

"I want to hire you for an assignment."

"Okay." So. After having engaged me anonymously for the past two decades to deliver flowers to Tim Holbrook's grave, he had something else for me to do. "What do you have in mind?"

"I need you to come here this morning to discuss it. I'm staying at my mother's house here in town." He told me where she lived.

"Sure thing." I grabbed a pen from the junk drawer and scribbled the address on a napkin. "What time?"

"Please arrive promptly at nine," he said.

I saluted the arrogant man. *Sir, yes, sir!* "Nine it is," I said. "You working from home this morning?"

"What? Oh. Yeah."

We said goodbye and I hung up. Martin asked about the call. "You're not going there alone," he said, when I told him about Porter's request.

"Oh, please." I was already heading out of the breakfast room.

"I'm serious, Jane." Martin was out of his chair, catching

up to me. "You're responsible for Vargas being accused, arrested, and possibly spending the rest of his life in jail. He's got to have it in for you."

"He sounded civil enough on the phone."

"How about the fact that the man is very likely a murderer?" he said.

"Nah, my money's on Lacey." When I realized he was following me up the stairs, I swung to face him. He bumped into me, which turned out to be more agreeable than it sounds.

"In which case Porter disposed of the body to cover his wife's crime," he said. "If you're right, he's still protecting her, pretending *he* killed Ernie in self-defense. You know how irrational he is when it comes to Lacey. He's capable of anything. It's blind, obsessive love."

My tone was arid. "Yeah, that's irrational, all right. I'm not having this discussion, Padre. And you're not allowed upstairs," I reminded him as I sprinted up the steps. For all the good it did me.

He trailed me into the master bedroom. "I'm going with you. No argument."

I opened my underwear drawer. "Do you mind? I have to shower and dress." He crossed his arms over his chest and stood his ground. I sighed. "I'll be careful, I promise, but I have no intention of showing up at a client's house with a bodyguard." My gut told me I had nothing to fear from Porter.

"I'm not giving you a choice, Jane. I'm going with you."

After a moment I tossed my hands in defeat. "All right, all right. Be ready to leave in forty-five minutes."

The instant he left the room, I threw on yesterday's clothes and hurried down the stairs, finger-combing my hair. When I entered the kitchen, I saw Dom standing over the stove, boiling water for his slow-cooking steel-cut oatmeal. A quick good-morning, a couple of scritches for SB, then I silently crept down the hallway, past the laundry room to the garage entrance opposite the maid's room where Martin was bunking. I heard the shower running in his bathroom and smiled to myself.

In less than ten minutes I pulled up in front of Mama Vargas's enormous, brick Tudor-style home with half-timbering and steep gable roofs. I was half an hour early, but if I waited to ring the bell, Martin would have time to figure out I'd given him the slip and come roaring up on his Harley before I got inside the door. Porter wanted prompt? Try thirty minutes early.

I made my way up the long brick walk and punched the doorbell. And waited. I rang it again. After a minute I tried the big brass door knocker. Porter could have been in the shower too, but then where was his mother? I couldn't ignore my tingling nape. Was it my imagination or had he indeed sounded stressed on the phone?

I descended the front porch steps and ambled around the house, peering as casually as I could into the first-floor windows and hoping none of Mama Vargas's neighbors decided to phone the local gendarmerie about a suspicious character casing the joint. There was nothing to see through the open drapes except traditional furnishings with an emphasis on genuine-looking antiques.

I rounded the back of the house and went straight for the multipaned bow window which projected into the backyard. Peering through the leaded-glass panes, I saw what appeared to be a great room, with a gigantic wood-and-stone fireplace mantel, Oriental rugs, floor-to-ceiling windows, and a steeply pitched, half-timbered ceiling with a couple of heavy timber cross pieces. A sturdy rope hung from the nearest timber, located some dozen feet from the window, with a dainty Louis XVI armchair positioned directly under it. Or maybe it was Louis Quatorze. I'm pretty sure it was some Louis.

Porter Vargas stood on the chair with—you're way ahead of me, I can tell—a noose around his neck.

He faced me, his expression clearly indicating that in fact he did not appreciate my early arrival. We locked eyes and I stood paralyzed for a long moment until he made his move, kicking the chair out from under his feet.

Acting on pure reflex, I spun around, not even knowing what I was looking for. I sprinted across the sprawling stone patio and lifted an ornate iron patio chair. In that instant, with my muscles marinating in adrenaline, that chair could have been made of Styrofoam. I got a running start and used my momentum and the aforementioned adrenaline rush to slam the chair through the bow window.

I followed the chair, leaping over the low sill through the shower of glass shards and lead fragments to reach Porter in about two seconds that felt like as many hours. Furiously he kicked out at me as I struggled to reposition the chair under him. His sneakered foot caught me in the temple and I went down with a cry of pain. Immediately I sprang up, wrapping my arms around his flailing legs while trying to drag the chair with my foot.

"Porter, don't do this," I shouted. "It won't solve anything."

His face was purple, his body twitching as he clawed at the noose—a reflexive action, I knew, and not a change of heart, since he still twisted and kicked and fought my efforts to save him.

Suddenly another pair of arms materialized, effectively trapping Porter's legs and lifting him several inches.

"Get the chair!" Martin barked.

I didn't pause to wonder where he'd come from but shoved the chair into place. Before Porter could mount a counteroffensive, Martin stood on the chair, restraining the other man with one muscular arm while slipping something out of his own back jeans pocket.

Sunlight flashed on steel as the switchblade sprang open. Martin sliced through the rope in one swift motion and caught Porter as he sagged. Together we lowered him onto the carpet. I loosened the slipknot at the side of his neck and pulled the rope over his head.

Porter gulped air as tears slid from his closed eyes down his temples. "Damn you," he rasped. "Damn you, Jane."

I slumped onto my butt, my own chest heaving, my heart jackhammering my ribcage. I looked at the padre and breathlessly mouthed, *Thank you.*

He placed a hand on my back. Had anything ever felt so good? So reassuring?

"Where... how...?" I said.

"You thought I didn't know what you were up to?" Martin wore a wry half smile. "'Be ready to leave in forty-five minutes'? Seriously?"

"Thank God you're sneakier than I am," I said. "But how did you get into the house?"

"I heard you holler as soon as I pulled up. Front door was unlocked." He glanced at the smashed bow window and gave me a once-over. "Hold still." He took my hand in his, which seemed a surprisingly tender if not unwelcome gesture until he turned my forearm to pluck a good-size piece of glass out of it.

He frowned as I pulled tissues from my pocket to try and soak up the blood. "You're a mess," he said.

I looked down at myself. It was true. I'd been so fixated on saving Porter, not to mention the adrenaline high, that I hadn't felt anything as I'd hurled myself through the broken window. That numbness was fast fading. When I touched my stinging scalp, my fingers came away red. A cut on my sandal-clad right foot and another, larger one on my shin dripped blood onto the velvety carpet, which was probably antique silk. I didn't even try to count the myriad smaller lacerations which made it look like I'd gone one-on-one with a giant blender. It could have been worse. At least I wore full-length jeans and not shorts.

Porter tried to sit up. Martin pushed him back down and said, "You owe this woman big-time, Vargas. You don't think so now, but you will."

I wasn't so sure. "Where's your mother, Porter?" I asked.

He scrubbed his hands over his face. A dark ligature mark encircled his neck, as well as scratches from his own fingernails. He took a breath to speak and coughed instead. His voice was hoarse as he said, "Breakfast meeting. She's on the board of a cancer charity." After a moment he added, "Didn't want her to be the one to find me."

"I get it," I said. "You figured a workable alternative was to let Jane Delaney, local Death Diva, discover your lifeless body swinging from the rafters."

Porter took note of my acerbic tone. He looked at me for the first time since we'd cut him down. "I figured you're used to… Anyway, I left payment." He indicated a small piecrust table on which lay two envelopes. He'd written my name on one and his wife's name on the other. I assumed mine contained a check, and Lacey's his suicide note.

He glanced at Martin. "I'm going to get up now." The padre made no move to stop him as he slowly sat up and looked around. His bloodshot gaze lingered on the smashed bow window as he told me what I'd already figured out. "I left the front door unlocked for you, Jane." Yeah, well.

When he took in the sliced-and-diced condition of yours truly, his expression morphed to something close to chagrin, as if it only just occurred to him what I'd gone through to save his ungrateful carcass.

Shakily he came to his feet. We did, too, and followed him to the other end of the spacious room. He slumped into an overstuffed armchair, tossed his hand toward me, and told Martin, "First-aid stuff's in the bathroom three doors down."

Martin hesitated, silently asking if I was okay with him leaving the room. I waved him away and went to Porter, gently touching his throat where the rope had dug in. He didn't seem to notice. I felt obliged to say, "You should go to the emergency room."

He ignored that. Big surprise. Well, his breathing seemed okay and he hadn't lost consciousness, so I didn't press the issue.

I said, "Porter, have you been drinking?"

He shook his head. "I want to die sober."

I believed him. He didn't smell like booze and I saw no telltale bottles. I suspected that at the first opportunity, he'd take another crack at dying sober.

Martin returned with the first-aid box. He pointed to the sofa across from Porter's chair. "Sit." I did. "How'd you get this?" he asked, running a finger over my bruised temple. I declined to answer and was grateful when he didn't pursue it. I doubted Porter even remembered kicking me.

The padre examined the cut on my scalp and declared it no biggie, adding that scalp wounds bleed a lot. He dabbed it with an alcohol wipe while I managed not to flinch, then began plucking shards of glass out of my hair, collecting them in an impressive little pile on the lamp table. He moved on to the gash on my forearm, digging around in the box for butterfly bandages to close it.

"When will your mother be home?" I asked Porter, who sat staring at nothing.

He flapped his arm in a gesture meant to convey the passage of a goodly length of time.

"Porter." I waited until he looked at me. "Why?"

His expression was heartbreakingly bleak. "I killed them, Jane. I killed them both."

If a heart can stumble over itself, mine did. Martin's fingers tightened on my forearm, ever so slightly, as he cleaned the cut. I willed calm into my voice. "Tim was a terrible accident, Porter."

"You were right what you said a couple of days ago. I was no kid, I should've known better than to get wasted on that boat, to get Tim wasted. I never should've let him dive in, much less…" He squeezed his eyes shut and barely managed to choke out, "I left him out there to die. I didn't mean for it to happen."

He did mean, however, for his good buddy Ernie to take the blame, by capitalizing on Ernie's unstated feelings for him.

I waited while Martin finished bandaging my arm. He then gently tugged up the right leg of my jeans and went to work on my lacerated shin. I'd been thinking I might need stitches, but the butterfly bandages seemed to do the trick.

I wondered how to ask the obvious next question. The padre did it for me. "So when you say you killed them both. Can I assume the other one is Ernie?"

Miserably Porter nodded. Martin and I exchanged a look. One of us was going to have to quietly leave the room and phone Bonnie.

"How did it happen, man?" Martin asked. "Did you guys have a fight?"

Porter didn't answer. Absently he touched the livid streak on his throat as if he'd forgotten what he'd just tried to do. His gaze was unfocused; he was somewhere else.

I decided a bluff was in order. "Okay, I have to tell you, Porter, the police already know Lacey did it."

He straightened and shot me a look of alarm. "That's not true. It was me, not her." He pointed to the piecrust table. "Read my note. It's all in there—my complete confession."

"Your statement to the cops had holes." I shrugged. "They know you're protecting your wife. They have evidence she was at Ernie's house the day he died."

"How could they know that?" He clamped his lips shut as if belatedly trying to take back his words. "I don't believe you. Bonnie Hernandez brought me in again last night. They're following a different lead now. Dean Phillips, Sophie's ex, concocted a story about me and Sophie—that we had a fling back then and killed Ernie. It's bull, of course. That loser's just trying to stick it to Sophie."

So that's what Bonnie wanted to talk to her about. They were meeting at that very moment. "You know Dean's story is bull," I said, "I know it's bull, and the cops know it's bull. They also know *your* story is bull, Porter. You might have disposed of Ernie's body and faked his suicide, but Lacey did the killing. You were trying to protect her, just like you were trying to protect her by hanging yourself and taking the blame for the whole thing in that note you left."

I watched conflicting emotions duke it out behind his bloodshot eyes, erasing any lingering doubts I might have had about Lacey's guilt. "If you really want to help your wife," I said, "you'll stick around and support her through the trial and whatever comes after. She needs you, Porter."

He held my gaze for long moments, then slowly sank back down in his chair. "She doesn't need me," he muttered. "I'd only get in the way. She has Colin."

"You're wrong," I said, not knowing whether it was a lie. "She's going to need you every step of the way."

He looked at us beseechingly, as if we were judge and jury. "It wasn't her fault. I drove her to it."

Martin said, "How?"

"I killed Tim and let her think Ernie did it," Porter said. "I let her think he got away with murder. When we got married she insisted I cut off all contact with Ernie, and I agreed."

"You didn't do it, though," I said, recalling Teddy's account of their ongoing friendship.

"The guy had been my best friend since kindergarten," he said. "And he hadn't actually done what she thought he did, so I figured, you know, what she didn't know wouldn't hurt her." He gave a weak shrug.

"But she found out," I said.

"Yeah." He sighed. "It was almost three years later and I was working from home one day, and Lacey gets a call from a friend who saw Ernie and me playing tennis the weekend before at this obscure club about ten towns away. I mean, what were the odds? Anyway, she hit the ceiling. Demanded I end the friendship for good."

"What did you do?" I asked.

"I felt like a slimeball for having deceived her, but what I did was act all puffed up and macho, like it's my business who I'm friends with and all that crap. Hoping to put an end to her tirade. She says, 'Well, if you won't take care of it, I will.' And she jumps in her car and takes off."

"This was the day Ernie died, right?" I asked.

"Yeah." Porter pushed his fingers through his disheveled black hair. "We'd just had lunch. Leftover lasagna and salad. Lacey makes amazing lasagna."

I recalled what Sophie had said about strong emotions sharpening memory.

"What then?" Martin asked.

"I waited a bit, hoping she'd cool down and come home. But the more I thought about it, the more I realized what a jerk I'd been. I mean, she didn't know Ernie wasn't responsible for Tim's death. I shouldn't expect her to tolerate our being friends."

"Did you ever consider fessing up?" I asked. "Telling her that it was really you and not Ernie at the controls of the boat that night?"

Porter averted his gaze. I had my answer.

Martin had finished bandaging my shin and the cut on my foot. He now took a pair of tweezers out of the kit and began extracting tiny glass splinters from my face. Yeah, I was a mess, all right.

"So is that when you headed over to Ernie's house?" I asked.

He nodded. "It wasn't Lacey's job to tell him our friendship was over. It was something I had to do myself.

Only, by the time I got there… it was too late."

"What do you mean?" I was pretty sure I knew, but I needed to hear him say it. Martin paused in his tweezing.

"I found him in his backyard. His head…" Porter swallowed hard. I'd never seen anyone look more haunted. "It was caved in. The blood…"

"Was Lacey there?" Martin asked.

Porter shook his head. "She must have freaked out and bolted. I know she hadn't gone there intending to kill him. I think they argued and she snapped. I wish I'd gotten there in time, but the fact was, there was nothing I could do for Ernie. I had my wife to think of. I had to protect her."

"Did you notice a weapon?" I asked. "I mean, did you see what she used to, um… what she hit him with?"

"He was lying close to the patio. I assumed she pushed him down and slammed his head against it. She was pretty athletic back then. Strong. Still is, in fact. You could tell there'd been a fight—furniture knocked over, stuff like that."

Martin asked, "But his head wasn't actually in contact with the patio?" His tweezers were busy again, having moved on to my right arm. "There was no blood on it?"

"No, the blood was on the grass. Figured she moved him. I hosed it down but didn't stop to straighten the furniture or anything. I was just trying to hold it together, figure out how to get rid of his body before a neighbor saw or Sophie came home early or something."

"So you put him in the trunk of his car," I said.

Porter nodded. "His car was in the old carriage house— they used it as a garage. Then I ran into the house, grabbed the boat key and wrote the suicide note on his typewriter, and drove to my folks' house. I told them Lacey and I had a fight and could I stay there overnight." He added, "It's not like it was the first time."

Martin said, "Didn't they ask why you were driving Ernie's car?"

"I parked it out of sight behind the guest cottage. Mom and Dad were snoring by ten. I stayed awake, working out what I had to do. Sometime after midnight I grabbed a shovel, a flashlight, and my old ocean kayak out of the storage barn and drove to the cemetery. I knew how to sneak in. Back in high school, Ernie and I used to do it for kicks."

"Why didn't you do the obvious thing?" I asked. "Tie something heavy to Ernie and dump him in the ocean when you took his boat out?"

"I wanted him… I know it sounds lame, all things considered, but I wanted him laid to rest in a real cemetery, not get turned into shark food in the ocean. It was dumb luck that they'd just planted those willow saplings. I buried him under one of them and said a prayer."

"The boat was discovered pretty far off Montauk the next morning," I said. "Did you go straight there from the cemetery?"

"Yeah. I took the kayak aboard so I could paddle back to shore. I left Ernie's car parked at the marina like he'd left it there."

Martin said, "Weren't you afraid someone would find blood in the trunk?"

Porter shook his head. "There were tarps in the carriage house. I put one under Ernie and tossed it overboard later."

"What did you do once you got back to shore?" I asked.

"I carried the kayak across Montauk Highway to Fort Pond and paddled to the northern end. The moon was nearly full. There wasn't another soul around. It was almost…" He gave a little shake of the head, his eyes glistening. "It was almost peaceful."

"How'd you get home?" Martin asked.

"It wasn't that far from the pond to the Montauk train station. I ditched the kayak in the woods and caught a train. Had to wait a couple of hours for it, and the ride itself was another four or five—it wasn't direct. I walked from the Crystal Harbor station back to Ernie and Sophie's street, where my car was parked."

"What time did you finally get home?" I asked.

"Around five p.m. I could tell Lacey didn't want to talk, so I figured I'd give her a little space till she was ready."

"How long till she was ready?" Martin asked.

Porter took a deep breath and let it out slowly. "I assumed she'd put two and two together after the 'suicide' news broke. She had to know what I'd done for her, but she never mentioned it, and neither did I. Things eventually got back to some version of normal and I was afraid to rock the boat. In the end, we never talked about what happened."

Not a peep in all those years. Talk about the proverbial elephant in the room. This was a whole darn herd of them perched on your chintz upholstery and sipping tea from your best china.

"Why didn't you go along with the story Dean spun for the cops?" I asked. "If you could get Lacey off while you and Sophie took the heat, why not go for it?"

"It's bad enough I faked Ernie's suicide, made Sophie believe her husband killed himself," he said. "For more than thirty years she thought that. I'll be damned if I help convict her of a murder she didn't commit. She doesn't deserve that."

"But you do?"

With heartbreaking sincerity he said, "I finally know how Ernie felt."

"What do you mean?"

"The huge favor he did for me all those years ago," he said. "Lying for me, saying he was the one who left Tim out there in the ocean. I never appreciated it at the time—his sacrifice, what he was willing to risk for me."

"You both knew his mother would take care of it," I said.

"We knew she'd *try*. There were no guarantees. Ernie could have been arrested. Done time." He took a deep breath. "Lacey will not go to prison. I'll do whatever it takes."

16

Wakey, Wakey, Janey

I TOOK A sip of sweet, cold Riesling and selected a salted pecan from a small, hand-glazed pottery bowl. Sophie had bought the bowl at that shop next to Janey's Place, the one owned by that young couple whose names I could never remember.

It was six p.m. and we were comfortably ensconced on Sophie's patio chaises. Sexy Beast lay dozing on the lawn. The evening was balmy and overcast. I just hoped if it was going to rain, it would hold off until I got home. Sophie had laid in some big citronella candles in ceramic tubs, and they did a decent job of repelling the mosquitoes.

She'd just gotten home from the Town Hall where she worked. She and her lawyer had met with Bonnie that morning while the padre and I had been saving Porter's bacon.

We'd waited for Porter's mother to return home before making tracks. She'd been shocked at the condition of her beautiful leaded-glass bow window, but once she realized what had caused it, her only concern was for Porter. By the time we left, his doctor and brother—who happened to be one and the same—was on his way to the house.

Sophie took one look at me and assumed I'd been in a car

accident. I'd told her about Lacey's certain guilt and how Porter had covered up the crime, but she was still worried about the damning story Dean had concocted. He must have laid it on Bonnie right after the town meeting the night before. It's why the detective had phoned Sophie for another meeting.

"Come on," I said, "how much credence do you think Bonnie's going to give a ridiculous tale like that? Especially considering Porter's much more believable version of events?"

"Well, Bonnie can be irritating as hell," Sophie said, "and she has a way of getting sidetracked, but I like to think she's too smart to be taken in by Dean's venomous nonsense."

"He's never let go of his bitterness toward you," I said. "That's what's driving his absurd lie."

"Be that as it may, she has a responsibility to follow up on all leads." Sophie tossed a few nuts into her mouth.

"Did you mention the time-sheet thing to her?" I asked. "You know, that Sten can probably produce the old records and show that you were in the office when Ernie was killed?"

"Got Sten to look for it last night and give it to Bonnie. For all the good it did me. She was like, right, no one ever fudges those forms."

"She's such a cynic."

"Comes with the job," Sophie said. "And she's right, a law-office time sheet alone doesn't count for much. Spend twenty minutes shooting the breeze around the water cooler, that time's got to be accounted for. Some client's going to pay."

"But the time sheet shows you didn't go home for lunch, right?" I insisted.

"Yep. Every little thing helps, Jane. Keep that agile brain of yours perking away."

I poured us each a little more wine. "What exactly does

your charming ex say happened the day Ernie died?"

"Says I went home at lunchtime, argued with Ernie—about his homosexuality, natch. Which we never did. I mean, I used to get after him about the clutter in his basement music studio, and he got after me about working too many hours, but once I got over the shock of marrying a gay guy, we never fought over that. Would've been like fighting over the color of his eyes."

"So you and gay hubby had it out," I said.

"In the fairy tale Dean spun for Bonnie, yeah. Then I snuffed gay hubby—with what variety of weapon, he declined to say—and called my lover Porter to get rid of the body for me." Sophie snickered. "Can you see that? Porter Vargas and me? He was Ernie's best friend, we used to get together with him all the time, but there was never that kind of sizzle between us. And anyway, neither of us would've done that to Ernie."

For Sophie, marriage to a man she could never be intimate with was still marriage. I had to admire her character, though I didn't think I could live with the same choices.

Of course, if said choices were sweetened with three million smackers, I might be tempted.

I said, "And why, pray tell, did your ex wait all these years to inform the law about the coldblooded killer he married?"

"Oh, he has an answer for that," she said.

"What a shock."

"Seems when Dean got home from Boston—the same day they discovered Ernie's suicide boat, but later—I wasn't all that broken up about my sudden widowhood."

"Oh no?" I deadpanned.

"Nope. I was pretty much okay with it, according to him.

Also, he says he had a few drinks with Porter not long after, and Porter told him it wasn't suicide and how the two of us did the deed. Meaning the murder, not sex. Well, that too. According to Dean."

"And he didn't come forward with this rather critical information back then why?" I asked.

"Because Porter had been drunk," Sophie said, "so Dean didn't believe his outlandish story. Also he didn't want to think that another man was doing it with his beloved Sophie. So he kept quiet all these years."

"He's still angry at you for not throwing your money away on his stupid schemes," I said. "That's all this is."

"No kidding," she said. "He says that after Ernie's murdered skeleton was discovered, he suddenly recalled Porter's drunk confession all those years ago and confronted me about my guilt. Seems I tried to pay him off, and when that didn't work, I threatened to bash his head in, too."

"Well, the whole thing's too preposterous," I said. "Bonnie can't possibly take him seriously."

"Think not?" Sophie said. "Porter's story isn't the final word by any means. Remember, he only came under suspicion when his wife claimed he murdered Ernie."

"Out of vindictive fury when she learned that he killed Tim," I reminded her.

"Yeah, but why would she have accused her husband if she herself was the murderer? You see what I'm saying? She risks Porter telling the cops who the guilty party really is—*her*."

"Except he loves her too much to let her take the rap," I said.

"Does she know that?"

"I think she does," I said. "And if she's capable of murder, she's not above letting her husband pay for her crime. Especially after learning he's responsible for Tim's death. Lacey has no perspective where Tim's concerned. In her memory he's larger than life, like some kind of god."

Sophie drained her wineglass. The way she looked at me, it was clear she was about to change the subject. "So here's the thing, Jane. Rumors are flying about Dom and Bonnie."

I'd always admired Sophie's directness. That admiration didn't keep my stomach from clenching. I set down my wineglass. "Okay, um… so what are people saying?"

She gave me a look. *What do you think they're saying?*

"He still wants to marry me again." Was that my voice, so weak?

"When's the last time he brought it up?" she asked.

"Well, I don't know, um…" When *had* he last mentioned it? At Jimmy's Sweet Shop, when he'd tricked her into going on a date with him? What a silly, sweet gesture. "Two days ago," I said. Was it possible for things to change so drastically in two short days?

"I'm not going to ask if *you* want to marry *him*," Sophie said. "It's complicated, I know that."

I sat up straight. "Right, and that's the thing he doesn't seem to understand. To him it's so *simple*. He wants what he wants, and that's all he knows."

Sophie let out a big, expressive sigh. "Well, you've got to talk to the boy. Sort it out."

"If he's been cheating—" I cut myself off. There it was again. That word that might or might not apply in this situation. "Anyway, that would be a deal-breaker."

"What about you and Martin?"

"Martin?" I tried to look astonished, but her expression

asked who I thought I was kidding. "There's nothing between us, Sophie, and that's the truth."

"Your choice or his?"

I opened my mouth to answer. My lower jaw just hung there for long seconds. Finally I said, "Damned if I know. I can't figure him out."

"I think that's by design," she said.

"What do you mean?" I flopped back down and rooted around in the nut bowl for another pecan. Settled for a hazelnut.

She said, "I can't find anyone who has any solid intelligence on that guy."

That was saying something. Sophie was the human embodiment of the FBI, the CIA, and Wikipedia all rolled into one. If she didn't know about someone or something in Crystal Harbor, it was because there was nothing to know.

"You think he's dangerous?" I asked.

She cackled, and okay, yeah, my question might have sounded more intrigued than scared. I recalled that the mayor herself hadn't been immune to bad boys at one time. She'd admitted it herself when explaining the illicit appeal of the young Dean Phillips.

"Dangerous in a good way or a bad way?" she asked. "If it means anything, I don't think Martin's going to slit your throat for asking him to pick up his dirty socks." She looked past me and gave a wave. "Good evening, Norman."

Sexy Beast awoke instantly and trotted over to check out the interloper. I turned to see Sophie's across-the-street neighbor make his way to us.

"Good evening, dear." Norman looked as dapper as ever in a long-sleeve dress shirt, bow tie, and argyle sweater vest, despite the heat. At his advanced age—I put him at well into his nineties—he probably welcomed the extra warmth. I rose to give him a hug and a kiss on the cheek, lifting SB so the old man could pat the little dog without having to bend.

"Good heavens, what happened to you?" he asked, alarmed by all my cuts and scratches.

"It's nothing," I said. "I, uh, fell off my bike."

I positioned a cushioned armchair for him, knowing from experience that he was more comfortable with a straight-backed seat. Norman propped his cane against the nearby patio table. He possessed an impressive collection of antique walking sticks, all passed down through his family. This particular one was crafted of some dark, burled wood and topped with a bent ivory handle carved in the shape of a naked woman. There was nothing remotely pornographic about the piece, which was elegantly sensual in an old-school way.

Sophie poured him a glass of wine without asking. Norman never turned down an evening libation.

Now that he was seated, it was easier for him to reach down and give some love to my obsequious pet. "This isn't a dog," he teased for probably the hundredth time in his cultivated Ivy League tones. I knew he had no idea he was repeating himself. "Father had a dog back in the late thirties that would put this animal to shame."

As if ninety-nine percent of the dogs who'd ever roamed the earth wouldn't put this animal to shame. I'd heard him wax poetic about Father's remarkable beast on numerous occasions.

"Her name was Candy," he said. "English setter, white with liver ticking. Best gun dog I ever saw. She had the sweetest temperament, but get her out there in the field and no grouse was safe. Broke my heart when Father eventually had to put the old girl down."

I asked, "Norman, I was wondering—did you get a chance to phone Detective Hernandez?"

He thought about that a second. "I don't believe I know a Detective Hernandez. Is he with the Crystal Harbor Police Department?"

"Yes," Sophie told him. "And the detective is a she. Bonnie Hernandez. She was at the town meeting Tuesday night."

Sophie and I shared a silent communication. We'd be surprised if he remembered the meeting, his short-term memory being what it was. As for long-term memory, however, his detailed stories about his family, historical events, and cultural references from decades earlier were, without exception, flawlessly accurate.

"Oh yes," he smoothly prevaricated, having had plenty of practice in concealing his diminished powers of recollection. "That was an interesting meeting."

"So I take it you didn't call her," I said.

He gave me a quizzical look. "Call who, dear?"

I waved off my question. "It doesn't matter. It was about Ernie." Norman had claimed to remember more from back when Ernie died, besides the price of gas and the abomination that was New Coke.

His expression turned sad. "What a terrible shame, a nice young man like that committing suicide in the prime of life."

I glanced at Sophie, letting my expression do the asking. Her shrug said he had indeed been informed of recent developments. Perhaps she hoped repetition would help the concept stick, because she said, "Actually, Norman, I'm afraid it was worse than that. Ernie was murdered. His body was discovered last week, after all these years."

Sadness turned to shock and dismay as he said, "No! How awful. I'm so sorry to hear that. Do they know who did it?"

"Not yet," she said, "but the police have a couple of leads."

"Well, I hope they catch the person soon." He shook his head. "I liked Ernie a great deal."

"He liked you too," Sophie said.

"He used to come across the street whenever it snowed and shovel my walk," he said. "Most young people nowadays would never think to do something like that for a neighbor."

Just as Norman would never think to fork over a few bucks to those wintertime entrepreneurs who knock on your door after every snowfall, shovel in hand. Like many old-money types I've known, he squeezed his pennies so hard you'd never guess he was sitting on tens of millions in stock, real estate, and in his case, Ched'r Wheelz With X-treme Cheese! and Picante Gigante Tac-O's.

Yeah, that's right, the guy was heir to the KrunchWorks snack-food empire. Then he'd gone and married Maud Miriam Shelby, heiress to the perennially popular Easter Buddy egg-dyeing kits, which had been around in one form or another since before the Civil War. Theirs had not, however, been a coldblooded, dynastic union. By all accounts, the two of them had been deeply in love.

"Ernie had a generous soul," Sophie said. She blinked and looked away for a moment.

"That last year when my Maud was so sick," he said, "we had a little birthday party for her in the upstairs parlor. Ernie composed a song for her. He brought his guitar over and sang it. She was so touched."

"I remember," Sophie said. Yep, her eyes were wet. "I was there."

"Yes, you were, dear. You gave her that beautiful alpaca shawl from Peru. Lavender and green, Maud's favorite colors. She loved that shawl. That was May eleventh, thirty-two years ago. Just a few weeks before Ernie committed suicide." He shook his head. "What a terrible shame, a nice young man like that taking his own life."

"It was a hard time for me," Sophie said, in a rare display of emotional vulnerability. She leaned forward and reached for his hand. "You and Maud were so kind."

"Well, it was nothing compared to how kind you've been to me all these years with her gone." He squeezed her hand.

Sexy Beast roused himself to get between them and nudge their joined hands. As far as he was concerned, humans had no business touching each other when they could be giving him scritches. Little Mr. Needy-and-Greedy got what he wanted before trotting across the lawn to patrol the property's perimeter, sniffing ferociously for the least sign of danger. It was a perilous, thankless job, but some pampered little lapdog had to do it.

I said, "Norman, this might seem like an odd question, but bear with me."

"My word," he said, taking in my sliced-and-diced appearance. "Whatever happened to you, dear?"

"Hawk attack. It tried to make off with Sexy Beast and I had to fight it off. So listen, on the day Ernie died—that is, the day before his boat was found—did you notice any unusual activity around here?" I knew that Norman had stuck close to home in those days, tending to his sick wife.

"Unusual?" He frowned, plunging into the crystal-clear depths of his long-term memory. "I do recall he had visitors that day, which surprised me at the time."

Sophie slowly straightened. She looked intently from Norman to me and back again.

"Why did that surprise you?" I asked.

"Well, because Ernie possessed an admirable work ethic—he spent most of every weekday writing his music." He turned to Sophie. "Isn't that right, dear?"

She nodded, as if she feared her voice might break the spell of remembrance.

"Do you recall who visited him that day?" I asked.

"Let's see… his friend Porter was here. I saw him arrive from up in my studio."

"Norman has an art studio on the top floor of his house," Sophie explained. "The third floor where it's all skylights."

"I've seen your work," I told him. A couple of his paintings hung on the walls of Sophie's house—large, dramatic landscapes executed in vivid colors. I wasn't just being polite when I said, "You're very talented."

"Thank you, dear," he said. "Painting keeps my old mind sharp."

Uh-huh. "Do you remember what time Porter arrived?"

"In those days I painted only for an hour or two after lunch when Maud napped. So it had to be sometime between one and three."

"Did you see him go inside the house?" I asked.

"No, he rang the bell, but then when there was no answer I saw him go around back. Ernie sometimes took that electric keyboard of his out here to the patio when the weather was nice. Why stay cooped up when you can accomplish the same thing while breathing fresh air?"

"Makes sense to me," I said. "You can't see back here when you're in your house, though, right? Even from your third-floor studio?"

"Oh no." He swept a gnarled hand toward the far reaches of the sprawling lawn. "I can see that area back there, and the woods, of course, but nothing closer to the house."

"Can you see the carriage house?" I asked.

"Certainly. Well, part of it," he said. "I can't see its doors from my studio. Too many trees in the way. Not that I try," he hastily assured Sophie. "I'm no snoop. Plus when I'm up there, my attention is on the canvas before me. I was working on a view of the salt flats in Death Valley that day. Maud and I had taken a trip out there the year before."

Sophie said, "That's right, I remember you showing me that painting shortly after Ernie died. It was still wet."

So even if Norman *had* been in busybody mode that day, from his vantage point behind his third-floor windows, he apparently couldn't have seen Porter carry Ernie's body into the carriage house and place it in the trunk of Ernie's car.

"Do you know how long Porter stayed here?" I asked.

Norman shook his head. "I didn't see him leave. I did see Ernie drive off, though."

Sophie jerked slightly. I asked, "You saw Ernie get into his car?"

He thought about that. "No, it was parked in the carriage house. But I glanced out the window and saw it come down the drive and turn onto the street."

With Ernie in the trunk and Porter behind the wheel. From Norman's vantage point, he wouldn't have been able to make out the driver.

"The young lady left then, too," Norman added, "but she was on foot."

Now it was my turn to jerk. "Young lady?"

"Oh, didn't I mention her? She slipped in through the gate and crouched among the bushes there. No doubt some sort of game the young people were playing." Chuckling, Norman pointed to the dense stand of hydrangeas that grew along one side of the property not far from where we sat. The bushes had been there as long as I could remember. It was the ideal hiding spot from which to observe the entire backyard undetected. And yes, the doors of the carriage house were clearly visible from that spot.

"What did this young lady look like?" I asked.

"All I recall about her," he said, "is long, dark hair and a pink headband. And eyeglasses."

Sophie turned to me and mouthed, *Lacey*. I wasn't surprised Norman didn't recognize her. That long-ago day when she hid in the hydrangeas would have been the first time she'd set foot on Ernie and Sophie's property.

He doesn't know I was there that afternoon, Lacey had said that night when she'd accused her husband of murder. Now we had a witness who could place her at the scene. But what had she been secretly observing from the cover of those bushes? Her husband covering up a murder he'd committed? Or her husband covering up a murder *she'd* committed?

"When did she get here?" I asked.

"I spotted her not long after Porter arrived." He sipped his wine. "Now I must ask *you* something."

"Shoot," I said.

"Why do you want to know who was here the day that poor boy took his life?"

Sophie fielded this one. "I was wondering about his final day," she said. "Who he interacted with, that sort of thing." It was the truth, just not every last little scrap of it.

"One never truly gets over the loss of one's dearest love." He gave her a smile full of compassion and commiseration. "I know that better than most. But it's been thirty-two years, dear. You need to look to the future, not dwell on the past."

This sweet speech would have had more oomph if not for the Big News of the preceding week. An unsolved three-decades-old murder demanded answers.

She squeezed his hand again. "Thank you, Norman. And thank you for answering all our dumb questions."

"Thank *you* for the excellent wine," he said. "It will help me get a good night's sleep."

"You be sure to give my best to your family." To me she explained, "Norman's granddaughter and her husband and kids have been staying with him for the past week."

He appeared happily surprised by the news.

"Ah, a full house," I said. "Great-grandchildren. That's wonderful. Listen, before you go, Norman, can I ask just one more question?"

"Anything, dear."

"You said 'visitors.' He had 'visitors' that day, as in more than one." Norman appeared confused, prompting me to clarify: "You told us that on the day Ernie died, Porter came by. Did anyone else visit him?"

"Why, yes," he said. "Dean dropped by in the morning."

Sophie frowned. "My husband Dean? My ex-husband, I mean. Dean Phillips?"

"Well, naturally. I don't think I even know another person by that name. There is a film actor, I believe, called Dean—"

"Are you sure it wasn't someone who just looked like him?" Her voice was tight. "Dean was in Boston the day Ernie died."

"You might not be recalling things too clearly." He patted Sophie's arm. "It can happen to anyone, dear. It was your Dean, all right. Well, he wasn't *your* Dean at the time, of course, he was merely a friend."

Sophie appeared at a loss for words, struggling to process this information. Norman seemed so certain, but could his recollection be trusted?

"Did he ring the front doorbell?" I asked.

He shook his head. "When I opened the bedroom drapes—it was after breakfast, around ten, I'd say—I saw him approaching from the trees back there and waving hello." He pointed toward the stretch of woods that bordered the back edge of Sophie's property. "I assumed he was waving to Ernie here on the patio, but from inside my house, most of your backyard isn't visible. Not that I look, mind you. I'm no snoop."

"Wait," Sophie said. "Dean came on foot through the woods? He didn't drive up to the house?"

"That's right," Norman said. "I assumed he was out for a morning stroll and decided to drop in on Ernie." As if the man who'd coveted Ernie's wife, not to mention Ernie's wife's fortune, would pay an impromptu social call on the man who was living the life he dreamt about. Well, except for the gay part.

"Do you know how long he stayed?" she asked.

"Haven't a clue. Ernie must have had a devil of a time trying to get any work done with people popping in all day." More somberly he asked, "You don't suppose that had anything to do with the poor boy's suicide?"

"No, I'm sure it didn't," she said.

He nodded, reassured, and glanced around for his cane. I

handed it to him. He noticed my myriad lacerations and said, "Good grief! What hap—"

"Who knew you shouldn't dry off a hand grenade in the microwave? Last question, I promise," I said, as we all rose. SB stretched luxuriantly, shook himself, and did his happy *where are we going now, what are we doing now* dance. "Do you recall anything else out of the ordinary about the day Ernie died?" I asked Norman. "Anything at all? Aside from the unusual foot traffic back here?"

He shook his head. "Just that and the mess those young hoodlums made. Otherwise it was a perfect June day. I was finishing up a landscape of the Death Valley salt flats that day. Took me forever to get the light just right. My daughter Margaret fell in love with that painting, so I gave it to her. It's hanging in her—"

"I'm sorry, Norman," I said. "Some young hoodlums made a mess? I don't think you got to that part."

"Didn't I? Well, it's hardly worth mentioning. I came over here in the late afternoon. The mailman had delivered a piece of your mail to us by mistake—" he directed this to Sophie "—and I didn't want to leave it in your mailbox. It looked to be official, a tax refund or some such. Ernie didn't answer the bell, so I assumed he was still outside."

"So you came back here," I said.

"And it's a good thing I did. The patio furniture had been overturned. The birdhouse knocked down. One of the cats had been pulled right out of the ground. Ernie's keyboard and music notebook were on the grass. I set it all to rights."

Sophie looked grim. To me she said, "I was wondering why he'd left his new keyboard outside. And then when he didn't come home that night… I didn't know what to think."

Until his boat was found floating off Montauk the next morning.

She said, "Why didn't you ever tell me about this, Norman?"

He gave a dismissive wave. "I didn't want you upset over nothing, especially the next day after…" He sighed. "No doubt it was a couple of delinquents showing off for each other. I'm just glad they didn't decide to—" he made spraying motions "—decorate the place with graffiti like you see on television."

I said, "What does that mean, 'one of the cats was pulled out of the ground'?"

Sophie pointed to the memorial cat statues. "Those guys."

"Yeah, but—"

"The white one." Norman strolled over to it and tapped it with the tip of his cane. "She's my favorite."

"What's to pull out of the ground?" I asked. "Don't they just sit on top of it?"

"Nope," Sophie said. "They have built-in pedestals. Only the actual sculpture sits aboveground."

My nape was doing that prickly, nagging thing. *Wakey, wakey, Janey,* it was saying. *You might want to splash some cold water on your gray matter right about now.*

The black cat still crouched, ready to attack. The white cat, the lazy one, still reclined in feline languor, licking that one pearly paw. I squatted by her and ran my fingers around her base, scraping away a little dirt. It was true. The marble extended belowground. I got a solid, two-handed grip on the thing and glanced up at Sophie. "Do you mind?"

"Knock yourself out."

I very nearly did just that. One good yank and that hunk of marble popped like a twenty-pound cork, leaving me sprawled in the grass and Sexy Beast yelping in alarm. I sat up, dusted myself off, and examined the statue's base, normally hidden from sight.

The pedestal was squared off, a perfect cube about six inches on all sides, with no shortage of hard, sharp edges.

One look at Sophie's face and I knew she was thinking the same thing I was. I asked her, "So when's the last time you pulled this thing out of the ground?"

"Never have," she said. "Bad luck."

"Bad luck, huh?" I gave her a wry smile. "You're the least superstitious person I know, Mayor."

"Yeah, well," she said, "I'll bet you anything it was damn unlucky for Ernie."

17

National Register of Historic Lawn Ornaments

"SO YOU KNOW what she said then?" I sat with Dom at one of the wood-and-chrome bistro tables next to the big picture windows at Janey's Place, facing Main Street. It was late morning and the lunch crowd had yet to descend. Behind the counter, Cheyenne texted nonstop on her phone with one hand while wiping incessantly at a nonexistent smudge with the other.

I'd gone into the shop for my usual papaya-ginger smoothie and had run into Dom. The Janey's Place headquarters where he worked were across town, but he'd dropped by the store that day as he often did, to check up on the flagship operation and relive the good/bad old days by slipping behind the counter and whipping up a Mediterranean quinoa salad or a predigested-looking tofu scramble for some lucky, pasty-skinned lettuce chomper.

Dom was struggling with the timeline. "Was this before you called Bonnie or after SB peed on the cat statue?"

"Both." I sucked up the last of the smoothie, a noisy operation that earned a lopsided smile from my ex. He'd always loved to feed me—it was how Janey's Place had been born. He'd felt certain that once I'd experienced bunny food in all its multifarious scrumptiousness, I'd become a lifelong convert to healthful eating. We all know how that turned out. "SB *tried* to pee on the cat," I said. "I didn't let him. It was starting to drizzle by then, so I shoved the base of the statue right back into the ground."

"Smart." Dom forked up a great big wad of something that looked like it had been peeled off the side of the road. Didn't smell half-bad, though. "Protecting whatever evidence might remain after all these years. Is that when you called Bonnie?"

I nodded. "While Sophie was making sure Norman got home okay. But first, let me tell you what she *said*."

"Sophie?"

"Of course Sophie. She told me that Dean, way back when they got married and he was living there? Dean insisted she get rid of the cat statues."

"Why?" Dom asked.

"The real why or his excuse?"

"Let's try both."

"Well, he told Sophie it was because he's allergic to cats and they creep him out and all that nonsense," I said.

"How do you know it was nonsense?"

"Well, the creeped-him-out part makes sense. If I'd bashed in someone's skull with a hunk of marble, I'd be creeped out every time I looked at it too. Plus he was probably worried that he'd left evidence on it."

"I take it Sophie didn't let him toss out the statues," he said.

"She told him she wasn't allowed to, that they're an inviolable part of the history of her house. You know, it's on the National Register of Historic Places. Of course, that's total BS. I mean, yeah, the house is a historic landmark, but Sophie can do whatever she wants with those cats. They might be old, but they're just lawn ornaments." I shrugged. "But she likes them, so they stayed."

"Aren't you getting a little ahead of yourself with this Dean business?" He gave that condescending smile I'd forgotten he was so good at. "From trying to ditch some old lawn ornaments to murder? Leave the investigation to the experts, Janey."

"Because they've done *such* a great job so far," I sneered.

"Hey, it's only been what?" he asked around a mouthful of vegetarian roadkill. "A week and a half? And the crime is more than three decades old. Give Bonnie a chance."

Something about the way he said that last part pressed a little alarm button inside me.

Don't judge me! It's complicated, like Sophie said. And anyway, I'm allowed to be conflicted about my ex. After seventeen years. And five months.

He said, "Speaking of which, did you call—"

"Yes! Yes, I called Bonnie! I *told* you I called her. Jeez."

"You could use a calming drink," he said.

I perked up. "Hey, it's five o'clock somewhere. Is Murray's Pub open yet, you think?"

Dom's indulgent chuckle said he knew I was kidding. Yeah, that's me, Jane the Kidder. He turned toward the service counter. "Cheyenne?" He waited. "Cheyenne!"

She glanced up from her phone, her dull-eyed annoyance revealing not the slightest comprehension of Dom's importance to her continued employment, or what her probation officer might have to say about the loss of said employment. She waited.

"Please pour Janey a cup of lavender tea," he told her.

I reared back in disgust. "*Lavender?* Why don't I just get my bridal bouquet out of mothballs and gnaw on that?"

My ex stared at me for a long moment while my face roasted to a nice, even shade of Holy Crap Did I Really Say That. In a murky little corner of my brainpan, I bitch-slapped the heck out of myself.

At last he said, "You still have your bridal bouquet? After all these years?"

The part he kindly left unsaid, which only amped up my mental self-flagellation, was: *After all these years, our divorce, my two subsequent marriages and three kids, and your pitifully lonely and childless state?*

"I, you know, had it freeze-dried." I gave an elaborate shrug.

He opened his yap to say, *And you still have it.* If he hadn't had the sense to snap it shut without speaking, I'd have had to grab another damn chair and hurl myself though another damn window.

After first beating him to death with the chair.

Not that I needed a calming damn beverage or anything.

"The bouquet's somewhere in the house." A careless toss of my hand. "Or not. You know what? Yeah, I think I tossed it out when I moved into that little basement apartment after the divorce."

It certainly wasn't parked in my attic in a fancy glass display dome, double-boxed with bubble wrap and Styrofoam peanuts, and plastered on all sides with big red stickers reading *FRAGILE! THIS END UP! KEEP DRY!*

Cheyenne plunked a steaming mug in front of me. No

joke, it smelled like lavender. Seriously, these people had issues.

"That'll be three ninety-five," she said.

Dom, the soul of patience, smiled at the girl. "It's on the house, Cheyenne." Her head tipped slightly to one side, and I swear her ears twitched at the mention of her name. He could have been talking to Sexy Beast.

"No charge," he explained. "For my friend."

At last, some animation. "So we can, like, give our friends stuff for free? Nobody told me."

"No, it's just..." *It's just that I get to treat my friends because I own the place?* I could see the instant he decided it was time to pass the buck. "Ask your dad to explain it." Cheyenne's father, Patrick O'Rourke, was the manager of the store. Not that Patrick needed a paycheck after a hefty recent inheritance, but he knew his own weaknesses well enough to welcome structure and responsibility into his life.

Cheyenne shrugged. "Whatever."

After she'd clopped away on her rhinestone-studded platform sandals, Dom reached into his wallet and slapped a healthy tip on the table. My lopsided grin accused him of being an old softie. His lopsided grin was accompanied by a helpless shrug.

If a clergyperson had been sitting at the next table, I would have married Dom again right then and there.

A priest, a rabbi, and a minister walk into Janey's Place. Insert your own punchline.

"So you called Bonnie..." Dom prompted, rolling his hand to steer me back on track.

"So she came out to Sophie's, and I could tell she thought I was wasting her time—*until* she laid eyes on the squared-off base of that cat statue," I said with a grin of satisfaction. "Then she went all crime-scene on us and got people out there and they set up this tent and lights and everything."

"Wow," Dom said. "Looks like you might have found the murder weapon."

"They're hoping to get evidence off the statue or the dirt it sat in. I mean, that thing has never been moved in all these years."

"DNA evidence?" he asked.

I nodded. "If they find hairs or, I don't know, dried blood or something, they can compare it to Ernie's skeletal remains— a tooth or whatever—and look for a match."

He nodded toward the lavender tea. "Drink up before it gets cold. Oh, don't give me that look. I bet you'll like it. Here." He plucked two raw-sugar packets from the table dispenser, tore them open, and stirred the beige crystals into the hot liquid.

"You've got some nerve calling this stuff tea." I slid the mug across the table to him. "I say it's potpourri soup, and I say it's all yours."

He sighed and lifted the mug. "Well, I'm glad you were able to help Bonnie with the investigation."

There it was again. That little alarm bell. Maybe because he directed his words to the mug rather than to my face.

"Oh yeah," I said, "she expressed her appreciation very eloquently. Her precise words were, 'Don't tell me how to do my job, Jane.' I'm telling you, I got all misty-eyed."

Dom lowered the mug. "I know I'm not getting the whole story here."

"I told her what Norman said about Dean being there the day Ernie died. She blew it off, said Norman's senile and besides, Dean was in Boston that day, which Sophie had verified by calling him at his hotel. And did I think Dean was in cahoots with Porter, because Porter's definitely the one who moved the body and made the murder look like suicide."

Dom spread his hands. "Well, is she wrong about any of that?"

"First of all," I said, "I hate that word, 'senile.' Norman's short-term memory is shot, it's true, but his recollection of stuff that happened way back when is spot-on. And hey, you know what? If Norman hadn't remembered about replacing the cat statue in the ground thirty-two years ago, Bonnie would never have found the murder weapon."

"If it *is* the murder weapon," he said. "Bonnie was right about the rest of it, though."

"Boston's, what, a four-hour drive from here. You're telling me Dean couldn't have slipped away from that seminar long enough to come down here and off Ernie? It's possible, right?"

"I thought he flew to Boston," Dom said. "He didn't have a car at his disposal."

The look I gave him was a plea not to go stupid on me. We both knew that if Dean had wanted to get hold of a car in Boston, he could have.

"Well, it *was* Porter who engineered the fake suicide, right?" Dom asked. "Not Dean."

"Yes," I said, "because he thought he was covering up for his wife. He thought Lacey murdered Ernie. He had no idea Dean had been there earlier."

"Maybe Lacey did murder Ernie," he said, "and maybe—"

"Yeah, I know, maybe Dean never left Boston that day." The simplest explanation was usually the correct one. Norman's eyewitness account was beginning to look like the delusions of a confused mind.

"Look," Dom said, "I know you like Norman. I like him too. But you have to admit he's not the most reliable witness. Short-term memory, long-term memory, whatever. A lot is at stake here. Someone's going to go away for life."

"Well, I still think Bonnie should bring Dean in for questioning," I said, "but she practically bit my head off when I suggested it. And she refused to even discuss the accusation Dean made—you know, about Sophie and Porter doing in Ernie."

I had become accustomed to Bonnie's cool civility toward me, her ex-fiancé's ex-wife. But the evening before, in Sophie's backyard, that polite façade had shown signs of wear. Which reminded me of watching her cozy up to Dom after the town meeting a couple of days ago. At least they'd looked darn cozy from where I'd stood.

Dom said, "A police detective can't be expected to share all the details of an investigation, Janey. You know that. How's Bonnie supposed to solve the case with some civilian running around playing—" He clamped his mouth shut.

I leaned back in my chair. "No, go ahead, Dom, finish the thought. With some meddlesome civilian running around playing detective and making a mess of the whole investigation."

"I didn't say 'meddlesome.'"

I scraped my chair back, shot to my feet, and grabbed my purse. Dom rewarded that with a gusty, put-upon sigh.

As satisfying as a grand exit would have been just then, my mouth had other plans. "Are you sleeping with her?"

His head jerked up. "What? Sleeping with who?"

A priest, a rabbi, and a minister walk into Janey's Place.

They restrain Janey's ex while she pours hot potpourri soup into his lap.

I commenced the grand exit. Dom leapt to his feet and clamped his fingers around my arm. "No!" he said. "No, I'm not sleeping with her. Why would you even ask that?"

Behind the counter, Cheyenne stared at us unashamedly, thumbs poised over her phone, while her texting buddy impatiently awaited the next *L8R* or *CU46*.

Oh, please. Just sound them out.

I stared straight into Dom's bottomless espresso eyes, willing him not to guiltily look away. He held my gaze, but his next words were far from comforting. He released my arm and said, quietly, "Bonnie wants us to get back together."

His words squeezed my chest. After a moment I said, "And what do you want?"

"You know what I want, Janey. I've waited three months for your answer."

Amateur, I wanted to shoot back. *I waited seventeen years for you to come around.* But Dom wasn't used to being single. He was a man who needed a woman. For him, three months without a significant other must have felt like being stranded on the moon.

A few months ago I'd been so certain my long... *infatuation?* Was that word even appropriate when referring to one's ex-husband? I'd been so certain my long, hopeless, helpless infatuation with Dom was a thing of the past. For the first time in my adult life, I didn't need this man in it.

And all he'd had to do was crook his finger at me for all that maturity and personal growth to evaporate. One part of me howled, *Why are you even stopping to think about it? He's the love of your life. You've waited the better part of two decades for this.* That part had never stopped fantasizing about a baby with Dom's dark, curly hair and my pale hazel eyes.

The other part of me asked why he was the one who got to call the shots, to demand answers at his convenience. Well, okay, it could be because he had smart, beautiful, desirable Bonnie Hernandez eager to share her life with him—while I had a toy poodle with OCD. Plus, even if there were no Bonnie, the man happened to be a sweet, sexy multimillionaire, which kind of, you know, tipped the scales of power in his favor.

But all that was just noise. Strip it away and it was just me and Dom, two lower-middle-class South Shore kids who'd found each other twenty-six years ago in Mr. Bender's eighth-grade Spanish class. One way or another, he'd always be in my life.

"Dom," I said, "how serious are you about wanting to remarry me?"

He blinked. "You know the answer to that, Janey. I love you. We're meant to be together."

"I have to admit, for me, it's not so cut-and-dried," I said. "We have so much history. It's complicated. If you really love me, you won't rush me."

A frustrated frown creased his brow. "What about Bonnie?"

"The hell with Bonnie," I snapped. "This isn't about Bonnie. It's about you and me, Dom. I'm telling you I need more time. Can't you understand that?"

"How much time are we talking about?" he asked. "A week? A year?"

"I don't know! For crying out—" I took a deep breath. "Not a year. Come on, I'm just asking you to be patient a little while longer, a few weeks maybe, so I can sort out my thoughts without feeling like I'm under the gun. Think you can do that for me?"

"Sure, Janey." He smiled and dropped a tender kiss on my mouth. I let him. "I think I can manage that."

After leaving Dom, I went next door to UnderStatements, hoping for a few words with Lacey. A young saleswoman I didn't recognize told me her boss had taken an early lunch break at the town park and wasn't I that satanic Death Diva person who'd made their shop famous? I learned that my humiliating television debut had been great for business. By popular demand, UnderStatements had added ugly, high-waisted, full-coverage, white cotton drawers to their inventory, and the granny panties were flying off the shelves—along with sexy thongs to wear over them. Seems I'd started a trend. She pointed to a prominent display near the entrance, then tried to shove a Sharpie into my hand. The idea was for me to autograph them. People would pay big bucks to own a pair of granny panties signed by the real Death Diva.

As much as I admired her business acumen, I declined the honor.

Nevins Park—named, as was Sophie's home, for the town's founding family—encompassed a dog park and the beach as well as a baseball diamond and bleachers, picnic tables and pavilions, a large playground, and plenty of wide-open green space. The park was typically busy for a summer Friday. The playground I'd passed was alive with the gleeful shouts of children overseen by a handful of young mothers and nannies, plus a stay-at-home dad. Under a pavilion decorated with balloons, about twenty preschoolers dug into birthday cake. The breeze shifted, blending the briny tang of the nearby Long

Island Sound with the scent of cut grass.

I found Lacey sitting alone at a wooden picnic table. A small white sack featuring Patisserie Susanne's distinctive white and gold label sat before her and she was nursing a large plastic takeout cup filled with black coffee and ice. Another one sat next to it, this one lightened with milk.

If she was aware of being Detective Hernandez's number-one suspect, I saw no sign of it in her calm features as she opened the sack and arranged a pair of pastries—chocolate croissants, my all-time favorite!—on paper napkins. Her placid expression closed down when she looked up and spied me heading toward her. "I don't want company," she said, when I seated myself across from her.

"Really?" I nodded toward the second iced coffee and the croissants. My stomach whined, despite the nice, filling papaya-ginger smoothie I'd just sucked down. "I think you mean you don't want *my* company."

"If that's how you want to put it," Lacey said. Was she meeting a guy here? Was it possible she'd moved on that quickly?

I knew I wasn't this woman's favorite person, despite my contribution to the newfound popularity—*notoriety* might be a more accurate term—of her lingerie store. I couldn't expect her to be grateful to me for revealing that her own husband, rather than his dead buddy Ernie, had been responsible for the death of her beloved Tim. The bearer of bad news makes very few BFF shortlists.

"Just let me run one thing by you," I said, "and then I'll be out of your way." I folded my arms on the table, squirmed my butt into a comfortable position on the hard wooden bench, and let my body language do the talking. *Hey, I can wait here all day. Who are we meeting today? Is he cute?*

Lacey shook her head in exasperation. "Okay, make it quick."

Now that I had the undivided attention of the prime suspect in the three-decades-old murder of Ernest Waterfield, I was at a loss for words.

That's right, I'd sought her out without having the slightest idea what I intended to say to her. Not a clue. Zip. Zilch. All I knew was, it was driving me crazy that Dean Phillips might be involved and that no one except Sophie and me—certainly not the detective in charge of the investigation—seemed to think the idea worth pursuing. Even Lacey's husband, who loved her beyond all reason, logic, or good old-fashioned common sense, was convinced she'd bludgeoned his old pal Ernie to death.

See how good I am at leaving the investigation to the experts? Okay, in my head that came out "the so-called experts." Probably in yours, too, am I right?

So that's how I found myself sitting across the table from Miss Congeniality, trying to formulate an intelligent question while eyeing those chocolate croissants and fighting the urge to cry, *Look! Behind you!*

"Okay, um," I started, "so here's the thing, Lacey. I mean… yeah, this thing is just so…" My urbane chuckle came out as a consumptive wheeze. "Well, you don't need *me* to tell *you*, am I right?"

She stared balefully, awaiting further elaboration on This Thing, before something over my shoulder snagged her attention. She looked up and waved. To me she said, "You can go now."

I turned to see Porter striding in our direction, as handsome as ever in a black polo shirt, khaki shorts, and boat shoes. He appeared surprised to see me sitting with his wife.

He greeted me before circling the table to lean down and kiss Lacey's cheek.

Her gaze zeroed in on his throat. She pulled the collar of his shirt aside to reveal the dark bruise left by his homemade noose. Her brow creased in concern. "What happened to you?"

Porter's tired eyes flicked to mine as he sat next to her. He looked worn down. I'd assumed Lacey knew about her husband's attempted suicide. Apparently not.

"Is this for me?" He tapped the iced coffee with milk.

"Yeah. Three sugars." She handed him a straw and one of the croissants, then seemed to notice I hadn't vamoosed as promised. "Goodbye, Jane."

"Don't run off on my account." Porter sipped his coffee.

"This is a family matter," Lacey said. "I didn't invite her here."

"Yeah, well." He tugged his collar back into place, concealing the livid streak on his neck as best he could. "Jane saved my life. I wish I could be grateful."

"Saved your…?" Lacey's startled gaze flew between me and her husband. "Somebody better tell me what's going on."

Suddenly I wished I had indeed vamoosed. Porter looked directly at his wife. "I tried to kill myself yesterday. Jane stopped me."

Color fled her face. She stared at his throat. "No. No, that's crazy. You wouldn't do that."

Sadly he said, "Yes, it's crazy, and yes, I'm afraid I did do it. Or tried to."

"But… why?"

His eyes briefly closed. "You know why."

Her mouth opened, but no words emerged. Her eyes welled. Finally she whispered, "Porter. Porter, no. It's not… That was…" Helplessly she shook her head.

"It's not just that." He swallowed hard, waging his own battle to retain his composure in this public setting. He took a deep breath. "They're going to arrest you, sweetheart. I can't protect you. I tried… I tried and I failed."

She shook her head in confusion. "That's insane. Why would they arrest *me*? You confessed."

"They didn't buy it. I wish to God they had. Lacey, I'm so sorry." He took her hand. "The police know you killed Ernie."

She jerked her hand out of his, eyes wide. "What are you talking about? *You* killed him. I saw you. I hid behind the rhododendrons in Sophie's yard and watched you put his body—" Her voice cracked. "I saw you, Porter. How can you say…?"

"Jane knows, sweetheart," he said. "You don't have to keep up the pretense with her."

"Pretense?" Lacey looked from one of us to the other. "This is insane. I had nothing to do with Ernie's murder. I went there straight from Teddy's house and saw you—"

"Wait, when did you go to Teddy's?" He frowned. "When you left our house, you were headed to Ernie's. You said if I wasn't going to end our friendship, you'd do it for me."

"Yeah, by going to his mom and getting her to set her son straight." Lacey winced at her own unfortunate choice of words. "I figured I'd have more success going through her. I was wrong."

I spoke up. "Porter, it's true. Teddy herself told me Lacey visited her that day, and for just that reason."

He appeared to be waging a mental battle, struggling to shoehorn new facts into three-decades-old assumptions. "How long did you stay at Teddy's?"

She shrugged. "I don't know, twenty minutes, a half hour? Just long enough for her to tell me her precious boy could choose his own friends and to get lost."

"I thought you went straight to Ernie's." He dragged his fingers through his hair, a habit that was becoming familiar. "After you left, it didn't take me long to cool down and decide I was an idiot, and then I went there looking for you. I was going to cut ties with him—anything to make it right between you and me. But when I got there he was already dead."

Lacey straightened. "You got to Ernie's before me. When I saw your car, I parked down the road and snuck onto the property. I thought maybe Teddy had called to tell him about my hissy fit, and that you guys were having a yok at my expense. Instead I saw you putting Ernie's body in the trunk of his car."

"What you saw," Porter said, "was me cleaning up after you, after the murder I thought you committed… the murder I'd driven you to commit."

"But—"

"I know," he said. "You went to Teddy's first, which means you wouldn't have had time to go to Ernie's and kill him before I got there. And all these years I thought…"

Lacey put a hand to her mouth, overcome. "And I thought you did it. I thought one of you started a fight and you ended up killing him."

Porter placed his hands on his wife's shoulders. He tipped his forehead to hers. They sat like that while I turned away to study the birthday-party kids, who'd finished their cake and were now exploring the finer points of Duck, Duck, Goose.

Eventually I heard a few sniffles, some soft whispers, and what sounded suspiciously like an actual kiss on the lips.

I turned back to see Lacey gently touch the bruise on her husband's throat. "I wondered why you weren't dressed for work today."

"I have to wait for the marks to fade. Officially I'm working from home for a few days."

The look she gave him was brimming with wonder. "You confessed to a crime you didn't commit to protect me. You were willing… you were willing to spend the rest of your life in jail. For me."

His voice was hoarse. "I messed up so badly, sweetheart. So badly. Starting with…" His throat worked. "Every time I looked at Colin, the whole time he was growing up, all I could see was Tim, and what I'd done. I wanted so much to be a good dad to him, but I knew I'd never deserve him. He'd never belong to me."

"Well, you picked a hell of a way to atone." Her half smile was an amalgam of tenderness, awe, and exasperation. "I wish to God you'd trusted me with the truth."

"I never set out to… to hurt Tim. I was young and drunk and stupid."

She gave a slow, sad nod. "For years I could never find it in me to forgive Ernie for what I thought he did. My hatred consumed me, it poisoned me and everyone around me even after Ernie was gone. Tim would've been…" She swallowed hard. "He would have been disappointed in me."

Porter stroked his wife's hair. "This is a good time to start over, what do you say?"

A smile creased the corners of her eyes, but swiftly faded. "The police really think I killed Ernie?"

He held her face between his hands. "We'll get the best lawyers. They have no case. It'll never go to trial."

"Oh God," she breathed. "I'm scared, Porter."

He wrapped his arms around her. I could barely make out the words he murmured into her ear. "It'll be okay, I promise, sweetheart. I will never leave your side. We'll get through this together." He stroked her back in slow circles. After a while something seemed to occur to him. He leaned slightly away. "So why are we here anyway? What's this important family matter you wanted to discuss?"

"What? Oh!" Lacey smacked her head. "My news."

"Please tell me it's good news," he said.

"It couldn't be much better." Her smile lit her from within, showing me the girl Porter had fallen in love with all those years ago. "You're going to be a grandfather."

A surprised grin softened his tired features. "No kidding. You're right, sweetheart, that is amazing news."

Lacey said, "Speaking of fresh starts." I knew what she meant. Here was Porter's chance to start over not just with his wife but with his stepson, Colin, as well.

Porter cast me a crooked sidelong smile. "We haven't forgotten you're there, Jane."

"Hey, don't mind me," I said. "I could sit here listening to good news all day."

"While you're listening, eat up." Porter handed his chocolate croissant across the table.

"Mine too." Lacey pushed hers across. "No appetite."

It took every scrap of my self-control not to rip into those buttery, chocolate-filled pastries right then and there, but at the moment, the Vargases needed privacy more than they needed to sit there watching me stuff my face.

"Well, you won't catch me turning down these bad boys. Thanks." I opened the sack and stuffed the croissants back into it. Rising, I said, "I'll eat these in the car. I, you know, have to be somewhere." I waved and started to leave.

Lacey said, "Jane?" I turned back. Her eyes glistened. She squeezed Porter's hand. "Thank you for saving my husband's life."

18

Keep Your Eye on the Ball

I TOSSED THE pastry sack onto the passenger seat and pulled out of the parking lot. I did not, in fact, have to be somewhere, at least not until three o'clock when I was scheduled to meet with a new client about arranging a Dixieland jazz funeral, complete with horse-drawn carriage, a lively brass band, and all those saints who go marching in. The client's recently deceased husband, a Chinese-American toy mogul, had never ventured farther south than Wall Street but had nevertheless been entranced by the idea of an authentic New Orleans sendoff. His devoted widow had mountains of dough and, more important, the willingness to part with a great big wad of it to honor hubby's final wish, so the only iffy thing would be securing a parade permit. Luckily for her, the Death Diva was on pretty good terms with the town mayor.

A spicy-sweet scent pervaded the car's interior, vaguely familiar but no competition to the dizzying aroma of chocolate. My hand snaked into the bag as I turned onto the road. Steering one-handedly, I shoved a big, messy hunk of chocolate croissant into my gaping maw. "Oh... *God!*" I moaned as the intense chocolate filling—Susanne's secret recipe, protected by a security system worthy of Fort Knox—

erupted in my mouth like the veritable embodiment of the best sex and food and love and sex and spiritual awakening and sex the universe had to offer, all rolled up into one flaky, buttery, irresistible choco-bomb.

Thank goodness I was alone in the car. I could create as much of a spectacle as I desired, with no appalled witnesses to concern myself with. No telltale crumbs either, once I'd sent in my intrepid poodle to hoover up the embarrassing evidence. Life was good.

Until the dark steel of a gun barrel tapped my right hip. A male voice said, "Keep driving, eh, and do what I say."

Half-masticated croissant sprayed the dashboard. Automatically I jerked around to see who was back there, though the accent kind of narrowed it down. Not to mention the nauseating cologne, which I belatedly recognized. I'd been so fixated on those stupid croissants, it had never occurred to me to check the floor of the backseat for Canadians with guns.

Plus it was a bright, sunny summer day. Things like this weren't supposed to happen on bright, sunny summer days. They were supposed to happen in rainy, deserted parking lots at midnight. Wasn't there some rule about that?

"What do you want?" A stupid question, but I had to start somewhere.

"Make a right at the corner." Dean remained on the floor, out of sight of other drivers and pedestrians.

I made the turn as my heart attempted to slug its way out of my chest. I'd tossed my purse, which contained my cell phone, onto the passenger seat. I watched Dean's hand slide between the seats to snatch it. "Why are you doing this?" I asked. "You don't have to do this."

"You did this to yourself. You just couldn't mind your

own business, could you? You had to go sticking your nose where it doesn't belong." He punctuated this statement with a hard punch to my seatback.

"So what?" I said. "Nobody listens to me. Certainly not Bonnie Hernandez."

"Oh yeah? That bitch had me in for questioning again this morning," he said. "All because of you and that demented old man."

A small part of me perked up at the thought that Bonnie had taken me, and Norman, seriously after all. Seriously enough to interview Dean again anyway. "I didn't have anything to do with that," I lied.

"Like hell. I've been watching you. You really thought I'd just hang back, eh, twiddling my thumbs while you got me sent away for life?" he sneered. "Turn in at that strip mall up the road. When you get there, drive behind the supermarket."

I was tempted to leap out of the car and scream for help, but I couldn't ignore that black semiautomatic pressed into my seatback. I wouldn't get one foot out of the car before he dropped me.

"Okay, what you need to do is stop this silly business—" I made an all-encompassing gesture meant to indicate the silly and ultimately homicidal business currently under way "—and hire yourself a good lawyer. The cops have DNA and, you know, all sorts of forensic stuff. I'm pretty sure they can prove you killed Ernie."

"Guy put up a hell of a fight for a homo," Dean said admiringly, "I'll give him that."

Oh, I would so love for this creep to spend the rest of his worthless life behind bars. Even better if I was alive to see it happen.

"I was going to make it look like a robbery gone wrong," he continued. "You know, sneak into the house through the back door, shoot Ernie, ransack the place, take a few valuables to make it look convincing."

"But Ernie wasn't inside when you got there," I said. "He was out back on the deck that morning, working on his music."

"Yeah, that threw me off," he said, "but I got the job done, eh, that's the important thing. Checked his pulse to make sure, then grabbed my gun and hauled ass out of there."

I envisioned Dean pulling a gun on Ernie, after having stereotyped and thereby underestimated him. I saw Ernie disarming his assailant, who, finding himself on the ground near the cat statues, made do with the weapon at hand.

"Why didn't you stay in Boston and hire a hitman?" I asked. "Less messy."

"I knew guys who would've done it," he said, "but the thing is, someone's always going to talk. Or shake you down for more money."

"So you leave Ernie lying dead in his yard," I said, "and then what, just turn around and drive back to Boston?"

"Like a bat outta hell, I don't mind telling you." Which is how he'd made it back in time to answer Sophie's phone call to his hotel room that afternoon. "So there I am, up in Boston, waiting to hear that Ernie's body's been discovered. Nothing. Next day, what do you know, they're saying he drowned himself." Dean snorted. "It was all over the news. The boat off Montauk. The suicide note. And me thinking I've got some kind of guardian angel."

"So all these years you had no idea it was your buddy Porter who moved the body and faked the suicide?"

"Not till a few days ago when his wife pointed the finger at him."

"That's some way to repay your guardian angel," I said. "By falsely accusing him of murder. But why accuse Sophie along with Porter? I mean, this whole story you spun about the two of them being lovers and killing her husband? He actually thought he was cleaning up after his wife's crime. Why not just say it was Porter and Lacey who did it?"

"I never knew Lacey," he said. "Why would she confess to me? I was *married* to Sophie. More believable this way, eh. Plus she's a cold, stingy bitch and I'll be happy to see her rot behind bars."

"You don't really think you're fooling the cops with that story?" I said. "I happen to know they're zeroing in on you as a suspect."

"Yeah, I'm shaking in my shoes. Thirty-two-year-old evidence and the rantings of that geezer Norman Butterwick? His story will be all hearsay anyway. Feeble old guys like that die peacefully in their sleep all the time."

I envisioned Norman dying peacefully in his sleep with a pillow held tight to his face.

Dean confirmed my suspicions. "Only thing, this feeble old guy will have help. The killer will leave plenty of evidence that she was there."

She. Sophie. He was going to make it look like she'd killed Norman to eliminate a witness to the goings-on at her place the day her husband was murdered. That would be damning evidence indeed. Sophie even had an emergency key to Norman's house. I doubted Dean would need it, though. He could probably break in to most houses as easily as he'd broken into my car.

"Where's that strip mall?" he demanded from the floor behind me. "You better not have passed it."

"It's right here." I turned in to it, passing Officer Geri Marvin behind the wheel of a black-and-white as she exited the mall. She lifted her cardboard coffee cup in a jaunty salute, pausing to squint in wonderment at the way my eyeballs kept jerking toward the rear of the car. A sharp nudge near the base of my spine got me moving once more.

The supermarket anchored the far end of the strip mall. I drove as slowly as I dared past the shoe store, frozen-yogurt parlor, hair salon, and children's clothing store. "Listen," I said, "you still have a chance to beat the rap on Ernie. If you drop what you're doing right now and focus on getting a good lawyer, like I said. I mean, no way am I going to mention our, uh, meeting like this. Who'd believe me anyway? Not Bonnie. She hates my guts. She's after my ex, only he's in love with me again and wants to remarry me, and she's, like, oh no you don't, that is *not* happening, you're still mine. 'Cause they were, you know, engaged until she broke up with him a few months ago. Well, he says he's the one who broke up with her, but please." Speaking of focusing.

Dean said, "I didn't follow most of that."

I moseyed past the nail salon, coffee shop, pizza place, and liquor store. "My point is, if you… do anything to me, or to Norman, you can't possibly get away with it. I mean, you're already on their radar."

"Yeah, thanks to you," he grumbled, "and my bitch of an ex-wife. I know the two of you have been conniving, eh, planning how to bring me down. Dammit, what's taking so long? Why do you keep stopping?"

"It's a parking lot," I said. "There are other cars around.

And pedestrians. You want me to run them over?"

"Get behind the damn supermarket!"

"Okay, okay, we're there." Reluctantly I steered the car around the end of the mall and found myself in the bleak stretch of asphalt where the store took deliveries of everything from turkeys to toothpaste.

Dean peeked above the seat at our deserted surroundings, then unfolded himself from the floor with a grunt of pain. His cologne assaulted me anew, along with the stale-tobacco smell of his breath. I took shallow breaths, wondering what he'd do if I vomited on him.

He ordered me to wait while he stiffly exited the car. He was perspiring under a light windbreaker, which I assumed he'd donned for weapon-concealment purposes. Plus duct-tape-concealment purposes, I realized as he produced a roll of the all-purpose silver tape from a pocket.

You can do anything with duct tape. That's what they say, and sure enough, I've seen pictures on the web of wallets made from the stuff, a hammock, even a prom dress. Oh yeah, and you can also tie up a Death Diva with it before stuffing her in the trunk of her car. This clever idea occurred to me after he pulled me out of the front seat and popped the trunk.

With swift efficiency he spun me around and taped my wrists behind my back, somehow keeping the gun pointed at me the entire time. It was an impressive maneuver that I would have appreciated more if I hadn't been quaking in terror. Which didn't keep me from babbling nonstop in a fruitless effort to change his mind.

"Seriously, Dean, I'm not going to say anything to—"

"You got that right," he said as he taped my mouth. And when I say he taped my mouth, I don't mean he placed a little strip of duct tape over just my mouth. I mean he wound that stuff around my head four or five times. He was taking no chance that I'd holler for help. Or kick my way out of the trunk. He wrapped tape around my ankles, as well, before lifting the trunk lid.

"Are you kidding me?" he asked, peering into it. "I sold you this car, what, not even a week ago. And just look at this!"

Okay, so I tend to use my car's trunk as a sort of catch-all. You have a junk drawer? Well, I had a junk trunk. As opposed to junk in the trunk, which is something completely different.

Oh, come on, be fair. What was I supposed to do with all the stuff that had piled up in my previous cars? Just throw it away? You never know when you're going to need a reflective blanket. Or a table hibachi. Or a twelve-can carton of smoked oysters for my mom which I kept forgetting to give her and which might have, you know, expired. I kept meaning to check the sell-by date. Or a yoga bag, complete with mat, blocks, straps, and all those other weird accessories. I tried yoga once five years ago and got a little carried away with the fun stuff that goes with it. Haven't been to a class since, but I *could*, any year now, and then I'd be ready.

And yeah, I blushed behind the duct tape, embarrassed to have my prospective killer *tsk-tsk*ing over my slovenly trunk-hoarding habits.

He lifted his free hand—the one not pointing that big old gun at my chest—and let it fall. "Is there even room for you in there?"

"Uh-uh," I grunted behind the tape, shaking my head vigorously. *You'll have to call the whole thing off.*

With a put-upon sigh he rearranged the junk, somehow managing to create a Jane-sized clearing right in the center.

While I mentally debated my next move, he made it for me, lifting me and tossing me into the trunk in one smooth motion. I had time only for a startled *Ooof!* before the lid slammed shut, leaving me curled up in blackness, facing the rear of the car.

A few seconds later, the vehicle rocked—Dean settling behind the wheel—then the engine started and we were moving.

I thought of Sexy Beast. I thought of my parents. I thought of Dom and, yeah, of Martin too. Then I thought, *All right, enough of that.*

My movements were of necessity limited due to the fact that my hands were bound behind my back and also that I was crammed in on all directions with My Stuff. It was impossible to say what all was in there, particular in the earliest, Mesozoic strata comprised of My Stuff that had accumulated in the third-hand Chrysler my dad had given me after my divorce and which had been tamped down in layers for ten years in said Chrysler before being blindly transferred to the trunk of my old Civic. There followed seven more years of further accretion, culminating in the latest transfer of My Stuff to the claustrophobic environs I now found myself in.

Fossil records differ, but I had to hope that if I dug long enough in this hellish midden, I just might be rewarded with some useful artifact capable of helping me survive my dire predicament. A long shot, I know, but Plan B was to lie there patiently awaiting a bullet to the brain, so, well, you know.

I wriggled to the extent possible, shoving my fingers into the mess behind me and scrabbling around for... I didn't know what, but I hoped I'd recognize it when I felt it. Obviously Dean hadn't considered anything in there to be of use to me, otherwise he'd have flung it out of the trunk before flinging me into it.

Meanwhile I could only guess where he was taking me. Long Island, once you got away from the populous towns, boasted no shortage of secluded areas where a body could be dumped, not to be discovered for months or years, if ever. Especially if the killer took the time to bury it.

Which would not be the case here, unless Dean had managed to conceal a shovel under that windbreaker.

Wait. A shovel. That was just the sort of thing I could see myself tossing into my car trunk at some point. If so, it might be good news for the man behind the wheel, but perhaps better news for me. Shovels have sharp edges. I could use a sharp edge.

I burrowed through the mess with renewed vigor, forcing my arms back at a painful angle. The temperature rose steadily in my cramped metal box. I blinked sweat out of my eyes—not that I could see a darn thing in the dark, but I felt the need to keep them open. I huffed through my nose, struggling to fill my lungs as the car ate up the miles between Crystal Harbor and whatever bucolic setting Dean had chosen as my final resting place. Occasionally the car stopped, for red lights, I assumed. I lacked the range of motion even to bang out an SOS signal with my cranium against the trunk lid.

My fingers worked steadily, identifying and discarding objects too banal and/or ridiculous to mention. I'll mention them anyway. There was the what-was-I-thinking booty-baring swimsuit I'd purchased a year or two back and kept meaning to return until it was too late. I found a snowbrush. Yeah, I know it was summer, but in a few months I'd need it again, wouldn't I? And then I found another snowbrush because I hadn't been able to locate the first one in the mess. And okay, so I found four snowbrushes in all. Plus three pairs of sunglasses: a John Lennon, an Elton John, and a Jackie O. Shades for every mood.

Then there was a doggie bag from some restaurant, mysterious leftovers still nestled in their Styrofoam box and enclosed in a plastic bag. Like most of the items in this trunk, I had no recollection of having lobbed it in there. I could only assume it must have been deep winter and snot-freezing cold at the time, otherwise the stink would have long ago caused me to root the thing out. By spring the freeze-dried contents had disappeared under mounds of other stuff.

What I did not find was anything sharp enough to cut through duct tape. No knives, scissors, pruning shears, hedge clippers, axes, or wire snips. Not one razor blade, tomahawk, letter opener, scalpel, or saw. Why couldn't it have been a Swiss Army knife I'd forgotten to return?

At last my fingernails scraped against a hard, wooden something. The shovel handle! With great exertion, growling and puffing, I finally grabbed hold of the object. It turned out to be the short handle of a tiny, automatic umbrella—the fifth one I'd excavated so far. I accidentally pressed the button, causing the umbrella to spring open, a wacky mishap that somehow failed to lighten the mood.

I lay there drenched in sweat, my lungs heaving as tears of hopelessness filled my eyes. Just then the ride grew rougher as the car left smooth asphalt and turned onto… what? A dirt road? I tried to calm my breathing and clear my mind as we slowly bumped along. Tree limbs scraped the sides of the car. I'd lost track of time during my ordeal. We must really be out in the sticks.

Even if by some miracle I managed to free my hands and feet, what then? I was still stuck in this trunk, and it wouldn't be long before Dean stopped the car, opened the lid, and—

No. I actually shook my head. *You are not giving up. Calm down and think, Jane!*

Okay, what did I know about the Easy-Bake Oven in which I currently resided besides the fact that an archaeological dig was long overdue? I thought back to the guided tour of my car that had been so thoughtfully provided by the man who was about to blow my brains out. I knew that if I managed to lift the floor mat beneath me, I'd find a spare tire and a tire iron. I knew I could change the taillights from in there.

My breath caught as I recalled something else Dean had shown me about this trunk. The interior escape cord. It was federal law now and had been for some time. All car trunks had to be manufactured with a way for someone to escape. He'd joked about it at the time, standing there in the used-car lot, smoking and treating me to a tediously exhaustive explanation of my vehicle's every feature, no matter how minor.

That escape cord didn't seem so minor to me now. I recalled him pointing out the gizmo in a small opening above the latch and telling me it glowed in the dark. I'd been in this trunk for who knew how long, facing that exact spot, and I didn't see anything glowing in the dark. There was nothing glowing in the damn dark!

The fact that this might be due to the heaps of My Stuff crammed in front of my face did not immediately occur to my overwrought brain. Then it did and I employed said face to shove and tamp down My Stuff, and what do you know, there it was. That square, glowing doodad was the Emerald City, dominating my field of vision, yet even more distant and unreachable.

Dean had known about the escape cord, of course, which is why he'd thoroughly immobilized me. He probably got a charge out of taunting my bound and gagged self with that bright little beacon.

Think. *Think!* If there was no sharp object in this trunk, then maybe there was an object that could be made sharp. Things could be made sharp by breaking, which I knew all too well from having flung myself through that broken window to save Porter. I was certain there were no glass objects in the trunk. But what else…?

I was moving before the thought had fully formed. One of the items I'd felt earlier was a gift bag from my friend Suze, a skilled potter. She'd presented me with a nested set of three serving bowls as a housewarming present this past April when I'd inherited Irene's house. They were beautifully shaped one-of-a-kind pieces that she'd finished with the distinctive Shino glaze she favored, an organic blend of cream and muted orange, flecked with charcoal-gray spots of carbon.

And no, you are not allowed to ask why this exquisite, lovingly hand-crafted gift was still in the trunk of my car several months after I'd received it. On the plus side, I was no longer in denial. There was no question I needed a serious intervention for my trunk-junk habit.

I dug behind me for the gift-bag handles I'd felt earlier, managing to drag the heavy bag closer once I'd located it. I burrowed past the carefully tucked tissue paper to the bowls themselves, each one meticulously swathed in bubble wrap and secured with packing tape. Of course. I found myself developing a profound aversion to tape in all its various forms.

My fingers were so sweaty I could barely grasp the tape on the largest bowl. It took several attempts, but I was motivated, and eventually, despite the bound wrists, I snagged it and peeled enough of it off the bubble wrap to allow me to free the bowl, which felt slick and heavy under my fingers. I repeated the procedure with the next largest bowl.

I was already exhausted. How could I deal with whatever came next?

By not thinking about it. *Don't think about it*, I commanded my inner wuss. *Just do it.*

Feeling behind me, I got a good grasp on one of the bowls, lifted it to the measly extent possible, and brought it down against the other one. Nothing. I had no leverage, no room to move. Meanwhile the rough terrain under the wheels was getting rougher all the time, tossing me around and making me lose my grip.

I wiped my palms on my jeans and repositioned the bottom bowl, exposing the delicate rim and bringing the heavy bottom of the other bowl down hard on it—or trying to. At the precise moment of impact, the car hit a rock or something and it slipped from my fingers.

I muttered a string of bad words behind the tape as I shoved the bottom bowl against my butt to hold it steady and lifted the other higher and higher until my shoulders screamed with pain. Gathering my strength, I slammed it with force against the side of the other bowl and was rewarded with the sound of shattering pottery. Without wasting a second, I turned the broken bowl, exposing the jagged edge to my taped wrists.

Every bump in the dirt road played havoc with my attempt to slice through the layers of reinforced tape. I ignored the blood dripping from the inevitable cuts. I barely felt them. This was a high-stakes endeavor—they didn't come much higher. I'd probably end up as dead as Ernie, but I refused to make it easy for my killer.

When I felt the tape begin to separate, I went at it with renewed vigor, sawing ferociously until I'd sliced all the way through. I twisted my wrists, pulling free of the tape. Reaching down, I found the end of the tape binding my ankles and started unwinding it.

The car stopped. I froze for a long moment, then yanked the rest of the tape off my ankles and reached behind me for the biggest, sharpest pottery shard I could find. I heard the driver's door open, felt the car rock as Dean exited, followed by the solid thunk of the driver's door closing.

I pictured him walking to the back of the car. I pictured his finger poised on the key fob, ready to pop the trunk. The instant he did, I'd be on him like a cobra, courtesy of our old friend adrenaline, prepared to launch a surprise attack on the first tender part of him to come within arm's reach.

I waited. I waited some more. The trunk did not pop. Layers of tape still circled my head. Cautiously I began to peel it until a big old hank of hair tore free from my scalp. Fortunately there was all this tape covering my mouth, so Dean didn't hear the earsplitting scream that reverberated through my skull.

So. Might be best to wait on that.

Where the heck was he? What could he be doing? Perhaps he'd thought ahead and left a shovel at this location and was even now digging my grave.

Somehow I doubted his mind was that organized. Then again, what did I know? The guy had managed to get away with murder for thirty-two years.

For all I knew, he could be silently standing over the trunk at that very moment, poised to shoot. In fact, he probably was. Nevertheless, I reached for the glow-in-the-dark doohickey, held my breath, and pulled.

The trunk lid released with a soft *clunk*. Fresh air rushed in through the gap, bringing the scent of green growing things. I squinted into the strip of daylight and saw an overgrown dirt road. I pushed the lid a little higher until trees came into view. I listened hard but heard only the thunderous whooshing of my own pulse.

I wiped my bloody fingers on my T-shirt, grabbed hold of the pottery shard, and eased the trunk lid all the way up. Silently I climbed out, my head swiveling like an owl's, eyes wide and unblinking. I latched the trunk and took stock of my surroundings. Thick woods as far as I could see, with a sun-spangled lake in the distance.

I glanced at the front seat, hoping to spy my purse, which held my cell phone. No purse. No gun. No keys. No Dean either, but I did notice that the bakery sack had been crumpled and tossed to the floor.

The bastard finished my croissants!

The Jane responsible for self-preservation seized the Jane now gaping in slack-jawed outrage and hauled her into a dense stand of trees several yards behind the car. The breeze shifted, bringing with it the scent of tobacco smoke. I squinted through the concealing foliage and finally spotted Dean standing about fifty yards away at the edge of the lake, smoking. His back was to me. He had my purse. As I watched, he withdrew my wallet and pocketed it. He removed the battery and SIM card from my cell phone, then hurled it and my purse far into the lake.

Great. Just when I'd finally joined the twenty-first century and gotten a smartphone. He stared for a moment as they sank, then produced a steel flask from his windbreaker and tilted it to his lips.

It struck me then. He was building up his courage. He hadn't killed in over three decades, not that I knew of anyway. He was working himself up to pop the car's trunk, put his gun to my head, and pull the trigger.

I recalled our first meeting at Sophie's house when she'd told him to take his complaint of police harassment to Teddy Waterfield, the person making the accusations. His wimpy response had been entertaining at the time. Ha ha, afraid of an old lady.

Never underestimate a wimp.

As much as I was tempted to take off running, I knew it would gain me nothing but a bullet in the back. I hadn't a clue where I was or how to get out of there without retracing the car's path along the miles-long dirt road.

Automatically I looked around for a weapon, something more effective than a chunk of broken pottery. A big rock, perhaps. My gaze landed on a fallen limb, larger than the softball bats I'd been accustomed to back in high school, but not so massive as to be unwieldy. I hefted it, weighed it in my hands. It would do.

Heavy footfalls and snapping brush alerted me to Dean's return. Peering from my hiding place, I noticed he looked a tad pale, but his hands remained steady as he produced his gun and the key fob. I got a firm, two-fisted grip on the limb as he approached the car trunk. I had a clear view of the back of his head, all those hair plugs laid out in orderly rows on his crown, and wondered giddily whether he used hairspray or a crop duster.

There were several buttons on the key fob, one of which

unlocked the trunk. I waited for Dean to press it. His back expanded with a calming breath. His finger caressed the trigger. Then I heard it. The slow double beep of the trunk-release button and the distinctive *clunk* as the latch disengaged.

I sprang from behind the trees, closing the distance between us as the trunk lid swung up. If there was one thing I'd learned during my trophy-winning softball days, it was how to keep my eye on the ball. Or in this case, on the uncultivated back forty of Dean's noggin.

He thrust his gun hand into the trunk, then stiffened. "What the—!"

He never got to finish the thought, but he did get a nice, long nap, snoring and drooling on top of My Stuff. Which turned out to be just the intervention I needed to finally throw it all away.

19

Dingos Ate My Drapes

I'D NEVER PAID attention to the unassuming door next to Murray's Pub, but now I found myself pressing the little doorbell button and waiting a few seconds to be buzzed in. The smell of fresh latex paint permeated the stairwell as I ascended the steps.

The door to the apartment stood open. Strolling inside, I saw paint cans and supplies scattered on a tarp covering the floor. Overhead, a ceiling fan turned lazily. The bare windows were wide open, except for the one housing a geriatric air conditioner, currently off.

Martin stood on a stepladder, painting the ceiling molding. He'd already done the ceiling itself—it was a snowy white. He wore jeans and a white undershirt, both paint-spattered. He'd tied a black bandana on his head, do-rag style.

"Grab a roller," he said, ignoring the fact that I was wearing a pretty linen sundress and chic platform sandals. "You can start on the walls."

"Sorry, I'm on my way somewhere," I said. "Where can I put these?" I lifted the grocery sacks I'd carried up the stairs.

"What's in them?" he asked.

"Your housewarming gift." I tugged down the edge of a

sack, revealing a box of Fruity Pebbles. "You got hooked on them staying at my place. Wouldn't want you to go through withdrawal."

That earned a grin. "How many of those did you buy?"

I shrugged. "Seven. At the rate you were eating mine, I figure these should last you about a week. Maybe less."

"Kitchen's through there." He pointed.

It was a worn time capsule of a kitchen, barely large enough to turn around in, but scrubbed clean. I deposited the bags on the Formica countertop. Out of curiosity, I opened the door of the fridge, a relic at least twenty years old but spotless. Inside were two six-packs and a porterhouse. "The last people left this place really clean," I called as I slid the cereal boxes into a cabinet.

He snorted at that. "It was a pigsty. The oven alone took me two hours and about a gallon of scary chemicals."

The image refused to form: Martin on his knees, scrubbing the scarred linoleum. I gave myself the grand tour, which took all of twenty seconds. One dinky bathroom. One sun-washed bedroom, where a king-size mattress lay on the wooden floor, covered with taupe-on-taupe striped sheets. "Hey!" I said. "Those are my sheets."

"They're not your sheets, they're Irene's sheets."

"Not since I inherited them." I stalked back into the living room. "You have some nerve."

"How can you be sure they're yours?" he asked. "Maybe you should crawl in there and give them a good feel, make sure they're the right thread count and everything. If you want—and I wouldn't make this offer to just anyone—I'd even let you strip down first so you could get a really good feel." He pressed his palm to his heart. "That's how much I admire and respect you."

I gave him a flat stare. "Are you finished?"

There was that impish grin again. "You want me to be finished?"

If I thought his words were more than goofy teasing, I'd…

Well, I don't know what I'd do, okay? So there. And anyway, he *was* just teasing. I'm kind of almost certain.

I asked, "What else did you steal from my house?"

"Towels, flatware, spices, cleaning supplies, canned soups and pasta, some pots and pans…" He paused, thinking. "And toilet paper. I like that expensive toilet paper you buy. Nice and soft but not linty. You want a beer?"

My crabby expression was answer enough. He shrugged and ambled into the kitchen. If I'd been at the house when he'd moved, I could have forestalled the pilfering, but he and Dom had cleared out at the same time two days earlier, when I was at the police department giving another statement to Detective Hernandez. It had been nine days since I'd beaned Dean with that tree limb and rifled his pockets to find his cell phone and call for help—a feat I'd accomplished only after managing to saw through the tape covering my mouth. My abductor was currently cooling his heels behind bars, having been denied bail.

"Admit it," he said, returning with a frosty bottle. "You never even missed the stuff I took."

Which said more about my powers of observation than his right to make off with said stuff, but I let it drop. "I'm surprised you didn't move closer to your job," I said. "This is even farther from Southampton than your mom's house."

"I'm working at Murray's now, starting tonight," he said. "Maxine rented me this place. You can't get much closer to your job than a short walk upstairs."

I thought of all those pretty padre groupies who were drawn to Martin like salt to a margarita glass, and wondered how often one of them would make the short trek upstairs with him. That thought left me a tad grumpy, so I cast about for a safer conversational topic. "Won't you miss the huge tips from those rich Southampton summer people?"

"I'll get by." He swigged from the beer bottle.

But why Crystal Harbor? I wondered. What was the attraction for him here? Most people, given their druthers, would choose to live and work near family or good buddies. His mom was on the South Shore and his daughter, Lexie, and her husband lived in Manhattan. He wasn't close to anyone in Crystal Harbor that I knew of. My face began to heat as I considered the obvious. Was that what he and I were? Good buddies? With the potential for… what?

I turned to hide my blush and scan the work in progress that was his living room. "So. What are you going to do for window treatments?"

"Why, are they sick?"

"You have to put something up on them. You can't just leave them bare. And I'm warning you right now, if I come home someday to find my drapes missing, you'll be in deep doo-doo."

"Relax," he said. "I have zero interest in drapes. That's one of those women's things."

"Spare me."

"Have you ever noticed that women are obsessed with things that start with *D*?" He ticked them off on his fingers. "There's diets, that's a big one. Drapes, of course. Divorce. Depression."

"I get depressed just thinking about diets and divorce."

"And diamonds." He leaned against the radiator and took a long pull on his beer. "Don't tell me you get depressed thinking about those?"

Well, yes, I do, if the diamond in question is a particular four-karat specimen, one I'd spied two days earlier on Bonnie Hernandez's dainty left ring finger. It was the same rock Dom had placed there last December and which she'd stopped wearing in April. Now here it was nearly August and that big old thing was once more on display, blindingly bright, Bonnie's own personal lighthouse beacon. I'd been struck dumb, unable to conceal my hurt, acutely aware of the smug triumph lurking beneath the detective's serene features.

A few weeks. Some time to think about Dom and me and the prospect of saying I do for the second time. That's what I'd asked for. That's what he'd agreed to.

Yet a mere seven days after that conversation, Bonnie was flaunting his ring. No wonder he'd slipped out of my house quietly, without so much as a text. Like a thief. Of course, the padre had done the same thing, but at least he *was* a thief. I think.

Martin's expression was too knowing. "The guy's a coward, Jane."

It was my turn to shrug. "Whatever."

"He should've talked to you first."

Dom and I had yet to speak since he'd moved out. I wasn't looking forward to that conversation. "Dirtbag exes," I said. "There's another *D*-word for you."

"Dingos," Martin said.

"Dingos?" I smirked. "Women talk about dingoes?"

"When they eat their babies, they do."

He had me there. "Dangerous dudes," I offered. I was

thinking along the lines of sexy bad boys, don't ask me why, but my words had a sobering effect on Martin.

He lifted my hand and ran his rough thumb over the scar still visible on my wrist, evidence of my frantic effort to hack my way through duct tape with a pottery shard.

I tried to keep the mood light. "On the plus side, my friend Suze has forgiven me for breaking her bowls. She promised to make me a ceramic AK-47 so I can shoot my way out next time."

"You should have brought me with you," he said.

"I didn't know it would get dangerous," I reminded him. We'd been over this. "All I did was go to the park to chat with Lacey. The rest of it…"

He managed a crooked smile. "Just don't let it happen again."

"Well, it won't happen again with Dean Phillips, that's for sure." If I had to guess, I'd say the likelihood of Dean being set free during his lifetime was somewhere between You've Got to Be Kidding and Hell No. "Sophie told me they matched the DNA in Ernie's teeth to the strands of hair they found under the cat statue."

"I think Phillips deserves a nice, friendly reception committee, don't you?"

"What, you mean in prison?"

"I know just the guys to make his stay in the joint extra special," he said.

"Oh, please don't do that." I didn't want to even imagine what he had in mind. "Life behind bars will be punishment enough."

"The son of a bitch tried to kill you, Jane." Martin's features were hard, his tone lethal. I'd never seen him like this.

He didn't add that Dean had succeeded in committing murder, and getting away with it for three decades. Apparently his attempted elimination of me carried more weight.

Which was kind of sweet. I know, I know, it was wrong, the whole reception-committee thing. But it was, you know, kind of sweet too.

Martin drained his beer and set the bottle on the floor. He lifted his hand to my hair and sifted it through his fingers. "I like it."

"Yeah? You didn't see it right after. Pretty scary." Tentatively I touched my new do: long, wavy, strawberry blond layers that reached my shoulder blades, with side-swept bangs. My hairdresser had blanched when she'd seen the mess I'd made of my hair in the woods, hacking at it with a chunk of broken pottery to remove the duct tape while waiting for the cavalry to arrive. In the end she'd worked a miracle. The result was charmingly messy.

"You've got a sexy bed-head thing going on here," he said, tugging playfully. "Do people still use that term? 'Bed-head'?"

Who cared? I could listen to this man talk about *bed*-anything all the livelong day.

He asked, "Still hooking up with losers on that doggie dating site?"

"For the record, I did not 'hook up' with any of them, and no, I suspended my membership."

"No more Dom to moon over. No more dog-loving losers." He gave a sad shake of the head. "If you get lonely, you can always swing by here for a shot of that añejo tequila you like so much."

I gave him the stink eye. "Did you steal my tequila?"

"You mean that bottle of tequila I bought you? Nope, I

purchased another one meant to lure you up here for my own nefarious purposes."

I knew he was kidding, but the mere idea of being the object of the padre's nefarious purposes made my tongue trip over itself. I responded with a witty riposte, but it might have sounded more like Sexy Beast hacking up part of a chew toy.

I heard the *ding!* of a text coming in and pulled my new phone out of my purse. "Sophie's getting antsy. I was supposed to pick her up three minutes ago."

"Antsy?" he said. "That doesn't sound like the Sophie I know."

I shoved the phone into my purse and headed for the stairwell. "If this doesn't go well, I'll be back later for some of that tequila."

Sophie was standing in front of her house when I pulled up a few minutes later. She refused to place her plastic cake carrier on the backseat and instead clutched it tightly on her lap. She was as dressed up as I ever saw her, in a flowing, summery tunic and loose trousers. Clearly she'd been to her hairdresser and even sported a touch of lipstick.

I tried to defuse her nervousness. "So remember I told you about Kyle Kenneally and his dead tortoise, Romeo?"

"Yeah."

"I just heard from the Smithsonian. They're taking him."

She looked at me. "No kidding."

"Brass plaque and all. Five grand in my pocket." I punctuated the news with a fist pump.

"Get cash," she advised. "Don't take a check from that guy."

"I'm way ahead of you. So," I said, "did you hear that Lacey and Porter are going to be grandparents?"

She snorted. "Bet I knew about it before you did. Colin and Samantha are good kids. Always liked them. They want to get out of their little rented apartment and into a house now that the baby's coming. I'm selling them that one over on Iris Street."

It took me a moment to make the connection. "You mean Dean's house?"

"The one I let him live in all these years, yeah. He won't be needing it anymore."

"I'm surprised Colin can afford Crystal Harbor on a teacher's salary," I said. "I mean, I know it's not the nicest part of town, but still. Are his parents helping out?"

"He wouldn't let them if they tried. It all worked out," she said. "I recouped my investment."

"Your invest… You charged them what you paid for the place?" I gaped at her. "Thirty years ago? In this part of Long Island? That had to be a fifth of what it's worth now. Maybe less."

"The kids aren't getting off so easy," she said. "You should see how Dean kept the place. Even the walls. Who knows how many coats of paint it'll take to cover up the nicotine stains."

Colin and Samantha were young. They'd have the place in baby-friendly shape in no time. I couldn't repress a grin. "You're a good person, Mayor Halperin."

She waved away the compliment. "Way I see it, it's an investment in Crystal Harbor. We need productive young people like those two raising families here. Good for everyone."

"I hope Porter's not in prison when his grandchild arrives." At her quizzical look, I added, "Moving Ernie's body? Faking his suicide? That's a lot of evidence tampering."

"Statute of limitations long ago expired on that. He won't

be prosecuted."

I was relieved, for his sake and his family's. "Porter and Lacey took a trip to Jersey last weekend," I told her. "They visited Tim Holbrook's grave. Together."

She nodded in approval. "Speaking of graves, Ernie's being laid to rest Sunday. In the proper part of the cemetery this time."

"Just tell me when." I reached over and squeezed her hand. "I'll be there."

She gave a ragged sigh. "I'm supposed to know everything that goes on in this damn town, Jane. How could I not have known... not even have suspected, what Dean did to Ernie?"

"It was made to look like suicide," I said. You had no reason to think—"

"I should have known!"

I gave her hand another squeeze and turned onto Wallings Drive. I pulled up in front of a house Sophie hadn't set eyes on in thirty-two years. She sat unmoving in the passenger seat.

I nodded toward the cake carrier in her lap. "What did you bring?"

"Hummingbird cake. Got the recipe out of a magazine back when I was in college. Not hard. One bowl and a spoon. Three layers. Cream-cheese frosting. Pecans. Teddy used to love it." She took a deep breath. "She still like sweets, you think?"

I recalled the cloying lemonade and cookies Teddy had served me, and chewed back a grin. "I think so."

"How do I look?"

"You look perfect, Sophie." I glanced at the house and saw a window curtain twitch. "Come on."

She kept a death grip on the cake carrier as we shuffled up

the walkway. The instant we stepped onto the porch, the front door swung open. Teddy Waterfield stood on the threshold. No apron and slippers today. She looked neat and ladylike in a white skirt and a pink-and-white striped blouse. And, yes, lipstick.

"Why, it's Sophie and Jane!" Teddy announced, as if she hadn't been preparing for our visit all morning. As if thirty-two years hadn't passed since she'd last set eyes on her daughter-in-law. She held the door wide. "Come in, come in, the air conditioning's on. I usually keep it off, but it's beastly out today, don't you think? Don't you think it's beastly out? My word, is that hummingbird cake?"

About the Author

Pamela Burford comes from a funny family. You may take that any way you want. She was raised in a household that valued laughter above all, so of course the first thing she looked for in a husband was a sense of humor. Is it any wonder their grown kids are into stand-up comedy and improv? Oh, and here's another fun fact: Pamela's identical twin sister, Patricia Ryan, aka P.B. Ryan, is also a published novelist. Patricia is the Good Twin, and yeah, Pamela knows what that makes her. But hey, Evil Twins have more fun!

It should come as no surprise that everything Pamela writes is infused with her own quirky brand of humor, from her feel-good contemporary romance and romantic suspense novels to her popular Jane Delaney mystery series, featuring snarky "Death Diva" Jane, her canine sidekick Sexy Beast, and a fun love-triangle subplot. Pamela's own beloved poodle, Murray, wants you to know that any similarities between himself and neurotic, high-strung Sexy Beast are purely coincidental.

Pamela is the proud founder and past president of Long Island Romance Writers. Her books have won awards and sold millions of copies, but what excites her most is hearing from readers. Swing by and say hi at pamelaburford.com.